Praise for *The Making of a Gentleman*

"The second installment of the Sons of the Revolution trilogy showcases Galen's talents for emotionally powerful romances that enchant readers... Galen gives her story wonderful twists and marvelous characterization that make it a standout."

—*RT Book Reviews*

"Replete with a lively wit, vivid descriptions, strong characters... filled with conflicts, emotional upheaval, a hint of mystery, and a dose of romance. Galen masterfully writes a witty, fun, mysterious, and intriguing tale of secrets, lies, and passion."

—*Rundpinne*

"A riveting story... The setting is impeccable, with just the right amount of detail while the characters, major and minor, sparkle."

—*Thoughts from Lady Tess*

"Fantastic historical romance, full of darkness and light."
—*Night Owl Romance*

"Totally absorbing... an adrenaline rush from start to finish! Shana Galen once again brings her characters to life through the expertise of her writing."

—*A Romance Review*

"A perfect read! If you love historical romances then you will enjoy this book.

—*Cheryl's Book Nook*

"Galen's trilogy, the stories of lost brothers, begins with a fast-paced, action-packed, cat-and-mouse spy thriller that will leave you breathless. Her engaging characters and strong plotline enhance the spirited dialogue and sense of adventure."

—*RT Book Reviews*

"Galen strikes the perfect balance between dangerous intrigue and sexy romance in her latest deftly crafted Regency historical."

—*Booklist*

"Delightful reading! Shana Galen creates a captivating tale... the dialogue, charming wit, the intrigues, and the steamy love scenes make the novel a page-turner."

—*The Long and the Short of It*

"Vivid, intense, and had me ensnared from the first line... Galen's book had me up until all hours."

—*History Undressed*

"Exceptionally entertaining reading with a cast of brilliantly written characters... Galen's descriptive writing and wonderful dialogue makes her novel impossible to set down... an all around delightful read."

—*Rundpinne*

"Intrigue, suspense, and romance wrapped neatly into a delicious story that will keep the reader going until the very last page."

—*Affaire de Coeur*

THE ROGUE PIRATE'S BRIDE

SHANA GALEN

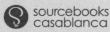

sourcebooks
casablanca

Copyright © 2012 by Shana Galen
Cover and internal design © 2012 by Sourcebooks, Inc.
Cover illustration by Alan Ayers

Sourcebooks and the colophon are registered trademarks of
Sourcebooks, Inc.

Published by Sourcebooks Casablanca, an imprint of Sourcebooks,
Inc.
P.O. Box 4410, Naperville, Illinois 60567-4410
(630) 961-3900
FAX: (630) 961-2168
www.sourcebooks.com

Printed and bound in Canada.
WC 10 9 8 7 6 5 4 3 2 1

For mothers, especially my mom, Nancy,
and my mother-in-law Cheryl.
How would I have done it without you?

One

France, 1802

"That's him," Percy whispered. "I'm almost certain of it."

Raeven Russell glanced at Percy. There was a fine sheen of perspiration on his pale, freckled skin, and his white-blond hair stood up in all directions as though he'd run a hand through it half a dozen times. Which he probably had. Percy Williams was purser for the HMS *Regal*, and while Raeven knew Percy adored her, she also knew he abhorred any action that violated her father's rules.

She reached over and slung an arm around him in the jaunty way she had seen men do time and time again. "You look nervous," she said under her breath. "People will wonder why."

"I *am* nervous," he hissed. "You're going to get yourself killed."

"That's my problem." She shifted away from him and scanned the men around her. Which one was Cutlass? There were several likely candidates.

Raeven stood like a man—legs braced apart and hands on hips—to survey the seedy Brest tavern. Dockside taverns the world over were the same, she mused as she studied the crowd. They were filled with sailors looking for wine and women, ships' captains hiring additions to their crews, beleaguered serving girls skirting men's too-free hands, and whores working to entice any man with the coin to pay.

She didn't know why she should feel so at home. She certainly didn't belong here and had gone to considerable trouble to disguise herself as a young man before sneaking off her father's ship and onto a cutter with the crew members going ashore legitimately.

If her father knew she was here... She shook her head. She could hear his booming voice in her head. *The daughter of a British admiral should behave with more decorum, in a manner befitting her station in life.*

But what was her station in life? Her mother had died days after her birth, and from the age of four—when the last of her relatives had given her up as incorrigible—she'd been sailing with her father. This certainly wasn't the first tavern she'd visited. It wasn't even the first time she'd sneaked off the HMS *Regal*.

It was the first time she'd found Captain Cutlass. After six months of searching for the murdering bastard, she was about to meet him... face to face.

"It'll be my neck when your father finds out." Percy swallowed audibly, and she suppressed a smile.

"Then you won't be long in following me to meet our maker. I'll put in a good word for you."

He gave her a horrified look, which she supposed indicated he didn't think she'd be a very good envoy.

He cleared his throat. "I prefer a little more time on this earthly world."

"I'm in complete agreement. Now, tell me which one he is again, but don't look at him or gesture toward him."

"Let's go sit at the bar," Percy said. "You can see him better from there, and we'll be less conspicuous."

"Fine." Remembering to play her role, she swaggered to the bar and leaned against it, trying to look belligerent. Percy ordered ale, and she did as well, though she had no intention of drinking it. She needed all her wits about her.

When the barkeep moved away, Percy studied his mug and murmured, "See the man in the far corner?"

Raeven allowed her gaze to roam lazily over the tavern until she focused on the corner he indicated.

"He's dressed as a gentleman in a navy coat, white cravat, buff breeches."

She saw him now and nodded. "A gentleman pirate." She shook her head. "Contradiction in terms."

"The rumor is he's a deposed marquis whose family fled France during the revolution."

She scowled at him. "Don't tell me you believe that rubbish. All the pirates concoct romantic stories. Just because one claims he's a duke doesn't make him any less of a thief and murderer."

"Of course I don't believe it. I'm telling you the rumor."

But she could hear in his voice he had believed the story, and now that she'd set her eyes on Cutlass, she could see why. The man did have the air of the aristocrat about him. It wasn't simply his clothes—any man could dress up as one of the quality, but there was something in Cutlass's bearing. He was sitting at a table, his back to the wall, facing the door to the tavern. That much told her he was no fool. There was a man seated across from him, and Cutlass was listening in a leisurely fashion to whatever the man was saying. Cutlass's arms were crossed over his chest, and his expression was one of mild interest. He had a glass of something on the table before him, but she hadn't seen him drink from it. Nor had she seen any whores approach him.

He was doing business then. It would have better served her purposes if he'd been drunk and whoring, but she didn't have the luxury of choosing when to strike.

Her gaze slid back to Percy. "He's handsome," she remarked and watched the purser's eyebrows wing upward. "I hadn't expected that."

The reports she'd had of him rarely mentioned his appearance. Captain Cutlass was known for his stealth, his agility, and his slippery escapes. It was rumored he'd boarded over a hundred vessels. That was obviously exaggeration, but even if his record was a quarter of that, it was an impressive feat. Of course, he claimed he was a privateer, and she knew he sailed under the Spanish flag and with that country's letters of marque. She didn't care for privateers any more than she cared for pirates, and made little distinction between them. Neither pirates nor privateers should dare attack ships of the British Navy. Neither should dare to kill a British naval officer.

She felt the anger and the blood pump through her and took a deep, calming breath. She couldn't afford to be emotional right now. She had to put emotion away. And she couldn't afford a schoolgirl crush on the man either. Yes, he was handsome. His dark brown hair was brushed back from his forehead and would have grazed his shoulder if not neatly secured in a queue. His face was strong with a square jaw, plenty of angles and planes, and a full mouth that destroyed the hard effect and hinted at softness. But the eyes—the eyes did not lie. There was no softness in the man. She couldn't quite see the eye color from this far away, but under the sardonic arch of his brow his eyes were sharp, cold, and calculating.

A worthy adversary, and she'd spill his blood tonight.

"I don't like the look in your eyes," Percy said. "Now that you've seen him, you can't possibly mean to challenge him. He's not a small man."

Raeven straightened her shoulders to give herself more height. She was well aware of her short stature, but size and strength were not everything. She was small and quick and deadly. "I do mean to challenge him," she said, brushing her hand against the light sword at her waist. "I'm only waiting until his business is completed." Though if it took much longer, she would have to interrupt. She wanted this over and done.

"I don't think that's wise. Perhaps if we wait—"

"I'm not waiting," she snapped. "I've waited six months, and that's too long."

"Timothy would not have wanted…"

Her glare cut him off. "Timothy is dead, and his murderer is sitting over there having a chat and sipping wine. Timothy would have wanted justice."

And because she knew Percy's next comment would be about justice versus vengeance, and because she did not want to hear it, she pushed off the bar and arrowed for Cutlass's table. It was a short trek across the tavern but long enough for her heart to pick up speed and pound painfully in her chest. She tried to calm herself with a deep breath, but she exhaled shakily. Her hands were sweating, and she flexed them to keep them loose.

When she stepped in front of Cutlass's table, he glanced up at her briefly and then back at the man seated across from him. Before she could speak, another man was beside her.

"Move away, lad. The captain's busy at present." The man was tall and lanky with a shock of red hair and pale, freckled skin. He was well dressed and spoke to her in fluent, if accented, French. English, she thought, and well bred. Probably Cutlass's quartermaster.

She stood her ground. "I think the captain will want to hear what I have to say." She said it to Cutlass, but he didn't acknowledge her.

"I'll tell him you wish to speak with him. In the meantime…" He made the mistake of taking her arm, and she responded with a quick jab to his abdomen. He grunted in surprise and took a step back.

"Problem, Mr. Maine?" Cutlass said smoothly. He had one brow cocked and a bemused smile on his lips. Obviously, he didn't see her as any sort of threat. "Is the lad giving you trouble?" He also spoke in French, but his was sweet and thick as honey. A native speaker, she surmised, and one with a polished accent. No wonder he played the deposed French marquis.

"No, Captain," Maine said, stepping forward again. "I'll get him out of your way."

Raeven put a hand on the small dagger at her waist. "Touch me again, and I'll slice your hand off." Her gaze met Cutlass's. "I want a word with you."

"Obviously." He lifted his wine, sipped. "But you'll have to learn some manners first. Come back when you've mastered the art of patience."

In one lightning-quick move, she drew her dagger, rounded the table, and pressed it under his jaw. "You want to talk about patience?" She pressed the blade into the bronze skin until a small bead of blood welled up. "I've been waiting six long months to slit your throat."

"Is that all?" he said, setting his glass of wine on the table. With annoyance, she noted his hand did not even tremble. "There are some who've waited far longer."

"I'm going to kill you," she said, looking directly into his eyes. They were cobalt blue and framed with thick brown lashes.

He raised a brow at her. "I don't think so." She should have seen it coming, should have seen his eyes flick down or his jaw clench, but he gave no indication he would move. And before she could react, he had her wrist pinned on the table, the dagger trapped and useless. Slowly he stood, his hand warm steel on hers. She watched him rise and rise and had never felt as small as she did in that moment. She realized the tavern had grown quiet as the patrons drank in the scene.

Percy's voice broke the silence. "Captain, the boy's had too much to drink. He's young. If you don't mind, we'll just be taking him back to the ship now."

Raeven scowled. She could imagine her father's men lined up behind her, Percy in the middle, his hands spread in a placating gesture. She kept her gaze locked on Cutlass's, saw him shrug and exchange a look with one of his men. Devil take her if he wasn't going to pat her head and shoo her away. She couldn't allow that. This was her last chance. Even now her father might have noticed her absence, and it could be months—*years*—before she had another opportunity to confront Cutlass.

"Coward," she said loud enough for her voice to carry through the tavern. "Too afraid to fight me, a mere boy?"

She saw the surprise in his face and then the irritation. "Look, lad, I don't want to kill you."

She laughed. "What makes you think you can? I'm good with a sword. Very good, and I challenge you to a duel." Now she did look away from him; she swept the room with her eyes, making sure everyone heard the challenge.

"Now you've done it," she heard Percy mutter. And she had. Cutlass could not back down from a direct challenge.

She heard a snort and whipped her gaze back to Cutlass. Or could he?

"Go back to your ship, boy. I don't have time to play sword fighting with you. Come back when you've grown a whisker or two"—he traced a finger over her cheek before she could jerk her head away—"and kissed a pretty girl." With that, he released her hand and shoved past her.

Raeven spun and drew her sword. She wasn't

surprised when, at the sound, he drew his own and faced her again. "Stupid little brat. Are you really going to make me kill you?"

"Not if I kill you first, you pirate bastard." She thrust her sword, but he parried easily, the weight of his heavier blade throwing her slightly off balance. She was in the corner, while he had the open space of the room in which to maneuver. She needed to push him back, to give herself more room. She was fast and agile, but those strengths required space.

She stumbled into a stool and kicked it back and out of her way. It didn't help much, but it was something. And not a moment too soon. Cutlass took advantage of her distraction to lunge, and she was almost too late in blocking him.

Not that the thrust would have done much more than scratch her. He was playing with her, still not taking her challenge seriously. Why should that irk her so? He'd see how serious she was when she gutted him.

"Go back to your ship, *enfant*," Cutlass said with a roguish smile that showed off a row of white teeth. For some reason, his perfect smile irritated her even more. The man should have some fault. Rotten teeth or a gap or... something! "Before you cease to amuse me."

"Oh, but I've only begun to amuse you, pirate." She made as if to lower her sword but jerked it up at the last minute, catching the sleeve of his coat and ripping a gash in the fine material. It was a move she'd perfected over the years, and she was not surprised it succeeded now. What did surprise her was that when Cutlass should have been gazing in astonishment at his torn coat, he was ready for her when she slashed at his throat. His blade connected with hers, the screech of metal against metal resounding through the stillness of the tavern. "Not laughing now, are you, bastard?" she ground out. Cutlass was strong, and it took most of her strength to keep his sword from slicing her own away.

"Do you think your little parlor trick impressed me, *enfant*?" he asked. "Now you owe me ten pounds for my coat."

"Ten pounds! Don't be ridiculous." She pushed back on his sword and leaned to the right. She could feel the walls behind her, crowding her. She needed to get out of this corner. Cutlass gave way, edging to her right, and she felt a small measure of victory. If she could just get him to circle…

He gave her borrowed clothes a distasteful perusal. "I assure you that you will pay me ten pounds for the damage you've done." His eyes narrowed, and she actually felt a shiver run down her spine. "One way or another."

"You'll have to pry the blunt out of my cold, dead hands, pirate bastard." She was sweating now and breathing heavily, but she'd managed to make him edge a little more to her right. Their swords were still locked in a stalemate, but she knew he was waiting for the right time to strike. She kept her weight on the balls of her feet, ready to defend.

Around her, she could hear the crowd exclaiming, could hear bets being placed and feel the men crowding in to observe. She wondered if anyone bet on her.

"I know we've not formally met," Cutlass said, "but might I ask why you keep referring to me as a 'bastard pirate' when I'm neither a pirate nor a bastard? It's rather impolite."

"I'll show you impolite!" She stepped back, moving quickly as his blade came down with a swish of hot air before her face. But before he could raise it again, she feinted to the left and skirted around him.

Ha! Victory! Now she had the open room to her back!

But Cutlass, quicker than she anticipated, spun around and thrust, forcing her, stumbling and pinwheeling, back into the crowd. One of the men caught her by the arms and shoved her forward again. She ducked and fell into a somersault as Cutlass's blade swooshed above her.

That was no swordplay. Cutlass was finally serious.

She sprang to her feet and, whipping around, paired her sword with his. The blades scraped together as she thrust and parried, and he followed suit. He was a good swordsman, she realized, as he matched her move for move. He'd studied the art, didn't just act on instinct. She too had studied, and mentally she went through her list of offensive maneuvers.

But the frustrating man blocked her every attack. He seemed to know what she would do before she did it. And the worst part was she was growing tired. When she'd left her father's ship, she'd been fueled by excitement and revenge. Now, Cutlass systematically wore away at her reserves. He defended but did not attack. And she couldn't help but notice he did not seem even slightly winded.

The crowd cheered at each of their advances, and she had the distinct impression they were rooting for her. But Cutlass would have his supporters as well. If she killed him—no, *when* she killed him—she needed to be ready for another attack.

"Devil take you!" she swore after another forceful lunge merely resulted in the two circling each other again.

"Not tonight." He smiled again, but she could see a faint sheen of perspiration on his upper lip. So he was not made of steel. He was tiring.

And that was the last thought she had before he attacked. Without warning and with great finesse, he switched stances and drove his blade toward her heart. She parried, of course, but it was a near thing. And then he was on her again, forcing her back into the throng, crowding her until she had little choice but to defend with quick, small movements instead of larger, more powerful ones.

"You're not going to win," he said, pressing her back.

"Then I die trying," she gritted out. She swiped at him to prove her point and had the satisfaction of seeing him jerk to the side to elude the sharp steel of her blade.

"And what are you dying for?" He struck back, and she struggled to hold her position.

"Revenge." She met his blade high, then low, then high again. She pushed hard, and he pushed back, and they stared at one another for a long moment.

"A noble cause. How did I offend?"

She opened her mouth and closed it again, unsure whether or not she wanted to answer. Finally, she said, "You killed my… friend."

"Doubtful. I kill far fewer than the rumors would have you believe."

The anger rose inside her like a tidal wave, and she brought her blade down hard on his. "You dare to mock me?"

His answer was a quick, triumphant grin, and just as she realized his intent, he brought his sword up and drove her back.

Into the tavern's support beam.

Frantic at the feel of the scratchy wood on her back, she tried to skirt around it, but Cutlass's blade caught her sleeve and drove into the wooden beam.

She was trapped.

Her right arm, that with the sword, was incapacitated, but she had enough presence of mind to toss her sword to her left hand and make a jab at him. She'd never been very good with her left hand—unlike those fencing masters who could fight with either hand—and he easily evaded her blade.

"I've beaten you," he said, leaning close. "Admit it, *enfant*, and I let you go."

"I'd rather choke on my own blood when you slit my throat."

He raised his brows at that, obviously not expecting such a vehement response. "Well, as appealing as that sounds, I don't want a reputation as a child killer." He gave her a speculative look. "But there is the matter of that ten pounds you owe me." He glanced at his torn coat, and she doubled her efforts to escape, but her sleeve would not tear. If her shirt had been made of fine linen, as Cutlass's was, she'd already be free. But this coarse homespun was not easily damaged. "I don't have ten pounds, so you'll have to kill me."

"Or…" He gave her a triumphant smile. "I've been looking for a new cabin boy. I think you might be right for the position. I'd enjoy seeing you empty my chamber pot each day."

The crowd hooted with laughter, but she was not amused.

"Never!" She tried again to strike him with her sword, but he plucked it out of her hands. She clenched her fist. If she lost that sword, there would be hell to pay. Her father had it made especially for her, and it had not come cheaply.

"Tut-tut." Cutlass grinned at the crowd, who were enjoying this little play. "You'll have to learn some manners. And we'll start with removing your cap when you speak to me." He reached for her.

"No!"

But she was too late. Before the words were out of her mouth, he'd snatched the cap from her head and was staring in shock as the mass of black curls tumbled down her back. She'd secured her hair tightly, but he'd ripped the hair pins loose when he tore the cap away. Cutlass stared at the cap, then at her, then at the cap again. For the moment, he appeared speechless. Then, slowly, he reached forward, wrapped a lock of her hair around two fingers, and tugged.

"Ow!"

He leaned close, peered into her face, and shook his head. "I must be an idiot. I can't believe I didn't see it sooner." She noted his blue eyes slid over her face with what looked to be appreciation. His gaze slipped down, and heat crept into her cheeks.

"So I'm a woman," she said, standing straighter. She managed to spare a glare for the patrons who were staring at her with expressions that ran from contempt to hilarity. "It doesn't mean I can't fight." She met Cutlass's gaze directly and ignored the spark of heat flooding into her. "It doesn't mean I won't kill you."

He raised a brow, glanced at her sword, which he held in one hand, then at his own sword, which still held her pinned to the tavern's wooden beam. The crowd chuckled.

"Devil take it!" She tried once more to free her shirt from his sword, but the material and the steel held fast.

"Such language from a woman. You really do need to learn some manners." He reached for her face, and she jerked away, but his touch was tender as he skated a finger down her cheek. She felt more heat burn across the skin he touched. Why was she reacting this way? He was a killer. He'd killed Timothy.

"I suppose I could hire you on as a cabin girl," he was saying, glint in his eye. "Though your duties might differ somewhat."

This brought cheers from some of the tavern's patrons, and, from the corner of her eye, Raeven could see the uneasy shuffling of her father's men. She did not want them to step in and save her. She'd rather let Cutlass take her and escape later than have to be rescued. She caught Percy's eye and shook her head. His white face paled further, and he looked ready to toss his accounts.

She glanced back at Cutlass, who was watching her. Had he seen her exchange with Percy? Doubtful.

Even if he had, he wouldn't make anything of it. "I'll be your cabin girl," Raeven said, her voice low and husky. She leaned forward, flirting, and Cutlass shook his head.

"I imagine you'll empty my chamber pot… right before you slit my throat."

She gave him a winning smile. "You know me so well."

"Well enough to make sure I don't turn my back on you." He gestured to his men. "Mr. Maine, see that she makes it aboard the *Shadow* and finds her way into my cabin. Untouched." He extracted his sword from the wooden beam, freeing her, but not before his man grabbed her arm. She could have fought, but Cutlass was playing right into her hands. She *would* kill him. Unaware of the danger he was in, Cutlass turned his back and strode for the tavern's exit.

"You're going to regret this, Cutlass!" Raeven called after him. "In more ways than you can count."

He waved a hand without looking back, clearly dismissing her.

"Let's go," Mr. Maine said, pushing her forward. Percy was instantly at her side, hissing in her ear.

"I can't let them kidnap you. Your father will kill me." He gestured to the other men of the *Regal*. "Kill all of us."

"If you intervene, *I'll* kill you," Raeven hissed back. "I'll be back on my father's ship before morning. You know I can escape anything and anyone."

Percy looked dubious.

"Besides," she added, "if you intervene now, everyone will know who I am. How do you think my father would like it known about Brest that his daughter was sword fighting in a tavern?"

"More than he'd like her kidnapped and—er—assaulted by Captain Cutlass."

"Enough talk!" Maine said, pushing her forward and separating her from Percy. Cutlass's men held the purser back.

Raeven called over her shoulder, "Give me six hours. If I'm not back by then, you know what to do."

Maine shoved her into the crisp, dark night, and quite suddenly she realized she was alone with half a dozen of Cutlass's men. A shiver ran up her spine as, one by one, she perused the seedy crew. One man with an earring and tattoos all over his face winked at her. Raven bit her lip.

What had she gotten herself into?

Two

SÉBASTIEN HAD NEVER BEEN SO GLAD TO STEP OUT OF A tavern. Usually he was more than pleased to step into one, but then nothing on this leg of his voyage had been what he'd term usual.

Least of all the girl.

Girl? He ran a hand through his hair and had a flash of the curve of her bottom.

No, not a girl. A woman.

Merde! What in the name of all that was holy—he thought of the fury in her green eyes—or perhaps all that was unholy, had caused the girl—woman—female! to attack him? She said she'd challenged him for revenge. But what could he have possibly done to her? He'd never seen her before. He would have remembered.

Ça alors! How had he not seen that the lad was no lad at all? The lashes framing those green eyes were far too thick and long. No boy had lashes like that. Or skin like that. Or a bottom like that.

Not that he'd been looking at her bottom… well, at least not until Bastien realized the he was a she.

He strode along the quay, heading toward the place where his ship, *Shadow*, waited. They'd be departing on the first tide, and he wanted to supervise the loading of the cargo. He trusted his men implicitly, but this cargo was precious, which was why it was being delivered in the dark of night. He checked his pocket watch and swore at the time. He would have been on board by now if the girl had not forced him to cross swords with her. He'd thought the whole incident ridiculous until she ruined his coat. Then he'd decided to teach the lad a lesson.

In the end, he supposed it was he who learned a lesson, not to judge by appearances. An annoying boy could turn out to be a beautiful woman—a beautiful woman intent on killing him. And what was he going to do about that? What was he going to do about her? He didn't need a cabin boy, and he sure as hell didn't need a cabin girl. All she'd do is distract him with her attempts to kill him, not to mention that luscious bottom.

And that was the kind of distraction he didn't need. He'd never needed to rape a woman to enjoy her bed, and he wasn't about to start now. But there was no denying the explosive attraction he'd felt the moment he pulled that ugly cap off her.

Well, he might not end up bedding her—though given time, he thought she might be persuaded. He'd been told more than once he was too charming for his own good, but at least she'd amuse him and keep him sharp. Nothing like waking up with a knife at the throat to keep a man's instincts honed. And, little as he liked to admit it, she was a good match for him.

An Englishwoman! Her French had been only adequate, and she couldn't disguise her heavy English accent. And who would have thought an Englishwoman so fiery? Not he. Cold and formal was how he'd always envisioned them. Perhaps he'd have to broaden his perspective...

Enough time for that later. Right now he needed to understand why she had come after him. He didn't have any connections to England. Their navy was a pest—at times pursuing and harassing him, but he dealt with them easily enough.

Unfortunately, now that England and France had signed a peace treaty, the English would have more time to harass him. Even so, he vastly preferred the English to the French. It riled him that he was docked here in Brest. He'd sworn never to return to France, and if there had been any other way to acquire this cargo, he would have pursued it. But there hadn't been, and now here he was, on French soil again. He looked down, surprised the ground wasn't covered in blood. God knew he'd seen enough of it shed during the revolution. His own family had been a victim of the bloodthirsty peasants, and now he was the only living member of the Valère family left.

Or perhaps the family had died out. He never used his surname, Harcourt, or his title, marquis de Valère. He was Captain Cutlass: a man without a history, and he liked it that way.

The bow of his sloop came into view, and Bastien smiled. With its three tall masts and eighteen cannon, the *Shadow* was a fine ship—the one thing in his life that had never let him down, the one thing he could count on. She'd gotten him out of more scrapes than he could count, made his fortune, and given him a purpose. His heart soared every time he saw her, and he felt free. His legs itched to board her and set sail, to rid himself of the confines of land.

A crate of cargo hung over the deck now, hoisted by several of his crew on the quay. On board, his bosun, Mr. Ridley, was calling orders and directing the operation. Ridley spotted him and gave a brief wave. Bastien returned it, pausing to watch as the cargo was lowered into the hold. As expected, Ridley had matters well in hand. The broad-chested, dark-skinned man was as efficient and orderly as he was fearsome. Bastien would have liked to claim that he'd never had a moment's fear of the man, but the truth was, the first time they'd met, the man had scared the hell out of him. Still did at times.

It wasn't the tattoos or the multiple earrings, it was the way the sailor—tall as a tree—could stare a man down and make the skin on the back of his neck itch.

Bastien had met Ridley in a tavern not so different than the one he'd just left. Ridley had been looking for work, and Bastien hiring on. He'd had reservations about making Ridley part of the crew of the *Shadow*, but how was he going to say no to a man who looked like a leviathan? Thinking it might deter the fearsome giant, Bastien had made a point of stressing that he wasn't a pirate. "I'm a privateer," he'd said. "I have letters of marque from Spain."

Ridley smiled, showing one gold tooth in the midst of a sea of white. "Sure, Cap'n Cutlass. Whatever you say. I'll call you a privateer, and you can call me… Ridley."

To this day, Bastien still had no idea what Ridley's real name was. He didn't care. The bosun was one of the best men he'd ever employed. He'd call the man Mary, if that's what he wanted.

With a wave at his crew to continue their work, Bastien strode up the gangplank, stepped onto the deck of his ship, and felt his world tilt, righting itself. The cargo was about half loaded, and he peered down the hold. Still plenty of room. The cargo would be tucked away in the next hour or so, and they'd begin preparations to sail. He was headed for Almeria, Spain on the Mediterranean. There, he'd deliver the cargo, take the money, and outfit the *Shadow* for an even more important task: sinking *La Sirena*.

There was nothing he'd like better than to see Jourdain's vessel at the bottom of the ocean—unless it was Jourdain going down with it.

"Cap'n," Ridley said, coming up beside him, dark eyes still focused on the cargo.

"Mr. Ridley." Bastien nodded. "Everything looks to be in good order."

"Aye, Cap'n," Ridley said, eyes shifting to the quay. "But I doan think that's the last of the cargo."

Bastien raised his brows then followed Ridley's gaze. He almost swore but caught the oath just in time. There, fighting his way toward the ship, was Mr. Maine and the black-haired hellion. She had an escort of six men and was giving every single one of them the devil of a time. They were all but carrying her, kicking, squirming, and swearing—if his ears did not deceive him—along the waterfront.

Merde. What had he gotten himself into?

He cleared his throat and glanced at Mr. Ridley. Bastien thought he could detect an underlying grin on the carefully neutral face.

"Last minute addition," Bastien said through clenched teeth as the crew hoisting his real cargo aboard paused to stare at the woman being carried up the gangplank.

"I see. Where you want it?"

Bastien cleared his throat. "Mr. Maine has orders to put it—er, her—in my cabin. She's the new... cabin girl."

Ridley's eyebrow arched ever so slightly.

"She won't be up on deck." Bastien tried not to cringe as Mr. Maine carried the woman past him. She'd caught sight of him, and the curses were flowing. Where the hell had she learned language like that? He raised his voice. "So she won't be in your way."

"Dat good." To his credit, Ridley kept his eyes on his captain and not on the scene behind him. "I best be getting back to work."

"Good man," Bastien said. The deck was calmer now, as the woman had obviously been taken below, and the loading of the cargo resumed. Bastien supposed he should get to work as well. He started toward his cabin then thought better of it. Perhaps he could find some work to do above deck. He needn't retire to his cabin directly. He could consult his charts and maps later... could make his log later.

If any of his belongings were still in one piece.

Merde. He supposed he couldn't get around her. Taking a deep breath, he set off to tame the savage beast.

❧

Bastien stood in the companionway outside his cabin and frowned. It was quiet. Too quiet.

He was tempted to search out Mr. Maine to see whether the quartermaster had put the black-haired hellion in his cabin as instructed. But Bastien knew Maine too well. The girl was in there.

He glanced down at his coat, at the ripped sleeve. Ah, yes. His cabin girl was going to work off the damage, even if it made both of them miserable. He'd guarantee she was the more miserable.

Best he instruct her on her duties so she could begin.

He opened his cabin door, noted a lamp had been lit, and glanced about. For a great cabin, it was small, but he didn't see the woman. His gaze scanned the neat, trim room: berth, trunks, desk…

Where the hell was she? Could she be hiding? Where? In the trunk?

He stepped inside and realized too late his mistake. He turned quickly enough to avoid the worst of the blow, but he still felt the force of the object slam into the side of his head. For a moment, bright white dots danced before a sea of black, and then he reached out and grabbed the little vixen.

She had the object raised! Damn him if she wasn't going to strike again!

But he had his hand wrapped around her wrist now, and he twisted it violently. She cried out, and he muttered, "Drop it."

"No."

The black sea was fading now, and he was able to focus on her face. It was set in a stubborn expression, those green eyes as turbulent as the ocean during a tempest. He tightened his grip and saw her jaw clench, but she didn't drop the candlestick she held.

C'est des conneries! The thing was brass and had to weigh two pounds. She really did want to kill him. Anger shot through him as his head throbbed again, and he wrenched her arm. The little hellion held on, so he pushed her up against the door, slamming it closed in the process.

Her eyes were watering with pain now, but she still held the candlestick. "Drop it."

"No!" The word was barely a breath.

He shook his head. "*Mon Dieu!* Are you always this stubborn?"

"Some might call it persistence," she gritted out.

He had her pinned to the door, one hand restraining her wrist and the candlestick she held aloft, and the opposite hand trapping her shoulder. In one quick motion, he released her, plucked the candlestick from her grasp, and tossed it over his shoulder. It thudded on the floor just as her fist came up. But he caught that too, grinned, and forced it back against the wood. Now he had both her hands pinned to the door. "I can be persistent as well."

He was looking directly into her eyes and realized, slowly, that their bodies were flush against one another.

"Don't get any ideas," she said.

He raised a brow. "What kind of ideas?" But his body had a mind of its own. He was more than aware of the warmth of her skin, the feel of her soft curves against his muscles, and the sweet, cherry smell of her hair. But something wasn't quite right...

He couldn't feel the swell of her breasts. He

glanced down, noted her white shirt was all but flat. He looked into her eyes again. "Bound them, did you? Clever disguise."

"It fooled you, pirate."

He sighed. "Are we back to that again? I told you, I'm not a pirate. I have letters of marque from—"

"I don't care what country's flag you fly under. I know what you are. And what you did. Now get off me!" She shoved back hard, taking him by surprise. But he was a good deal larger than she and much stronger. He held her in place, rather liking this position and the view it afforded him of her eyes. They were undoubtedly her best feature... well, the best of the ones he could see at the moment. Her nose was a bit too snub, her lips too small—or perhaps that was because she had them firmly compressed—and her chin jutted too sharply. But those eyes were amazing. He'd never seen anyone with such vividly green eyes. They reminded him of a lush pasture or of a shower of emeralds.

And now he was reminding himself of some god-awful poet. He shook his head and hopefully rid himself of all poetic urges.

"Do you have a name?" he asked.

"What?" She blinked at him. "No."

"And you say I'm the bastard. Very well then, I shall call you Cabin Girl."

She snorted. "You can try it."

"You need some sort of name. How else will you come running when I call?"

Her mouth dropped open, and she let out a short, incredulous laugh. "Oh, you're just full of delusions."

"We'll see." He glanced about the cabin. "And your first task, Cabin Girl… is to empty my chamber pot."

She smiled sweetly. At least he supposed that was her version of a sweet smile. "Of course," she cooed. "Release me, and I'll empty it."

He narrowed his eyes.

"You're hesitating." She challenged him with an arch of her brows. "Afraid of something?"

"Not afraid. Merely… concerned."

It was late, and he was beginning to realize he could be fighting her all night. If he released her now, she might wreak any manner of damage. He glanced over his shoulder, checking for blunt objects nearby, and jerked back as he felt her shift.

Too late.

Pain cut through him, and without thinking, he reached for the shin she'd rammed her boot into. Quick as a cat, she wriggled free and darted around him. He grabbed for her, catching her elbow. With an oath, she pulled away, careening into the berth then tumbling to the floor. He watched helplessly as her legs tangled with his and brought him down on top of her.

His first thought was that she was surprisingly soft. He didn't have time for a second thought. He caught her fist a half inch from his jaw and—once again—forced her wrist down. No fool, he caught the other wrist and pinned it before she had time to strike.

"This is becoming something of a habit," he huffed.

"Get off me, you bastard!"

He had to give her credit. She was fighting like a hooked shark. She clawed, bit, kicked, and bucked.

One of her knees came perilously close to his balls, and he'd had enough. He pushed her arms down viciously and rose over her until he was straddling her. "Look at me."

She continued to fight, her black hair flying about her face. He squeezed his knees into her side and pushed her arms down again. "Look at me, little hellion!"

She stiffened in midflail and glared at him. He could see the hate in her eyes—deep hatred, something that went much farther back than anything he'd done in the past few moments.

"Calm down."

"Get. Off. Me."

"I will. If you calm down."

She clenched her jaw. "I'll calm down if you get off me."

"*Mon Dieu*, but you are impossible."

"This is only the beginning."

He shook his head. "Don't tempt me, *ma belle*. I like a challenge as much as you do."

"What challenge? If you want to kill me, then do it. I'd rather die than bear your touch a moment longer."

He raised a brow. It was the first time a woman had ever said such to him, and it was a bit disheartening. "I think I could persuade you otherwise."

She rolled her eyes. "I'm swooning with passion. Go ahead and try to rape me. You'll regret it."

Now he was truly offended. Rape her? Who the hell did she think he was? "I'm insulted, *chérie*. I have no intention of raping you."

She glanced down at the juncture where their bodies met, and he had the sudden realization that he was hard. He shrugged. "You're an attractive woman. I can't control that."

"Get *off* me, pirate!"

But now he was aware of his reaction—and really his attraction to her had been simmering for some time—he had the urge to test it. What would it feel like to kiss her? To tame that defiant mouth and make it bend to his will? He leaned closer.

"No!" She turned her head to the side. "Get off!"

"One kiss. If you don't like it, I'll release you."

"Release me?" She sounded too hopeful.

"To begin your duties as cabin girl."

She sighed and rolled her eyes. "You might as well let go now."

"Wait." He trailed a finger over the palm of one of the hands he held captive. "If you *do* like it—"

"I won't."

"*If* you do, then you follow my orders without further argument."

She stared directly at him, those green eyes intent. "Fine."

He blinked. "Fine?" Her quick compliance made him uneasy.

"Yes, fine. Hurry up and kiss me."

"Hurry up…" He shook his head. "*Ma belle*, I do not kiss that way. A kiss should be soft and slow and—"

"Are you going to talk, pirate, or kiss?"

He laughed in spite of himself. She was constantly surprising him. In answer to her question, he bent and brushed his lips over hers.

"No, not impressed." She shook her head. "You may release me now."

He frowned at her. "That wasn't the kiss."

"Your lips touched mine. That was it."

"No." He leaned down, but she turned her head away.

"The agreement was one kiss. This is two."

"*Merde*, but you are exasperating."

"I resent—"

He closed his mouth over hers, effectively silencing her. Her lips were tense in protest, but he forced them open. He was tired of her games, tired of the push and pull. He would show her who was in control. This would not be a soft, slow kiss, but one that demanded her submission. Her lips finally parted, and he dipped his tongue inside her mouth, twining it with hers, overwhelming her resistance.

She tasted surprisingly sweet. If her hair had smelled like cherries, her mouth was more of the same. Ripe. Dark. And a little tart. No surprise, as she had spirit, what the English called pluck. It maddened and drew him. Even now, as she fought his kiss, he alternately wanted to tame and free her.

But taming won. His body thrummed as his lips slanted over hers again and again, kissing her deeply and without mercy. Finally, he felt her give. The tension drained out of the wrists he was holding until they went slack in his grip. Her mouth yielded to his, her lips becoming full and lush under his. But when her tongue joined with his, he almost jumped away.

A zing of pleasure raced through him, the strength of which caught him off guard. He tightened the reins of his control, reminding himself that *he* was taming *her*. But then she let out a soft sigh, arched, her hips against him, and stroked his tongue expertly. Suddenly, he couldn't get enough. His blood was drumming in his ears, and his body felt tight as a sail in a storm.

He released her wrists and fisted his hands in her hair. It was thick and luxurious. He used it to tilt her head upward to give him better access. He wanted to explore her mouth fully, explore *her* fully. If he could just pull away from her mouth long enough, he could have her naked and under him on the berth. If he could…

Three hard raps on the cabin door echoed through the room, and Bastien jerked away from the girl like a man struck by lightning.

"Cap'n, come to let you know the cargo is loaded. We ready to sail."

Cargo? It took a moment for his mind to clear, a moment before he recognized Ridley's voice and made sense of the words.

"Cap'n?"

He made the mistake of looking down, saw the cabin girl beneath him. Her mouth was red and swollen, her cheeks flushed, but her eyes still flashed that same hatred. What the hell had just happened?

There was another rap at the door, and Bastien jumped up. "I'm coming, Mr. Ridley." He strode to the door, took a moment to right his clothing and sweep his loosened hair back out of his face. He put a hand on the knob and, without turning toward her, murmured, "You might want to get up off the floor."

He opened the door and nodded at Ridley. "Good work. Ready the ship to sail. I'll be on deck in a moment to supervise the last preparations."

"Yes, Cap'n." To his credit, Ridley's eyes never

left Bastien's face, apparently seeing nothing. And still, Bastien had the feeling Ridley saw everything.

Bastien closed the door and turned back to the cabin girl. She was standing on the far side of the room, looking cool and composed. "I'd say I won that wager," he drawled.

"You *would* think so."

He opened his mouth to retort and shut it again. He didn't have time to exchange verbal ripostes with her. Not to mention he couldn't seem to focus. She had done something to him with that kiss. Bewitched him somehow. Between the first touch of their lips and that last fervent joining, the kiss had become less about her emptying his chamber pot and more about taking her to bed.

But he was still the captain of this vessel, and she was under his command. She would do his bidding.

"Empty the chamber pot," he commanded. She raised a brow, and he added, "And tidy the cabin." Nothing save the candlestick she meant to use to dash his brains in was out of place, but he felt more orders were needed. "We'll speak again when I return."

And he strode from the cabin, stopping outside the door to lock it securely. On his way to the main deck, he rubbed his face several times, trying to clear the lingering haze. He had no idea what the hell had happened. One moment he was in control; the next he was little more than a bumbling youth who couldn't wait to get his breeches off.

He strode on the main deck of *Shadow* and felt instantly better. This was his ship, his place. Even though the ship rolled with the motion of the water, he stood on solid ground again. The girl had definitely bewitched him, but his senses were rapidly returning.

Ridley approached him, nodded. "Everything to your satisfaction, Cap'n?"

He nodded. He hadn't inspected so much as a thumb knot, but he had faith in his crew. "Won't be long before the tide goes out. Lower the boats."

"Yes, Cap'n. If you got a moment, Mr. Maine been wanting to speak wit you."

Bastien raised his eyebrows then nodded.

"He in the wardroom."

"Thank you." Bastien turned and strode across the deck, taking a ladderway to the lower deck. When he reached the wardroom, he saw the door was ajar. Maine stood with a lean, black-haired youth. Bastien recognized the boy as one of his crew, but he couldn't recall the lad's name at the moment. He and Maine were speaking earnestly, but their conversation ceased as soon as Bastien entered.

"Captain, you know Jack Smith. He's one of the deckhands."

"Of course."

The boy had a nervous look on his face, and Maine knew as well as Bastien that having the captain know who he was would put Jack at ease.

"Jack has some interesting news to share."

Bastien nodded and crossed his arms over his chest. "I'm listening."

"I–it's about the girl, Captain. The one you brought on board." Bastien noted Jack had an English accent, lower class. Perhaps he'd known the hellion in England? Except that now that he thought about it, the hellion had a refined accent. He was no expert on English accents, but he knew her speech was educated. Why hadn't he considered that important until now?

"I know that girl, Captain. She's trouble."

Bastien smiled. "You don't have to tell me."

"No, sir. I mean, she could get *us* into trouble. Her father…" He swallowed, tried again. "Her father is Admiral Russell with His Majesty's Navy."

Bastien felt as though a mast had fallen on his head. He blinked slowly.

The boy must have seen something in his eyes, because he took a step back. "I used to be in the navy, Captain. Before I deserted." He glanced at Maine as though wondering if this admission would cause him trouble. But Bastien couldn't have cared less about his crew's former lives. Hell, half of his men had probably deserted some navy or other.

Maine put a hand on the boy's shoulder. "Go on."

"I wasn't part of Admiral Russell's crew, but I seen him from time to time. And I seen his daughter with him. She sails with him, Captain, and it's a bit of a scandal."

Bastien nodded but still did not trust himself to speak.

"Her name is Raeven, Captain, like the bird. Raeven Russell, and she was engaged to Captain Timothy Bowers."

Bastien waited for the lad to continue, but he seemed to think this explanation sufficient.

"What the hell does Captain Bowers have to do with me?" Bastien looked at Maine. "And why the hell is Admiral Russell's daughter seeking me out and challenging me to a duel in a Brest tavern?"

The lad's eyes were huge now. "I heard she has a bit of a temper."

Bastien laughed. "That's an understatement, but it doesn't answer my question."

"It's Captain Bowers," Maine said, "her fiancé. He was captain of the HMS *Valor*."

Like lines on a map, everything took shape as soon as he was oriented. "The HMS *Valor*."

"Yes, sir."

"The ship we… had a run-in with last spring." The *Valor* had come after them and gone away the worse for it. But as the *Shadow* hadn't sunk the 32-gun frigate, Bastien didn't consider the incident much more than a skirmish.

Maine nodded.

"And am I to assume that Bowers was wounded in the fighting?"

"Killed."

Bastien already knew this, but he wanted it confirmed. So the little hellion, Raeven Russell, wanted revenge for the death of her fiancé. He could hardly blame her. Bowers had not died a hero. The British captain had chosen the wrong ship to trifle with and had, after a series of clumsy maneuvers, almost lost his own vessel. Bowers's error, as Bastien recalled, was engaging the *Shadow* in stormy weather. The *Shadow*'s guns were mounted on the upper deck. The *Valor*'s guns graced both the upper and lower decks. In the storm, the seas grew so rough, the *Valor* had been forced to close its gun ports on the lower deck, evening the odds against the *Shadow*.

Bastien remembered the *Shadow* had fired the first

volley, but the *Valor* was far from innocent. If Bastien hadn't fired first, Bowers would have. The *Valor* had pursued him, and everyone knew the British Navy was notorious for attacking ships and pressing their crews into service. The *Valor* hadn't had a full crew—one of the reasons they'd been so easily defeated—and if Bastien hadn't attacked, young Jack would be serving on Bowers's ship now. Bastien himself would be dead.

Bastien's gaze met Maine's. "It appears we have something of a problem. I've just kidnapped the daughter of a British admiral."

"Aye, Captain."

"No matter that she attacked me. I didn't go looking for her. And she never identified herself."

"It's a dilemma, Captain."

"And we sail in… what? An hour? Less?"

Maine gave a curt nod.

"*Merde.*"

"Aye, Captain."

Bastien raked a hand through his hair, swore again, and flung open the door. "Mr. Maine, I intend to leave on the tide. How's the wind?" Brest was the best port France had to offer, but it was situated on a lee shore, and the westerly wind could make outward passage difficult.

"It's shifted, Captain."

"Good. Make final preparations to cast off, but wait for my command."

"Aye, Captain."

Bastien stormed out the door and strode quickly back to his cabin. How the hell had this happened? How the hell had he kidnapped an admiral's daughter?

He'd have the whole British Navy after him as soon as the word was out. He'd have to let her go. Turn her loose as quickly as possible. But he couldn't exactly set her on the quay and leave her to fend for herself. Miss Russell would need an escort back to her ship. Could he hire a cutter that quickly?

He didn't have time for such niceties. The cargo was loaded, and he needed to be on his way. He had his own agenda, and it didn't allow for deviation. Especially not those due to silly girls who fancied themselves avenging their dead lovers.

Merde, but it was like some ridiculous fairy tale. And, somehow, he had ended up playing the villain.

Well, if he was the villain, then he need not have any qualms about Miss Russell. He'd set her ashore and be done with her. As he reached his cabin door, he checked his pocket watch. Still forty minutes or so until the tide would come in.

He replaced the watch, took out his key, and unlocked his cabin. He pushed the door open, prepared for anything except an empty room. "What the…" He spent five minutes searching the tiny cabin only to conclude it was, as he'd first noted, empty.

"Maine!" he called. "Maine!

When a deckhand came running, Bastien waved his hand and roared, "Get me Mr. Maine."

"Yes, Captain."

While he waited, Bastien stood with hands on his hips. How the hell had she done it? How he she gotten out? If someone had assisted her…

But he knew no one on his crew would dare speak to the girl, much less help her escape. Still, he would have Maine organize a search of every inch of the ship, question every crew member.

His gaze caught on the white bowl on his bed. His chamber pot, which, for all his insistence she empty had been, ironically, already empty. But he did not usually keep it on his berth.

He strode to it, glanced down. Inside was a slip of paper from his desk. In small, feminine handwriting she'd scrawled: *I am afraid you shall be obliged to empty your own chamber pot, pirate. But take heart. You shall not live so long that the task becomes tedious. The next time we meet, I will have my revenge.*

Bastien crumpled the paper and threw it against the wall.

Three

HE WAS GOING TO BE SORRY HE'D TRIED TO MAKE HER empty his chamber pot. He was going to be sorry for quite a few things, the least of which was that abominable kiss he'd forced on her. Raeven swiped at her mouth, but she could still taste him. Could still feel his lips there. She'd kissed him back, but only because she'd realized that was the way to beat him. And it had been working. He'd been distracted and had even released her hands. A moment more and she could have kneed him between the legs, incapacitated him, then slit his throat.

And she would have done it too.

She *could* have done it. For Timothy.

She clenched her hands. It was ridiculous to feel any qualms about killing the pirate. After all, had he paused even a moment before murdering Timothy? Most decidedly not.

But then again, he didn't know Timothy. He'd ordered his cannons to fire, and Timothy had died after one of the explosions. It hadn't been a personal thing, like between her and the pirate. Now she'd stood eye to eye with the man. She'd liked the idea of killing him more before she'd been so… intimately acquainted with him.

She took the much-discussed chamber pot, opened the lid, and noted it was empty. Too bad. She would have emptied it on his berth. She set it there anyway and went to the pirate's desk. He had paper and quill, which meant he was literate, and that shouldn't have surprised her.

But he did surprise her. She looked about his cabin and had to admit she was impressed. She'd seen many great cabins, and while this one was small, it was well appointed. The furniture was mahogany and polished until it gleamed. The berth was large and adorned with a plush coverlet. The desk was solid and practical, but the legs had a decorative arch, and the feet were fashioned as lion's paws. The wardrobe was tall and stately, and his trunk looked as though it were new.

On the floor, on top of the gleaming wood, was a thick Turkey rug in blues and greens, the green of which matched the coverlet on the berth. On the walls hung pictures of landscapes and countrysides. She was no judge of art, but she thought they were well done.

The entire cabin was quietly tasteful and surprisingly neat and tidy. The man did not need a cabin boy.

It seemed everything about the man was different from what she had imagined. He wasn't ugly or stupid. Loathe as she was to admit it, he was actually quite handsome and intelligent.

And, if she was honest—and she was always honest with herself—Raeven had to admit he'd mastered the art of kissing. She had not enjoyed the kiss, but if she hadn't hated him so much, she might have.

As it was, she could only lie there and think of poor Timothy and what he would have said had he seen her in such an embrace with a man who was not only a pirate but his murderer.

She wouldn't think of that. Instead, she put quill to paper and scrawled out a note to the murdering pirate bastard. Satisfied, she placed it delicately in his chamber pot and tugged a hairpin from the nest of curls around her shoulders. She didn't have to imagine that she looked a fright. Cutlass had a mirror nailed to the wall next to the large wardrobe she supposed housed his expensive clothing. She'd caught a glimpse of her reflection earlier and had no desire to look again. She looked like a banshee.

She twisted the hairpin and knelt in front of the cabin door. With a smile, she saw the keyhole was similar to those on the *Regal*. She was in luck—not that she needed it. She could pick any lock, a talent she had learned at age thirteen from a young pickpocket her father pressed into service. She'd had six years to practice the skill. Mostly she picked locks for fun, but found it a useful skill when her father ordered her locked in her cabin and she would rather be enjoying a sunny day, high in the rigging.

She went to work quickly now, unsure how much time she had before Cutlass returned. The *Shadow* was most likely sailing with the tide, and that would be out soon. She had no desire to be stranded on a ship with a band of rogues. She had to be off the pirate ship before it sailed, or the only way back to the *Regal* was a long swim, and the sharks would get her if the currents didn't.

She heard a snick as the lock gave way, and she twisted the hairpin again, ever so gently, until the door popped open. She stood, dusted off her hands, and pocketed the hairpin. She eased the cabin door open and peered into the companionway. A sailor was disappearing up a ladderway; but for him, the companionway was empty. Raeven could not have picked better timing. The crew would be busy on deck, making the final preparations. No one would notice one small boy—she tucked her hair in her collar—shimmying across a dock line. If only she had her dagger, she could cut a piece of rope, knot it, and make her escape where she chose. As it was, her best bet was the anchor cable.

She skulked up the stairs and onto the deck, ducking behind a gun carriage then peering out to survey the deck. It swarmed with activity. Men were aloft preparing the sails; others lowered the ship's boats or stowed provisions. The pirate crew looked unexpectedly efficient and orderly. Still, it was a pirate crew. She wished she had her sword. Her thigh felt naked without the familiar weight against it. But whatever Cutlass had done with the sword, he had been smart enough not to leave it in his cabin. She had no choice but to depart without it.

Yet another reason to detest the man.

She scurried forward along the deck, glancing over the side, looking for the lines mooring the ship to the quay. She only wished she could see Cutlass's face when he discovered his cabin was empty.

But she would see him again—soon. And then she'd make him pay both for Timothy's death and the theft of her sword.

She edged along the deck, smiling as she caught sight of the forward dock line made fast to the quay. The crew hadn't cast off yet. Luck was with her tonight, and she had one leg over the side when she glanced over her shoulder and caught a glimpse of the open cargo hold. She paused, leg dangling precariously.

She'd seen the crew loading cargo when she was brought on board, but she had been too busy cursing the men dragging her up the gangplank to note it. It was probably only foodstuffs and rum. Perhaps powder and solid shot. But then why hadn't the *Shadow* anchored in the harbor and had the provisions delivered via cutter?

Because the cargo was too heavy or too difficult to load from a cutter. Cutlass had needed the dock cranes to load it. And that meant it was more than salt pork and ship's biscuit.

She pulled her leg back over the rail then hesitated. Was it worth risking capture again to investigate this cargo?

Probably not.

On the other hand, if she discovered something of use to her father or the navy, then her little excursion might be more easily forgiven. And at this point, she had little hope her absence from the *Regal* had not been noted. She might need an extra measure of forgiveness.

She took another quick glance about the ship to be certain she hadn't been spotted then ducked down and dashed toward the cargo hold. Several crates were stacked on deck, still waiting placement, and Raeven stooped behind these. Cautiously, she lifted her head and peered over the crates and into the hold. The men working there had lanterns, but the light was far too weak for her to ascertain the nature of the cargo.

Devil take it! She had risked capture for nothing. Now she would…

She stared at the crate right in front of her. Nondescript and unlabeled, it could be anything. Peering about the deck, she saw a mallet one of the deckhands had set aside. She had to venture out from her hiding place to snatch it, and she did so quickly, dropping back just as two sailors walked past. One was the man Cutlass called Maine. He was shouting orders, telling the crew to finish securing the hold and prepare to cast off. That meant the mallet and these crates would have to be stowed soon. She had better hurry.

She'd opened a fair number of crates in her time, and she made quick work of this one. Some men found her skill with men's tools and her less-than-soft, pretty hands unattractive, but Timothy had only laughed when she did something women were not supposed to. He would laugh now if he could see her hiding on the deck of a pirate ship and hoisting open a crate of… medicine.

She studied the little vials, packed securely in straw. Pulling one out, she noted it was morphine. Another, laudanum.

She sat back on her haunches and considered. Of course a pirate ship had as much need of medicines as any other vessel. But usually the ship's doctor took charge of it. She moved that crate aside and opened another. More vials.

These two crates alone were worth several hundred pounds, and she counted seven more of the same size yet to be stowed in the hold. Beyond that were the larger crates the sailors were handing down into the hold. She did not think they were medicine vials. Weapons and ammunition? But how many weapons did a pirate ship need?

"Is that the last of the rifles?" one of the sailors loading the cargo asked another.

"Should be. Then we just have those." He gestured to the crates sheltering Raeven, and she tried to squeeze herself into a shadow. It didn't surprise her that her guess had been correct. She'd seen too many boxes and crates of rifles, bayonets, swords…

They were the trappings of war. And that begged the question: was Cutlass going to war?

She shook her head, knowing she needed to shimmy along that dock line before it was cast off but unable to stop staring at the *Shadow's* cargo hold.

Its too-full cargo hold.

Perhaps Cutlass wasn't going to war. But Cutlass sailed for Spain, at least under its letters of marque. Had he acquired this cargo for Spain? Why? Spain had signed the Treaty of Amien, just as Britain had. But perhaps Spain did not intend to honor that treaty. Perhaps while it made gestures of peace with one hand, with the other it gathered the weapons of war, supplied by its privateers, of course.

Could Spain be looking to attack Great Britain? The treaty returned Minorca to the Spanish, but Britain kept Trinidad.

She fisted her hands, fresh anger at Cutlass churning

through her. The sailors finished loading the last of the
rifles, and she knew she had to move. As much as she
wanted to punish Cutlass, it would have to wait.

With a last look around, she crept back to the deck
rail. She hoisted one leg over, grasping the dock line
with one hand. Perhaps she could...

"Maine!" she heard Cutlass's voice cut above the
din of the sailors working. "Maine!"

Devil take it! She released the dock line and ducked
down again.

The thump of boots shook the deck as men
scrambled to get out of Cutlass's way.

"He's on the fo'c'sle, Captain," one sailor offered.

"Go get him," Cutlass ordered, and more boots
thumped. "And search the ship. I've lost my cabin girl."

Raeven ground her teeth to keep from spewing
venom at him. She was *not* his cabin girl. Not
his anything.

But she was out of time. She peered over the rail
again, saw the dock line and, beneath it, the long drop
to the water. But she'd been raised on a ship and was
a veritable monkey. She easily latched onto the line
with both hands, her feet swinging up to wrap around
the rope. She made her way across the line toward the
quay, hand over fist, looking behind her several times
to judge the distance to the bollard.

Finally, she dropped her feet into the water beside
the quay and, transferring her grip from the dock line
to the dock, she swung her legs onto it. But she must
have been more fatigued than she realized, because
she misjudged the distance and smashed her knee.
With a curse, she crawled onto the quay and rolled

into a ball, closing her eyes against the scream of pain in her knee.

Finally, she groaned and stared up at the *Shadow*. The next time she saw the vessel, she vowed it would be in pieces.

Cautiously, she rose to her knees. She was bruised but not badly injured. She was relatively certain her knee would be sore for a week, and her gloveless hands were raw and bleeding. But nothing was broken. She limped away from the ship, heading for the cutters ferrying sailors to and from the ships in the harbor.

She couldn't wait to tell her father what she'd seen on the *Shadow*. Now he'd have a reason to pursue and destroy the pirate ship. Despite her throbbing knee, her battered hands, and a dull headache, she smiled.

∼

"I don't care if the rogue planned to assassinate the King!" Admiral Russell boomed, hands cutting the air in front of Raeven. "I don't care if the blackguard plotted to kidnap the Regent—though we might all be better off if he did," he muttered. "It's no excuse for your reckless behavior. Your behavior is impulsive, undisciplined, unrestrained, un…" He gestured violently, face red, too angry to form the words.

Raeven pursed her lips and waited. "Unacceptable?" she ventured.

"Damn it, girl!" He slammed a fist down on the cherrywood desk in his cabin, sending a sextant crashing to the floor and several maps flying into the air like startled seagulls. From behind the admiral, Percy gave her a pained look. She knew what he was thinking: why did she try to help? Why didn't she keep her mouth shut? There was no reasoning with her father when he was in this state. In her opinion, there was never any reasoning with him.

It had taken her three hours to return to the *Regal*, and as she'd feared, in the five or six hours she'd been away, her absence had been noted. From her chair on the opposite side of the desk, she could just see the face of her father's little clock. Devil take it, but he'd been railing for almost thirty minutes.

He shoved his palms down hard on the desk and leaned over until his face was level with hers. "Do you find this tedious, girl? Am I keeping you from another, more pressing engagement?"

"No, but—"

"Good, because you and Mr. Williams will be busy swabbing the decks and emptying the buckets all day."

Percy closed his eyes and shuddered. It wasn't the first time her actions had caused him grief. But she'd find a way to make it up to him. Just as soon as she had Cutlass.

"Fine, but—"

"Fine? *Fine?*" He was about to speak again, but before he could form the words, he erupted into a storm of hacking coughs. It was three or four minutes before he recovered, and drawing the handkerchief from his purpling face, he wheezed, "You don't feel even a moment's remorse. Do you comprehend the trouble you might have gotten into? The pirate could have raped you, girl! Worse, he could have decided to have you keelhauled or flogged or—" He dissolved into another coughing spell.

"No, he couldn't. He was too eager to be underway," Raeven said, taking advantage of her father's incapacitation.

"Oh, well that's even better! At this moment you could be somewhere in the middle of the Channel with no one but Mr. Williams the wiser. That blackguard could sell you into slavery or take you to—"

"Sir."

But he was still listing all the horrors that might have happened. Horrors of which she was well aware. Horrors she had escaped. Easily escaped, at that.

"Sir... *Father!*"

"What?" He stared at her, arms locked at his sides. "What have you to say for yourself?"

"He's getting away."

Behind her father, Percy closed his eyes and sighed heavily, like a man doomed to the gallows and resigned to his fate. Her father, obviously similarly exasperated, sat heavily in his chair. "Since we're not chasing the rogue, dear daughter, he can't be getting away." He dabbed at his forehead with the handkerchief.

"But that's what I've been trying to tell you." Now she stood and braced her hands on his desk. "We *should* be chasing him. He has arms and medicines for Spain to use against us."

"That may be."

"*May* be? I'm telling you what I saw with my own two eyes!"

"And it's valuable intelligence. I will grant you that, though the manner in which it was obtained is completely un—"

"—acceptable. Yes, I know. I know." She pressed

her fingers lightly over her eyes. It was almost dawn, and she was exhausted. Her headache had developed into a full-blown military tattoo. She was tired of talking, tired of arguing. She wanted something to eat, a glass of wine, and her warm berth, and she knew she was unlikely to have any of them for some time. Worst of all, Cutlass was getting away. She could feel the distance between them growing, and the farther he ventured, the more tense she became. She felt like a ship straining against its anchor. She had waited six months for the opportunity to challenge him as she had last night. Now it might be years before their paths crossed again. If she didn't avenge Timothy's death, no one would.

Something of her thoughts must have shown on her face, because her father sighed loudly. A gruff, bold man who had served on a ship since the age of eight, George Russell was uncomfortable with the emotional proclivities of women. Raeven was well aware he'd been surrounded by men for as long as he could remember. From what she could determine, he'd loved his wife but hadn't minded the long voyages away, either. And then she'd died in childbirth, and it had been Raeven and the admiral for as long as she could remember.

Raeven wasn't the kind of woman given to tears or fainting spells. If she had been, she would never have made it ten minutes on a ship, much less the last fifteen years. Still, she could feel the tears—tears of exhaustion and frustration, not weakness—pricking behind her eyes. She would rather die than allow them to fall. So she swallowed and looked her father directly in the face. "I saw medicines, sir. Crates of them. I saw crates of what the crew identified as rifles. There may have been other arms, as well. It was dark, and I didn't have the time or opportunity to explore the cargo hold."

"You damn well shouldn't have been on the vessel in the first place. If I ever get my hands on that Cutlass—"

"That's precisely what I'd like to give you the opportunity to do, sir. I can't prove the medicines and arms were meant for Spain, but he sails under their letters of marque. Perhaps the Spanish and the French are forming an alliance and will soon attack Britain. It's worth investigating, if nothing else."

"I agree."

Raeven's heart leapt.

"And I shall report it to the Secretary as soon as we return, but we are not going to chase after this pirate. We have our orders, which are to escort merchant ships across the Channel. We have a duty to keep their crews and cargo safe, and I will not disregard my orders."

Her stomach tightened, and she could feel the ball of icy despair lodged there growing. It had been wedged in her belly since Timothy's death but had shrunk when she knew she'd have the opportunity to challenge Cutlass. Now it was growing again. The tears stung her eyes, but she gave a curt nod and kept her voice level. "Yes, sir. I understand. If you'll give me leave, I'll start on the decks right away. No need to punish, Mr. Williams, Admiral. He's not to blame for my foolish actions."

"You have my leave, and Mr. Williams *will* assist you."

She nodded and started for the door. Percy was

through it and waiting in the companionway for her, but her father's voice caught her before she reached him. "I know Bowers's death is painful, Raeven."

She didn't turn to face him, too afraid the tears would break loose if she saw any hint of sympathy on his ruddy, lined face.

"It will be painful for some time. But we're not vigilantes. We are His Majesty's Royal Navy, and we will do our duty. Now, go get a few hours of sleep before your punishment."

She turned abruptly. "With your permission, sir, I'd like to begin now."

"No, you need your rest and..." He frowned and shook his head. "Never mind. Permission granted. I can see you need to do something to keep your mind—and hands—occupied."

She glanced down and saw that her hands were twisting the tails of her shirt. The materials was stretched and wrinkled where she'd worried it. She released it and put her hands at her sides. "Thank you, sir."

A few moments later they were on deck, watching a glorious morning unfold. Raeven supposed she had been out and about this morning when the sun rose, but she hadn't even noted it. She paused to take in the harbor. From this vantage point, she couldn't see the place where the *Shadow* had been docked, but she knew it would be empty. Cutlass was gone.

"I'm sorry you have to swab the decks," she told Percy. He was standing beside her, looking every bit the officer he was in his crisp wool navy coat and stark white breeches.

He sighed. "What were you thinking, Raeven?

You told me you only wanted to see the man. I should have known better. You might have gotten yourself killed."

She put both hands on the ship's rail and stared out and over the water. She never tired of seeing it lapping on the ship's hull, never tired of the smell or the sound. "I might have."

He made a sound of disgust, but she didn't turn from the view of the water. "And then what would your father have done? It would have broken his heart."

As mine is broken, she thought and clenched the rails more tightly.

"Do you think putting yourself in danger would have made Tim happy?"

She looked up at Percy now.

"Tim was my friend too, or have you forgotten? And he would have wanted me to look out for you. He would have wanted you to live a long life, not die at the hands of some pirate in a tavern brawl."

He was right. She knew Percy was right.

"I'm going to get started on the decks." He turned to go, and she reached out and grasped his sleeve.

"I'm sorry, Percy."

He shook her hand off. "You always are. Do you ever think of anyone besides yourself?"

His rejoinder stung, but she couldn't argue with it. She didn't think of others. Not anymore. Maybe she never had.

No, that wasn't true. She had thought of Timothy often enough. She would have done anything for him. She had done.

Her hands were aching from her white-knuckled

grip on the rail, so she let it go, tried to allow some of her anger and hurt to go as well. But like the mist on the harbor, it clung and permeated. She wished she could let Timothy go so easily. It had been six months since his death. Why could she not put it behind her?

Because she had loved him more than herself, more than life, more than… well, not more than the sea. But then he had probably not loved her more than the sea or his ship, either. And that was just one reason they had been so perfect for one another. They understood one another. He understood her the way no man ever had. Rather, the way no man had ever tried.

She knew she was pretty. Some had even called her beautiful, and so there had been men trying to understand her for quite a few years now. When she'd been a few years younger than her now wise nineteen, she had sometimes mistaken their lust for genuine love. But something would always happen—she would swear or best them at swordplay or don breeches and scamper up the rigging like a monkey. Then their true feelings were revealed.

What kind of woman was she? Women didn't drink rum or chart a ship's course or know how to prime and fire a cannon.

But Timothy had appreciated her talents. He didn't think women were to be seen and not heard. He didn't think she should wear dresses all the time, though he complimented her when she did. At twenty-six, he was one of the youngest captains in the navy; and no son of fortune, he had worked his way up through the ranks. Her own father, though born into a well-off family, had also worked his way up through the ranks. He'd refused to buy a commission and was proud of what he'd accomplished on his own. He'd drilled that work ethic into Raeven, and it was one of the qualities that drew her to the young, handsome Captain Bowers.

If pressed, she might also admit she was drawn to Timothy's recklessness. He was brave and daring, which was one of the reasons he'd been given command of the fifth-rate ship-of-the-line. Timothy had wanted to advance quickly, and the glamorous frigates offered the best opportunities for engaging enemy ships, acquiring prize money from their capture, and all-out glory. But duties assigned a frigate captain could be mundane, as well—convoy duty, reconnaissance, and ferrying her father's orders to the fleet.

Timothy, of course, preferred the action and would, more often than not, seek it.

With a sigh, she leaned her elbows on the oak rail and stared into the water rippling against the ship. She thought she must be a disappointment to her father. How could she be otherwise?

He'd wanted a son. He might never have said so, but what man didn't want a son? And instead he had been saddled with an unruly daughter. Timothy might have been his son, had she married him. She might have been able to give him grandsons. Now she couldn't imagine what the future held for her.

Nothing. No one.

With a shake, she straightened from the rail and rolled her shoulders back. She wasn't usually prone to maudlin moods, and she certainly wasn't about to mope around the ship like a lovelorn puppy. The crew would tease her unmercifully.

No. She notched her chin up. She would do her duty, just as her father and the rest of the crew would do theirs. And when the next opportunity arose to punish Cutlass—and she had no doubt that it would—she would make sure the murdering, thieving pirate got what he deserved.

Four

Gibraltar, six months later

BASTIEN SURVEYED THE PASHA'S BALLROOM, TAKING care to appear to do so leisurely. He held a smoking cigar in one hand, a glass of champagne in the other. The white marble gleamed coldly in the candlelight, but the silk draping falling in waves from ceiling to floor and the jewel toned velvet pillows scattered about on low benches created an air of sumptuousness. He sipped his champagne again. It was fine champagne. As any good sailor, he preferred rum, but he would take champagne if it were offered.

And Kemal Muhammed Mustafa, the local pasha, was offering. Cigars, champagne, a rich meal of delicacies, if the trays Bastien had seen servants carrying toward the ballroom earlier were any indication. There were perhaps fifty men and women in attendance tonight. The majority hailed from Britain, as the pasha was smart enough to court their good graces. The others were locals, most of Arabic descent.

There were several other privateers making an

appearance. Two Americans and a Moroccan. They studied Bastien as closely as he studied them. The pasha had yet to explain why he'd invited them, but Bastien had no doubt the man wanted some favor or other. Probably to run the American blockade of Tripoli or some other errand for Yusef Karamanli, Tripoli's pasha and Kemal's superior. Bastien would have been happy to oblige, if he were not otherwise employed.

And that was the reason he'd agreed to attend. The little information he garnered in Spain and then Greece indicated Jourdain was in Gibraltar. And so Bastien was in Gibraltar and had been for a fortnight. Unfortunately, despite the money he'd spent paying local boys to find Jourdain's whereabouts, he'd come up empty-handed. This ball was his last hope. The cargo he'd delivered in Almeria fetched him enough to outfit the *Shadow* as he'd hoped. He had cannon, powder, and cartridges aplenty. He had foodstuff, medicines, cutlasses, and rifles spilling out of the holds.

He had everything he needed to sink *La Sirena,* except the ship and its captain.

And he was running out of time. He'd spent the past three months searching for Jourdain, and he was well aware his crew tolerated the diversion only because of their deep respect for him. But he couldn't expect them to sit twiddling their thumbs indefinitely. Not when there were blockades to run and profitable cargoes to sell. His band of—oh, hell, he might as well call them what they were—pirates had limited amounts of patience and unlimited greed.

But they possessed loyalty, and that was what he was riding on these past few weeks.

He saw his quartermaster approaching and finished his champagne. "Well?"

"I've been through the entire ballroom and inspected each and every guest, sir," the Englishman said with his usual matter-of-factness. "He's not here. Yet." The last sounded like an afterthought. It was late, and obviously Maine didn't think Jourdain was coming.

"Let's give him another quarter hour." Bastien offered Maine a cigar he'd pocketed for later.

"Yes, Captain." Maine took the cigar and put it in his coat. A man of few, if any, vices, he would probably sell it to a crewmember later.

"Bastien."

"Sir?"

"We're not onboard. Call me Bastien."

Maine gave him a perplexed look and scanned the room again. A waiter passed with a tray of champagne, and Bastien took another glass and one for Maine. "Here. Drink this."

The quartermaster glanced at it as though it were poison. Bastien sighed. "Alan, how long have we known one another?"

"Four years, six months, and..."

Bastien waved a hand. "Close enough. My point is we've known one another long enough to be friends. And friends can enjoy a glass of champagne and"—he reached into the man's coat—"a cigar together."

"Yes, sir—Bastien."

Bastien sighed.

"It's just that I'm on duty. It doesn't feel right."

"Then I relieve you of duty for the next ten minutes. This isn't the British Navy, *mon ami*."

"Old habits die hard, I suppose."

They drank and smoked in silence for a moment, watching the room as the last of the polished and plumed guests arrived. The range of colors and the dress reflected the diverse guest list. The Brits wore their silks and satins, their cravats and waistcoats. The locals wore the loose-fitting robes common to the region. Good Muslims, they left their wives and concubines at home. The other privateers dressed as gentlemen, as did Bastien. His coat was of the finest wool, his shirt the best linen, his leather boots highly polished. He'd forgone the formality and stuffiness of a cravat, but he thought the spill of lace at his throat and wrists worked to good effect. He wanted to look wealthy without pretension. And perhaps he wanted to look a little bit dangerous. He'd worn his sword—his dress sword, of course—and his pistol was tucked under his coat. If they did meet Jourdain, he'd be ready.

He listened idly as the pasha made a welcoming speech. Dinner would be served at ten. Bastien checked his pocket watch. It was half past nine, and he would not be staying.

"Are you ready?" he asked his quartermaster, though he knew the man had probably been ready twenty minutes ago.

"We're leaving? You haven't spoken to the pasha."

And he wouldn't. Not tonight. "I hadn't intended to, but perhaps I will call on him tomorrow. After all, if his endeavor is lucrative, we might take him up on it."

Maine raised his eyebrows. "But we haven't found Jourdain."

Bastien shrugged, as though the failure meant nothing to him. "Peering into cobwebbed shadows and chasing every stray rumor won't make our fortune. And"—he held up a hand when his quartermaster would have objected—"the crew has been more than patient. Tomorrow we embark on more profitable ventures. I'll want to speak with the crew at..." He trailed off, his gaze caught by a flash of emerald. The gown was in perfect harmony with the pasha's jeweled theme, and the woman wearing it the loveliest creature in the room. But that wasn't a fair description in a room of less than fifteen ladies, most of whom were well past childrearing age. This woman would stand out in any room, and several other men turned their heads appreciatively as she entered.

"Oh." Maine wheezed out the sound, and Bastien glanced at him, surprised. Alan had told him once that he was married, and Bastien had never known the quartermaster to show interest in other women. But now he was staring.

"She's pretty," Bastien said.

"She's more than that, sir."

With a frown, Bastien glanced back. She was moving through the crowd now, her dress rippling like a lagoon. "She looks... familiar."

"Yes, sir. You're acquainted."

And as he watched, someone near her made a remark that had her green eyes flashing, and Bastien groaned. Why here? Why now?

It was his cabin girl. How had he not recognized her immediately? He hadn't forgotten her. On the contrary, he thought of her daily. He'd hung her delicate yet deadly sharp sword on his cabin wall: a reminder that appearances could be deceptive. But he hadn't thought to ever see her again.

In particular, he hadn't thought to see her looking so… feminine. So… glorious.

It wasn't just the lavish gown she wore, though the emerald green silk matched her eyes perfectly. *She* was glorious. The kind of woman who turned every man's head. And she had—she *was*, he corrected as he watched her move through the room.

Her dark hair was swept up in what looked like a careless mass of curls. Long tendrils had escaped their moorings to caress a neck and shoulders of exposed honey-colored flesh. Her face was that same honey color with just a little blush about the high cheekbones. Her mouth was full and lush, something he did not remember from before. But perhaps that was because right now she was relaxed and smiling whereas before… well, she had not smiled that he could remember. She still had the snub nose and the sharp chin, but it didn't look quite as sharp when she wasn't jerking it at him. And then, of course, there were those amazing eyes. Impossibly green, impossibly expressive.

Now that she wasn't dressed as a boy, he could admire her other features as well. She was petite but voluptuous. The dress showed her rounded shoulders, her creamy skin, and the soft, half moons of her breasts. It didn't taper to her natural waist, as the style currently favored higher waists, but he imagined her waist was trim and flared nicely to accent shapely hips.

He already knew she had a shapely bottom and

lovely legs. Her masculine dress had shown him that much. But how refreshing to see that, in spite of her precision with a sword and her rough language, she was soft and very female.

"Sir, I think it best we leave before she sees us. If I'm not mistaken, that's Admiral Russell with her."

Bastien's gaze focused on the older man at her side. He'd never seen Admiral Russell before, but the man with the salt-and-pepper hair, the ruddy complexion, and the bowlegs had to be he. He looked every bit the British naval officer, even out of uniform as he was now.

"Mr. Maine, I look to you to lead the way." Bastien indicated a side exit with a hand, and Maine started for the door. They were halfway across the room when the pasha and his entourage stepped before them.

"Leaving so soon, Mr. Cutlass?" The pasha's voice was soft and silky, as was the rest of him. He wore European clothing but for the white turban on his head. His small hands were bejeweled with rings on every finger. His skin was the color of café au lait, his eyes a soft, rich brown.

He was small and soft-spoken, but as Bastien knew well, appearances could be deceiving. The man was influential, and he had the ear of the powerful Yusef Karamanli.

Bastien made a sweeping bow. "Ah, you have caught me, my lord. Mr. Maine and I find that we are called back to the *Shadow* unexpectedly."

The pasha gave a silken smile. "But you have not had time to eat, and we have not had the opportunity to speak. Perhaps you can send your man back and join your crew later." There were two burly men dressed in flowing robes behind the pasha, and now they crossed their arms over their massive chests, indicating that the pasha's wishes should be obeyed.

"I'm afraid that won't be possible," Bastien said, spreading his hands apologetically. "This is a matter that requires my personal attention. You understand, my lord."

"Please." The pasha shook his head slightly. "We are old friends, Sébastien. You should call me Kemal."

Bastien smiled. He was neither friends nor enemies with Kemal Muhammed Mustafa, and he intended to keep it that way. "I shall call on you first thing in the morning, Kemal. I can promise you I'm anxious to hear all you have to say."

"I think you might want to hear what I have to say tonight. After all, it concerns a friend of both of ours—a friend for whom I hear you have been searching."

Bastien's pulse kicked, but he kept his expression neutral. "I see. And still, I'm afraid we will have to discuss this friend tomorrow." But a quick glance about the room—a last search for Jourdain, their mutual friend—convinced Bastien he was already too late. Miss Russell was moving toward them and would spot him any moment.

The pasha followed his gaze, and obviously seeing an opportunity to delay Bastien further, spread a welcoming hand toward the Russells. "Admiral and Miss Russell. Allow me to introduce you to Sébastien… Cutlass." He glanced at Bastien with a tolerant smile as he gave the false surname. "Like you, Admiral, the captain shares a love of the sea."

Bastien watched as the Russells' polite smiles turned to ice at the mention of his name. His gaze caught and held Miss Russell's, and he was fascinated by the play of a thousand emotions over her face. He spotted anger, excitement, wariness, and finally worry. The last was punctuated by one of her slim, fair hands catching her father's sleeve and tugging him back.

"What the hell is the meaning of this?" the admiral sputtered. "You're dealing with thieves and rogues now, my lord?" He turned an accusing glare on the pasha, and the man feigned astonishment. But if he was surprised the navy man and the privateer didn't get on, Bastien would cheerfully eat his boot.

"Captain Cutlass is an old friend of mine, Admiral. I assure you he is neither a thief nor a rogue."

"And I can assure you, your lordship, he is both. And to those crimes I add kidnapping and piracy."

Bastien had hoped to avoid this drama, but since doing so now seemed impossible, he put a hand to his heart. "Oh no, sir. You wound me. I am no pirate."

With a roar, the admiral lunged, but his daughter danced before him. "Sir, please! Not here."

Bastien could feel the gazes of all in the room on their little party, but he couldn't take his own from Raeven Russell. Was she actually protecting him? The idea made him laugh. She was probably only saving him for her own homicidal plans.

The admiral was about to object, but before he could speak, he doubled over into a fit of coughing. His daughter bent as well, assisting the older man who fumbled with his handkerchief. But she was not so concerned she didn't have a moment to flash emerald daggers at him with those eyes. Bastien raised a brow, indicating he was hardly responsible for an old man's cough.

"Miss Russell," the pasha began, "might I offer one of my men to assist you and your father? I think a comfortable chair and a glass of brandy might help."

"Yes." She nodded as one of the pasha's burly men came forward, but her attention was on Bastien. "I think you are right."

"Another time then, mademoiselle." Bastien reached out, took her hand, bent, and kissed it. He moved out of the way just in time to avoid her up-thrust knuckles. He chuckled. "I see some things never change."

She gave him a contemptuous shake of her head. "No, they don't."

"Good night, my lord. Admiral. Miss Russell." He bowed to each, turned on his heel, and followed Maine out of the room. The side corridor he'd chosen was stark and cold, gloomy compared to the bright, colorful ballroom. Still, it bore the marks of the pasha's wealth. Turkey rugs lined the marble floors, and gold sconces held stub candles whose dancing light illuminated various objets d'art. But he made it no farther than the first sconce before he heard the shush of slippers behind him.

"Wait just one moment, sir!" a woman's voice called after him.

Miss Russell, of course. He turned and smiled. "*Sir?* I've moved up in your estimation, then."

"Hardly." She stalked down the corridor, the light flickering off her gown. "I want a word with you."

He raised his brows. "Only a word? What, no dagger hidden in the folds of your dress? I was certain you were only out for my blood, *ma belle*."

In the shadowy corridor, he had difficulty seeing her face. Even as she moved closer, he could discern only that her expression was cloaked. "I will have your blood, pirate." Her voice was as hard as the marble surrounding them. "But first I'd like my property back."

"Do I have something of yours?" he drawled.

"My sword." Her voice was ice, her mouth once again thin and tight.

"Ah." He drew out a cigar, stepped toward one of the candles, and lit it. "It's a beautiful piece. Handcrafted?"

Behind him Maine cleared his throat, and Bastien waved at him. "Go ahead, Mr. Maine. I shall see you back aboard shortly."

"Yes, Captain." His boots clicked as he marched away.

Bastien drew on the cigar and faced his cabin girl again. Her eyes were hard emeralds. "I noticed you didn't send him to fetch my sword."

He blew out smoke. "Why would I intentionally arm you again? No, Miss Russell. I think we are all much safer when you are weaponless, though your eyes are shooting flaming arrows at me this moment. You have dangerous eyes."

She shook her head and scowled. "Do statements like that charm other ladies, pirate? They don't charm me."

He shrugged, drew on his cigar again. In fact, statements like that *did* charm other ladies, but he didn't imagine they would work on his cabin girl. In fact, he was glad that they didn't. "I hadn't expected to see you in Gibraltar. Your father's ship isn't usually assigned to these waters."

She smiled. "I see in my absence you've done your research."

"I like to know something about my enemies."

She glanced back over her shoulder, toward the ballroom. He supposed she would have to return to her father, and he actually found himself disappointed their conversation would end. "Are we still enemies?" he asked.

"Oh, most assuredly." She stepped closer, looked him directly in the eye. "I made you a promise, pirate, and I will keep it."

"For what it's worth," he said quietly, "I didn't intend to kill Captain Bowers. It was an unfortunate incident."

She stiffened, and he saw her clench her gloved fists. "An unfortunate incident? Is that what you call assault and murder? I suppose I shouldn't be surprised, knowing you're a pirate."

"Hmm. Privateer. Would it make any difference if I told you Captain Bowers engaged my ship? I didn't go after him."

He could see in her face she hadn't considered that possibility. She opened her mouth, closed it again, and swallowed. "That's not the report I was given."

"And who gave you the report? An impartial observer or one of the men from the *Valor*?"

She notched her sharp chin up. "I have no reason to doubt the report I was given or the man who gave it me."

"And every reason to doubt me." He tossed the butt of the cigar on the floor and dashed the last embers with the toe of his boot.

"Of course! You're a lying, thieving, murdering pirate. You have no sense of honor, of honesty. You—"

"I see you haven't done your research in our absence. You still know nothing about me."

She put her hands on her hips. "Do you have my sword?"

He thought of the object hanging in his cabin.

"Then that makes you a thief. Did you kill Captain Bowers?" She didn't wait for an answer. "Then that makes you a murderer. Do you attack ships on the high seas, confiscate their cargo, and sell it for your own profit? Then that makes you a pirate. Do you deny all of these accusations? That makes you a liar."

"How old are you, Miss Russell?"

She blinked, seemingly taken back by the question. "Why?"

"Because your view of the world is startlingly naïve. It would be charming in a girl of eleven or twelve, but as my sources put you closer to twenty, I think we might safely call it ignorance."

Her jaw dropped, and he could see her reach for her side where her sword was absent.

He nodded at her. "You see, *ma belle*, better if you are unarmed." A movement at the other end of the corridor caught his attention, and he squinted to see through the shadows.

"But I won't be unarmed forever, and when you're least expecting it, I'll be there to slit your—"

"Shh." He grabbed her wrist and pulled her into a shadow.

"What are you doing? Release m—"

He clamped a hand over her mouth, effectively

silencing her. For his pains, he received an elbow jab to the abdomen and a slipper thrust down hard on his foot. But as she stiffened after the impact, he decided she received the worse part of the blow. Soft slippers were not made for warfare. He wrapped his other arm around her middle to keep her arms at her sides and bent close to her ear. "I'm not kidnapping you, mademoiselle. I need you to be silent a moment."

She said something against his hand, which he took as a refusal because she began to writhe and struggle against him anew. The men at the far end of the corridor were drawing closer, and he had no option but to drag her into a nearby alcove. He did so, ignoring her flailing until he had her out of sight. Using his body to anchor her, he peered around the corner.

Bon Dieu! He hadn't been mistaken. It was Juan Victor de los Santos. Jourdain called him El Santo, The Saint. He'd been serving with Jourdain for as long as Bastien had known the man. And where he went, Jourdain could always be found. So his information had been correct! Jourdain was in Gibraltar.

A sharp kick to his shin reminded him he had other concerns at the moment. He ducked back into the alcove. "Be still for one moment." She kicked him again. "*Merde!*" With his arms covering her mouth and holding her wrists still, he had no way to contain her feet other than to press against her. She objected immediately, twisting her face back and forth and attempting to cry for help. The effect was that he quickly became intimately acquainted with her lovely breasts. She must have bound them quite tightly to pass as a lad before.

"Stop moving," he growled, attempting to ignore the warmth the motion of those breasts was beginning to ignite. The last thing he wanted was to be spotted by El Santo. If Jourdain knew Bastien was searching for him, and given the lengths Jourdain had gone to conceal himself, he probably did, Bastien knew the only way to find the Barbary pirate was to follow El Santo undetected.

He risked one last glimpse around the corner and swore again. El Santo had not gone into the ball as Bastien had anticipated. Instead, he was coming this way. In a moment, he would pass Bastien and the struggling Miss Russell. Bastien looked down at the woman, and even in the darkness he could see murder in her eyes. "*Je suis désolé*," he murmured, lowering his mouth to hers.

He kissed her passionlessly, more intent on shielding their identities from El Santo and the men with him. He wanted them to see nothing more than a couple engaged in a romantic rendezvous.

A somewhat tumultuous rendezvous, as his cabin girl was fighting him with everything she had. She was petite, but she was feisty and strong. It took all of his concentration to keep her under control. He might have had a moment to enjoy the kiss—she still tasted of cherries—but she bit his lip, and he had to suppress a bark of pain.

He heard the men passing, heard the remark, spoken in Arabic, about the lovers, and then their boots clicked away. He drew back from his cabin girl, careful to cover her mouth again before she could protest. He peered out from the alcove again and saw

El Santo turn a corner down the hall. Immediately, he released the woman and started after him.

At least he tried. The little hellion stuck out her foot and caught his ankle. He would have sprawled across the floor if he hadn't caught himself. He tossed her an impatient frown. "I don't have time for your games, *chérie*. But if you're good, I promise to play with you again later."

"Bastard. What the hell is going on? What was that about?" She pointed to the alcove where he'd just been embracing her.

He glanced impatiently at the corner down the corridor. "Once again I succumbed to your many charms, mademoiselle. I assure you it will not happen again." He took her hand, kissed it. "Now I must be away."

He started after El Santo, but she was right behind him. *Merde!* But he did not want her following him, and every moment he spent with her meant El Santo was getting farther away. "Isn't your father in some need of assistance?"

Her eyes narrowed. "Oh, so now you want to be rid of me. Is there something you don't want me to see?"

He stopped himself from glancing over his shoulder again, but she must have caught the movement nonetheless.

"What are you looking for? *Who* are you looking for?"

He gritted his teeth and tried to remain calm. He had to get away from her. "Why don't I explain everything tomorrow? I shall call on you and your father in the morning. I'll bring your sword."

Her eyebrows winged up. "You must want to be

rid of me quite badly if you're willing to go to all that trouble."

"No, but…" He could see she didn't believe him. He might as well stop wasting time and tell the truth. "Very well. I spotted someone I have been looking for, someone I need to see very badly. Now if you'll excuse me…" He started down the corridor, but she was right by his side. At this point, he had no choice but to continue with her beside him, else he would lose any chance of finding El Santo again.

"Who is this man?"

He gave her an impatient look and continued walking.

"Oh, perhaps it's a woman."

They were nearing the corner, and Bastien did not know what he would find when he rounded it. "It's no one you need concern yourself with. I assure you."

"Oh, but I want to concern myself, pirate. After all, you did say I needed to do more research."

The smug look on her face devastated the last of his patience. He pushed her up against the wall, disappointed to see the action didn't seem to faze her at all. "This isn't a game, Miss Russell. This is serious. Now go back to your father and your ball."

"And you can continue to treat me like a child," she said, green eyes searing him, "but you're wasting your time, and the man you're seeking is getting away. Now, who are we following?"

A hundred thoughts raced through his mind; most centered on how to be rid of her, if not for good, for a good long time. His hands itched to circle her neck and throttle her. She was like a plague he couldn't seem to be rid of—one who infested him at the most inopportune times.

Unfortunately, she was right. He was out of time. "Stay out of my way. If you can't keep up or get into trouble, don't look to me for assistance."

She sneered at him. "As though I would need your assistance, pirate."

He was about to release her but leaned close instead. A hint of cherries teased his senses, but he resolutely resisted inhaling more deeply. "And if you do anything to jeopardize my plans—anything at all—I'll make sure you are very, very sorry."

She tilted her head coyly, and the movement of her hair stirred up the cherry scent again. "I like this side of you. The desperate, bargaining side."

On an oath, he released her and started after El Santo. He rounded the corner and spotted the exterior door at the far end. There were several doors throughout the corridor, undoubtedly leading to various rooms. He would have to try each, a time-consuming and potentially dangerous process, or he could go straight for the exterior door.

"I think the exterior door," his cabin girl said decisively. "The rooms in this hallway are used for storage and by the servants."

Again, she was correct. He'd seen servants coming and going from this corridor earlier in the evening. But it galled him to acknowledge she was correct. Instead, he stalked down the corridor, aware she was right on his heels. Aware, too, she had to scamper to keep up with his long strides.

Compared to the corridor behind them, this

hallway was spartan and dark. A few guttering candles sputtered in dark wall recesses, casting shadows over the bare floors and unadorned walls.

He reached the exterior door and tried the handle. It was unlocked, and he pushed it gingerly open.

Merde. No sign of El Santo.

He leaned back, prepared to order Miss Russell to return to her father, carry her all the way, if necessary, when the shot exploded and he felt a hot spray of wooden splinters. Belatedly, he ducked then glanced up at the hole in the wooden door.

If he hadn't turned back...

If he'd been standing just a fraction to the right...

"What are you doing!"

He felt her hand claw at his shoulder, then she reached past him and pulled the door closed.

"Someone's shooting at you! Get down!" she cried, falling back against the wall as another lead ball hit the door, sending a shock reverberating through Bastien.

Bastien clenched his fist. El Santo had seen him after all. But Jourdain must be frantic to avoid Bastien if El Santo was willing to kill him so openly. And that made Bastien all the more eager to get his hands on the man—on both men. He reached into his coat and pulled out his pistol. A swish of green satin beside him drew his attention in time to see his cabin girl hike her skirts and draw a dagger from a belt strapped to her thigh.

A quite shapely thigh...

He blinked. "Put that away, and go back to your father."

She shook her head and flipped the dagger into throwing position. The move was smooth and practiced, and Bastien would have liked to see if she could throw and how accurately. Judging by her skills with a sword, he had a feeling her aim was deadly.

"Get out of here," he ordered.

"I don't think that's possible."

"Yes, it is..."

But she was looking over his shoulder, down the corridor through which they'd come. "No, it's not. I believe that man with the pistol means to block our passage."

Bastien closed his eyes. *Merde*.

Five

RAEVEN STARED AT THE BROAD-SHOULDERED MAN sighting his pistol on her. She was beginning to think she should have left Cutlass to his own devices, but when she'd seen him again, so unexpectedly, her pulse had kicked, and she hadn't been able to leave well enough alone. One look at his too-handsome face, one word from his too-charming mouth, and she didn't know if she wanted to kiss him or kill him.

But she knew she had to follow him.

Now, here she stood, on the wrong end of a pistol. Killing or kissing Cutlass would have to wait.

She didn't like the look on the thug's face or the way his finger wavered over the flintlock's hammer. She wasn't going to allow him to put a lead ball in her head. She caressed the smooth hilt of her dagger. No pretty jeweled showpiece, the dagger was ugly and functional. She'd worn the hilt down over the years with hours of practice, but the blade was still deadly sharp. Given half a chance, she could take out the thug's eye.

But first she needed Cutlass to get out of her way.

The ridiculous man was trying to shield her with his body. Hadn't she told him she didn't need his assistance?

"El Santo," Cutlass said, after turning to face the man—and pushing her farther behind him.

"Get out of my way," she said through clenched teeth. "I can't aim with you standing there."

His response was to take her wrist and force the dagger down at her waist, using her skirts to cover it up. She hadn't been about to show the man the dagger, but she had to raise it in order to throw it.

"Captain Cutlass," the man called El Santo said with a sneer. As Raeven would have said his name with the same sneer, she raised her brows with interest. The man wore boots, tight breeches, and white shirt open at the throat to display several gold chains. His ears were similarly adorned with three or four gold hoops each. His close-cropped beard was a dark smudge on his face, and his hair was thinning, leaving a tall dome of a forehead. His gaze drifted over her quickly, and she noted his eyes were two-toned, one brown, the other green.

He quickly dismissed her and returned his glare to Cutlass. Apparently, this El Santo had no more love for Cutlass than she did. Still, Cutlass was hers to kill—if she so chose. She didn't want to hurt El Santo, but she wasn't about to allow him to fire a shot at her... or her pirate.

"Trying to follow me?" El Santo said with a smile. His teeth were large and bright white against his olive-toned skin. Two of them were gold. "It seems as though I've turned the tables on you. Again."

Cutlass ran a hand through hair that had escaped the thong holding it back. She could tell he was still a

bit shaken by how close he'd come to having his head
blown off. She didn't fault him for being shaken. She'd
seen other men dissolve into hysterics over less.

"I assume those are Jourdain's men outside."

El Santo smiled again. "A small surprise for you.
One of many we can spring, *señor*."

"Traps? Is that the way your captain operates now?
I thought Jourdain was a man of courage."

Raeven watched as El Santo's jaw worked. Cutlass
was making him angry. It wasn't the tactic she would
have chosen, considering the man was pointing a pistol
at them, but she had little choice but to trust Cutlass.

For the moment.

He was still holding her wrist, and she could feel
him pressing into her skin with strong fingers, telling
her not to move. To wait.

"Jourdain has more courage in his little finger than
you have in your entire body, *señor*."

Cutlass gave him a dubious look. "Then why does
he hide?"

El Santo straightened and raised the pistol. "We are
not hiding now, *señor*."

"Good point." Cutlass raised his own pistol. "It
seems we are at an impasse."

"I am not afraid to die, *señor*."

"Neither am I, especially because I doubt your aim
is much better than that of your men. They missed
me by a foot."

Raeven did take a small step back now. El Santo's
face flushed purple, and he sputtered a Spanish
obscenity. The pistol wavered for a moment as he
strove to contain his rage, and Raeven held her breath.

She didn't like having a flintlock pointed at her, but she especially did not like it when the man holding said flintlock was incensed.

She hoped her father had believed her when she'd said she was going to the ladies' retiring room. The last thing she needed was the admiral stumbling into this powder keg. But even if the ladies' retiring room bought her some time, the clock was ticking.

Suddenly, El Santo's eyes met hers. He smiled, the gold teeth glinting in the gloom. "I see you keep better company these days, *señor*. Who is *la mujer*?"

Cutlass gave her a cursory glance. "No one. A whore I found in the city." The casualness of his words was belied by his punishing grip on her wrist. She thought she might have bruises later. She would have to check... if she lived.

El Santo shook his head. "This one is no whore." He looked back at Cutlass. "I shoot you, and you shoot me. We are even."

"If your aim is any good."

"Oh, don't worry about my aim, *señor*." Without warning, his hand snaked out and captured Raeven's free wrist. With a jerk, he yanked her to him.

For a moment, Cutlass held on to her opposite wrist, and she felt like a rope in tug-of-war. But she was no simpering miss, and she wrenched her hand free of Cutlass's and allowed herself to be pulled flush against El Santo's broad chest. She could feel his wiry chest hair on the back of her neck, and she stifled a shudder of revulsion.

"Would you like me to demonstrate my aim now?" El Santo said, and Raeven felt the barrel of the pistol dig painfully into her temple. Devil take it! First her wrist, now her temple. She was going to be black and blue.

Cutlass shrugged. "Go ahead. As I said, she's only a whore. She means nothing to me."

Raeven knew he was trying to help her. She was almost certain El Santo was a Barbary pirate. The waters of the Mediterranean all but choked with the vermin right now. And the Barbary corsairs liked nothing better than captives to ransom. As the daughter of a British admiral, she'd be a fine prize.

Still, she thought Cutlass might have managed to look a tad bit concerned.

El Santo cocked the pistol, and Raeven decided she would have to be the one to end this stalemate. In a single move, she loosed the dagger from her skirts, slipped free of El Santo's hold, and plunged it into his thigh. She caught a glimpse of pure surprise and shock on his face. He truly hadn't expected her to be any danger. But then she wrenched the dagger deeper and the shock faded, replaced by pain and anger. He howled and grabbed for her. She side-stepped, bent, yanked the dagger back out, and dove for the exterior door.

"No!" Cutlass yelled. "We'll be shot."

She glanced back, saw El Santo fumbling with his pistol. "I'll take my chances!" She pushed the door open, ducked and rolled, raising her head long enough to spot a small wagon laden with produce. The silence of the night was shattered by the echo of pistol fire, but she was counting on the encroaching darkness to obscure the sniper's shot. She sprinted for the wagon and landed in a heap behind one blessedly large wheel.

A moment later, Cutlass landed beside her, kicking up sand and gravel so she had to close her eyes to keep them clear. When she opened them again, she saw Cutlass peering around the wagon. "I think he's over in that cluster of buildings."

Raeven crawled beside him and peered over his shoulder. The pasha's kitchen area was located here, as evidenced by the fires and smells of food coming from across the small courtyard where they hid. But the area was void of servants—not surprising, given shots had been fired.

"I think you're right," she said, judging the angle of the buildings and where the first shot hit. "By now one of the kitchen staff must have alerted the pasha. If we wait, his men should come to our aid."

"And if the kitchen staff is huddled in a corner with a pistol trained on them?"

She shrugged. "My father must be wondering how long I can spend in the ladies' retiring room."

Cutlass ducked his head behind the cart again and rested his back against the large wheel. Raeven dared not relax and remained on her haunches. She felt sand and gravel in her slippers and could imagine the state of her gown. She'd ruined another one now, and her father would never let her hear the end of it.

"You should have gone back to your father when I told you," Cutlass said. In the darkness, she could make out the frown on his face and see the hard glitter of his eyes.

"You're right," she conceded.

He blinked at her, obviously surprised.

"But if I'd done that, I wouldn't have been able

to save you from El Santo. You'd probably be dead by now."

He arched a brow. "Unlikely. Besides, I thought you wanted me dead."

She brushed at the sleeve of her dress, dismayed to find it was ripped. Her father was going to lecture her for hours! "I do want you dead." She leaned close. "But *I* want to be the one to do it."

He chuckled. "Well, you might yet get your chance."

"Oh, you can be certain I will."

"But not if I sit here waiting. The pasha or your father may or may not come this way. In the meantime, El Santo's men are making plans."

"What do you propose?"

"I'll make a run for it, through that gate"—he pointed to a large wooden gate where wagons made deliveries in and out—"and draw them after me. Then you'll be safe to go inside."

"What about El Santo?"

"Find another door. There must be more than one way in and out. If nothing else, go around the front again."

Raeven could picture the startled looks on the faces of the pasha's guests as she made a second grand entrance: her hair disheveled, her dress torn, and her face smudged with dirt. The reactions might be amusing… if she couldn't imagine her father's enraged face among them. Perhaps she could send him a note to meet her outside…

In any case, she and Cutlass needed to act. They had been sitting in one spot too long. "All right, go ahead and make your diversion."

He rose to a crouch, but before he could spring away, she grabbed his arm. The muscles underneath his coat were sleek and hard, and she immediately released him. But it was too late to staunch the flow of heat shooting through her belly. He looked at her, and she remembered another time, remembered his cobalt eyes warm with passion.

She shut her own eyes and blocked out the image. "Just don't get yourself killed."

"I would thank you for your concern," he whispered, his breath feathering against her cheek. He smelled faintly of tobacco and champagne. Thinking of their kiss of a few moments before—what seemed hours after the events of the past few minutes—she recalled he had tasted of champagne. His mouth had been cool and sweet. "But I know you want me to live only so you can kill me later."

She smiled. She did want to kill him. But she wouldn't mind kissing him once or twice first.

"Wish me luck, *ma belle*." And as though reading her mind, he leaned forward and brushed her cheek with his lips. She shivered involuntarily, and when he pulled back, she could have sworn his expression was smug and knowing.

She clenched her fists. "Good luck," she said. "I think you'll need it."

She watched as he moved, catlike, from the protection of one wheel to that of the other, closer to the gate. She could feel him tense, prepare to move, and then the door to the palace burst open, and the courtyard shone in the torchlight. Raeven turned in alarm and expectation of seeing her father or the pasha, but

El Santo stood in the doorway. He had a tourniquet around his leg, blood on the hand holding the torch, and three armed men with him.

"*Merde*," Cutlass said beside her.

"Exactly," she breathed. "Any other suggestions?"

One of the men pointed to the cart, and Raeven's eyes locked with El Santo's. With a roar, he charged them.

"Run!" Cutlass yelled, and taking her hand, pulled her toward the gate. A shot burst out, then another, and she felt the heat of one near her shoulder. She tried to run in a zigzag, but running at all was difficult in the cumbersome skirts, and she could barely keep up with Cutlass. Despite his earlier threats of leaving her behind, he pulled her forward, all but yanking her arm from her socket. When they reached the gate, he paused and kicked it hard.

Raeven gasped in horror when it didn't budge. Cutlass let forth a stream of French epithets and rammed the gate with his shoulder. Raeven didn't want to look behind them, but she was compelled.

El Santo and his men were advancing, the men loading their half-cocked guns. "Come here, little girl," El Santo called, his voice echoing against the walls of the courtyard. "You like to play with sharp objects. I have something for you to play with!" He gestured grotesquely to his groin, and Raeven had to swallow the bile in her throat.

"Hurry up," she hissed at Cutlass.

He rammed the gate again, but it didn't move. "Let's climb it," he said.

"There's no time." Not to mention, she'd never be able to scale the gate in those skirts. She glanced back over her shoulder and saw El Santo's men taking aim. "Get out of my way." She pushed Cutlass aside and made a quick study of the gate. A wide beam of wood rested over the double doors, barring outsiders from entering. It was far too thick to snap when kicked or rammed, but she lifted it quickly, thrust it over, and pushed the gate open.

She dove through just as fresh shots rang out.

Her skirts wound around her ankles, and she had a moment of panic when she tripped and went down, but strong hands lifted her and all but carried her into the alley and behind a heap of trash. He practically dumped her on her bottom, and Raeven knew the dress was beyond salvageable now. She coughed at the stench of rotting fruits and meat, tried not to think about their close call, and gave Cutlass a long glare. "You didn't think to simply lift the gate's bar?" Men and their reliance on brute force.

"I should have left you in a tangle of skirts back there," he retorted.

"Why *did* you help me?" She scanned the alley, looking for an escape. It would not take El Santo long before he realized where they were hiding.

"Glutton for punishment. Come on." He pulled her to her feet, and keeping hold of her wrist, dragged her down the length of the alley, staying in the shadows. A moment later they heard the unmistakable sound of boots scuffling, and she knew they were being chased. Her father was definitely worried about her by now, and what was she going to tell him if—no, when—she returned? She could hardly tell him the truth. She realized she didn't even know the truth. Why were they being chased?

They neared the end of the alley, and Cutlass pulled her into a wider street toward what appeared to be an open-air market. It was deserted in the evening, but the tents housing the stalls were still in place, their brightly colored patterns muted by the night. It was a good hiding place, and for that, she had to give Cutlass credit.

They ducked behind one of the tents, and Raeven bent to catch her breath. The smells of fruit and livestock lingered in the air permeated by the scent of incense and spices. She'd been in the Gibraltar market-places several times since their arrival a few days ago, but she hadn't noted the scents like she did now. Too much to see, she supposed.

A man shouted, and she braced herself to run again. But the sounds of pursuit faded momentarily, and she breathed a sigh of relief. She glanced at Cutlass and saw he had his head back against the material of the tent and his eyes closed. The moon was full tonight, and she could make out the long curve of his strong throat. With his shirt open at the throat, she could see the muscles of his neck, the cleft where his neck met his chest, and the smooth skin beneath which beat the vessels pumping blood to his body. One slice of the dagger she held in her sweaty palm, and he'd be no more. She could picture the blood pumping out of the artery, spurting down his shirt to drench the white fabric in a swath of crimson.

All that blood... Her stomach roiled.

"Why don't you just do it?" he asked, eyes still closed, face still relaxed. "You're thinking about it so hard, I can almost hear your thoughts."

She certainly hoped he couldn't hear her thinking about bloodless ways to kill him. Perhaps poison might be better...

"I'm curious," she said, avoiding his topic of conversation. "Why exactly are we running?"

He opened his eyes. "Someone starts shooting at me, I shoot back. Five men start shooting at me, I run."

"Yes, but why are they shooting at you?"

"Just a popular man, I suppose." He winked at her.

She shook her head. Ridiculous man. He really did think he was charming. And she might have agreed under different circumstances. Very different circumstances. "The man in the pasha's palace, El Santo, he mentioned someone called Jourdain. Who is he?"

Now Cutlass's eyes grew hard. She could almost see the wall come up. "An old friend."

"Not much of a friend, if he wants you dead."

"It's a complicated friendship." He looked at her. "Much like ours, *chérie*."

"There's nothing complicated about our relationship. I hate you and want you dead." *After I kiss you half a dozen more times.*

He shrugged. "I suppose it's much the same with Jourdain. The difference is I'm going to kill him first. Toward you, I have no ill will." He reached out and traced a finger down her cheek. Before her traitorous skin could warm to his touch, she snatched his hand away.

"I'm touched by your sentiments. Exactly why do you want this Jourdain dead?"

He cocked his head. "Do you know you get a

little line right here"—he touched the space between her brows—"when you start asking questions? You remind me of one of your English barristers."

"And you remind me of a guilty client. You won't answer my questions."

He grinned. "How can I concentrate on questions when I'm in the presence of such beauty?"

She rolled her eyes. "Cutlass—"

"No, really. I cannot believe I ever mistook you for a boy." His gaze traveled from her face to her neck to her breasts, and she had the sudden urge to put a hand over them to keep them safe from his warm glance. She resisted and fisted her hands at her sides instead. She still wore her gloves, and she set about removing them. She could handle her dagger better without a layer of kidskin between the handle and her palm.

"Bowers was a lucky man."

She jerked her head up, her bare fingers clutching the dagger tightly. "Shut up, pirate. Don't look at me, don't touch me, and don't speak his name."

"You really loved him." The look on his face was incredulous, and she wondered if he'd ever loved anyone. She doubted it. He was too full of flattery, too full of sweet phrases.

"Let's concentrate on getting back to the palace. My father must be frantic by now."

Cutlass chuckled. "Somehow I doubt that. I imagine he's used to your disappearing."

That was true, but she'd promised him she wouldn't do it anymore. She'd sworn if he allowed her to go ashore in Gibraltar, to attend the pasha's ball, she would stay right at his side. It had seemed an easy promise on board the *Regal*. She'd been bored and willing to do anything to get off the ship: promise to stay at his side, even don this uncomfortable dress. And she had intended to keep her promise, too. The admiral had been coughing quite a bit the last few months, and though he passed off the fits as nothing, she was beginning to worry. More than once she'd seen him pull a bloody handkerchief from his mouth.

She'd pretended she hadn't noticed the blood, of course. But inside, her heart constricted painfully, and panic swept through her. If he was sick if he... no, she would not think of that. But what would she do if she didn't have him? She had no family other than a handful of aunts and uncles in Portsmouth she'd seen only half a dozen times since she was four.

She'd been a fool to go after Cutlass. She should have stayed with her father, especially given that she was too afraid—or filled with lust—to do what she'd gone after Cutlass to do in the first place.

"All right, I'll get you back," Cutlass said, taking her hand.

She wrenched it free. "I told you not to touch me. And I can get back on my own. I don't need your help."

He raised a brow. "Going alone is not wise."

"Why?" She crossed her arms defiantly. "Because I'm a woman?"

"A lone woman, dressed as you are"—he glanced at her breasts again—"wandering the city at night? Even if El Santo doesn't find you, someone else might take an interest."

"I can protect myself."

"All the same, I'll see you back."

She opened her mouth to protest then closed it
again. There was no need to act the fool simply to
prove she didn't want his company. Once she was
back at the palace, she'd be rid of him for the moment,
and she could start planning how to best enact her
revenge. Or satisfy her lust.

Devil take it! Revenge, not lust, was priority.

"Very well. Let's go," she said. And without
waiting, she stepped out from the tent and stared into
the grinning face of El Santo.

Six

BASTIEN SWORE, RAISED HIS PISTOL, AND FIRED. BUT EL
Santo was too quick, and he'd ducked behind the tent
beside them. Bastien pulled his cabin girl back to their
hiding place and tried to think of an escape. El Santo
might have men hiding throughout the market. They
could be trapped.

"Come out, come out, wherever you are!" El Santo
called. "You might as well surrender now, *señor*. A
dagger and a used pistol won't get you far."

She looked at him, those green eyes accusing.
"Do you have more powder or another ball for
the pistol?"

"No." He'd brought his pistol only as an afterthought. He hadn't planned to kill Jourdain on land.
He wanted to destroy him at sea, destroy *La Sirena*,
and watch Jourdain sink to the bottom of the ocean
on its burning timbers.

"Well, we can't surrender." She crossed her arms as
though this was the final word on the subject.

And he agreed with her on that point. He never
surrendered. But he had no desire to die in a Gibraltan

marketplace, and they were hopelessly outmatched. "We can't exactly stand and fight."

She nodded. "So we run."

"Any particular direction? He probably has men at both ends."

"The far end," she said. "His men didn't cut through the market, so they must be going around. That will take time. If we hurry, we might beat them."

"Stick to the shadows," he ordered.

"Stick to the tents," she said, and leaned down, pulled the material of the tent at their back apart, and ducked inside.

He followed, knowing this was a paltry hiding place. El Santo would have them in a moment. But once inside, he saw his resilient cabin girl lean down and lift the material at the other end. She ducked through, and when he peered after her, he saw her scamper into another tent. Well, she was smart. Damned obstinate and too persistent for her own good, but smart.

He followed, noting she was already on her way into another tent when he entered. So she wasn't waiting for him. She didn't need him to save her. He didn't plan to.

So why should it irk him that she so obviously didn't need him?

He plunged into the next tent and saw her standing at the far side, peering through the flaps. "There's another tent just past those open stalls," she said without looking back at him. "It's a bit of a sprint, and the moon is full."

He stood beside her and took in the scene. A crude wooden rectangular structure swayed a few feet away.

It could house four or five vendors selling fruits or vegetables. The next tent was on the other side. The rickety structure would give them some cover, but not much.

She turned sharply at a nearby sound of rustling fabric. "Are we playing cat and mouse. Cutlass? Why don't you stop playing the coward and come out and face me like a man?"

"All the easier to shoot me," Bastien murmured.

She nodded. "But we can't stay here. He's close."

The tent where they hid must have been owned by a clothing merchant. He'd left several robes hanging in the back. "You could stay here. Hide behind those robes. I'll run for it and lure the men after me."

She nodded. "Fine. Once I'm sure they're after you, I'll go back the way we came."

"Be careful," he said. "Put on one of the robes." He tugged down a veil. "And it wouldn't hurt to disguise your face."

The sound of fabric ripping jolted through the tent. She clutched his arm. "That was close," she hissed. "You'd better go."

He nodded and started for the slit in the flaps, but she pulled him back. "Be careful."

He grinned. "Don't worry, *ma belle*. I'll save my neck for you."

With a frown, she turned away from him, but he grabbed her shoulder, turned her back, and kissed her hard. She sputtered a protest, but he silenced her with a finger on her lips. "For luck," he murmured and was gone.

Bastien swore as soon as he exited the tent. The

moon was full and bright and provided him no cover whatsoever. He wasn't even lucky enough to be afforded a smattering of cloud cover. He heard another rip and saw El Santo and one of his men tear into the tent across from the one he'd just occupied. They each held cutlasses, and they were slashing through the fabric as though it were butter.

Bastien ducked behind one of the meager boards comprising the stall, but it did almost nothing to conceal him. El Santo stumbled out of the tent and turned for the one Bastien had just vacated. In that moment, Bastien clearly saw his escape. While El Santo and his man tore the tent apart and found Miss Russell in the process, he could secure a better hiding place. They'd take his cabin girl to Jourdain, and he'd follow. Of course, they might decide to rape the girl first. They might even kill her if she put up much of a protest—and knowing his cabin girl, she would.

But that wasn't his problem. She had insisted on coming after him. He told her numerous times to turn back. He'd *ordered* her to turn back, but she hadn't listened. Her situation was her own fault, not his.

"*Merde,*" he swore. Of course he wouldn't allow El Santo to touch her. And like a fool, Bastien stood up when El Santo reached the cabin girl's tent. "Looking for someone?" Bastien taunted.

El Santo whirled for him, and Bastien drew his sword. "Why don't we stop this game of chase, and fight like men?"

El Santo didn't lower his pistol, and Bastien cursed his misplaced sense of honor. He should have let them find the girl. She would only try to kill him for his pains.

"*Mon ami*," Bastien said, spreading his arms in a peaceable gesture. He was certain he made a perfect target for El Santo's pistol. "Do you remember that time in Algiers? It must have taken quite a bit of catgut to sew you up. Maybe you'd like to pay me back."

"I'd rather just shoot you, *señor*." The sound of the hammer locking into place cut through the silence, and El Santo's man laughed.

"But Jourdain wouldn't like that." He was reaching, but the shadow that crossed El Santo's face told him he'd hit on something. "He wants me alive."

"Alive," El Santo said, "but not necessarily in one piece." He lowered the pistol, aiming it between Bastien's legs. Bastien's groin tensed, but he kept his legs braced apart.

"Shoot me, then," Bastien said with a shrug. "I just hope I don't die before you get me back to Jourdain."

The man with El Santo said something in a language Bastien didn't know, and Jourdain's lieutenant answered him harshly. Obviously they had differing opinions as to Bastien's fate. While they argued, Bastien's mind raced

There had been four men with El Santo earlier. Were the other three searching the marketplace, or had the group split? If he did take El Santo in a sword fight, what chance of escape did he have?

"Very well, *señor*." El Santo gestured with his pistol. "Put down the sword and come with us. We'll let Jourdain decide what to do with you."

Bastien cocked a brow. "You want me to surrender? You'll have to kill me first."

"Fine." El Santo aimed and fired.

With a curse, Bastien flew back, searing white pain in his left shoulder. He stumbled to the ground on one knee and shook his head. He could see a haze of stars in front of his eyes, and the pain was spreading through his body like some kind of virulent disease. "*Fils de salope*," he muttered. The bastard had actually shot him.

If the ball had hit his right shoulder, he'd be doomed, but he still had his sword clutched in his right hand. Now he pivoted and came up with a roar. El Santo's eyes widened in surprise, and he fumbled for his own sword. His henchman wasted no time, however. He raised his own pistol, and Bastien closed his eyes.

Something zipped past him and struck the man with enough force to cause him to drop his pistol and clutch his abdomen. Bastien had a moment to look behind him and saw his cabin girl, his beautiful cabin girl, standing there with arm outstretched. He'd known she'd be accurate with that dagger.

He grinned at her, but she gave him a look of horror. He turned in time to deflect El Santo's first strike. Their blades clashed, and Bastien figured if Jourdain's other men weren't in the marketplace by now, they would be soon. The whole city must have heard the gunfire and now the clash of sword and cutlass.

But when El Santo thrust again, he had little time to worry about the future. Bastien had to concentrate on deflecting the blow. His shoulder felt as though it were on fire, the pain making it hard to concentrate or move as quickly as he would have liked. He could feel a stream of wetness soaking his shirt and coat, dripping from his hand onto the ground below. Still, he managed to push back El Santo and put him on the defensive. But the man charged him like some kind of berserker, and Bastien, worried he couldn't stand up against such a strong assault, was forced to sidestep. El Santo pivoted and went for him again, and this time metal crashed with metal. Bastien clenched his teeth and forced his sword back against El Santo's cutlass. Sweat streamed down his face and into his eyes, and he blinked. From the corner of his vision he saw a flurry of green. Was it just his blurred vision, or had his cabin girl gone to retrieve her dagger from El Santo's man?

He saw her crouch beside the wounded man and doubled his efforts against El Santo. Jourdain's lieutenant had his back to the man, and Bastien preferred to keep him occupied until she had the dagger in hand again. He met El Santo's blade with his own, the clash of steel reverberating through his body painfully. But it wasn't the pain he thought of. He'd just decided that if his cabin girl regained that blade, he was going to have to seriously consider marrying her.

⁓

Raeven had thought the man was dead, but when she reached for the dagger jutting from his abdomen, he grabbed her hand with his own bloody one. She let out a small screech, as much from surprise as the revulsion of his blood on her skin. Her vision wavered and went dark, then she bit hard on her lip and forced her hand free. The man reached for her again, but she punched him hard, and he rolled to the side. She leaned over him and freed the dagger with a sickening squelch. She wished she'd kept her gloves on because she was pretty certain there was some part of the man's intestine on the hilt of the dagger, and it was slippery on her fingertips.

The sound of clashing swords drew her attention, and she watched as Cutlass deflected another of El Santo's blows. Even in the moonlight, he looked decidedly gray. His blood dotted the ground, darkening the sand as the men's feet trampled it. He fought valiantly, but she could see the tremor in his arm and hear how heavily he was breathing. He wouldn't last much longer.

She didn't know why she should care. She should let this El Santo take him, let this Jourdain finish him off. She was probably too much of a coward to do it anyway.

But she owed him now. She'd been peeking through the tent slit when El Santo angled for it. She had known then she was in trouble and thought Cutlass was long gone. But then she'd heard him call out. There was no good reason for him to have done so, other than to save her.

So now she'd save him and they'd be even. Then she could kill him with a clear conscience.

"El Santo," she called.

He turned at her voice, and she raised the dagger.

"Put down the sword, or I give you another taste of my dagger." She looked pointedly at the bloodied tourniquet on his thigh.

El Santo seemed to consider. She could all but read his thoughts. On his one side, Cutlass stood huffing and panting. Killing or seriously incapacitating the wounded man would be easy. He looked at her, at the dagger. She could see him judging the distance.

Could he reach her with his cutlass before she could let go the dagger?

But before he could make his decision, the sound of boots and men's voices filled the night air. At first Raeven tensed, certain El Santo's other men had found them, but then she recognized the language as English. "My father's men!" she said, recognizing Percy's voice among the others. "He's probably sent them out to search for me."

"You're not hard to find with all the gunfire," Cutlass rasped.

"What is this?" El Santo pivoted toward her then back toward Cutlass.

"*Les Anglais sont ici.*" Bastien smiled at her. "The British are here."

El Santo still looked confused, and the pirate added, "They're looking for her. You've been chasing Admiral Russell's only daughter."

"I knew she was no whore."

"I'd run now, while you have the chance."

But El Santo was already backing up, moving away from the sound of boots and men's voices.

"Tell Jourdain we're not through," Cutlass called after the retreating Spaniard. "And the next time we meet, he'd better be man enough to face me on his own."

Cutlass lowered his sword, and she saw him lean on it heavily. She went to him, putting her arm around him to support him. "I'm fine." He waved her away.

"You're shot."

"I have a good ship's doctor. I'll make it." He lifted the sword, attempted to sheath it, but missed. She took it from him and sheathed it for him.

"Can you make it back to your ship on your own? If my father's men find you here—"

"I understand and have no desire to swing from the *Regal*'s yardarm."

And yet she noticed he didn't move away. He stood looking at her, his expression unreadable. She looked back, feeling uncomfortable. For some reason she kept thinking about the kiss they had shared—not the hard, perfunctory kiss at the pasha's palace, but that kiss six months before on his ship. She wanted him to kiss her like that again, and yet she knew if he tried, she'd hit him rather than kiss him back.

"You'd better get out of here."

He nodded. "I'm waiting to see if you're going to kiss me good-bye."

"Kiss you? I'd rather—"

He took her chin with his clean hand. "Just do it, Raeven." He nodded toward the growing commotion. Her father's men were moments away. "This might be your last chance."

It wasn't. She knew she'd see him again, find some way to exact her revenge. He was wounded, and she could kill him now. She could have killed him ten times over tonight. And yet, she hadn't.

She didn't want to.

She was intrigued by him and, truth be told, she wanted him. And so she stepped into his arms, wrapped her hands around his neck, and pressed her lips to his.

His body was hard and warm. She could feel his muscles tense and bunch then release as his arm came around her to pull her hard against him. His mouth opened for her, and she plundered its depth. He still tasted of tobacco and champagne, and she thought the flavors suited him. His mouth slanted over hers, his tongue mating with hers, and she let out a small moan. One touch of his mouth and she was breathless; her head was spinning, and she felt as though she were sinking in quicksand.

What was wrong with her? Kissing Timothy had never felt like this...

The horror of what she was doing hit her, and she pulled away. He allowed it, though she could tell he was reluctant to release her.

"Get out of here," she said and raised her dagger. "While you still can."

He was still holding one of her hands, and he raised it, brushed his lips against it. "*Adieu, chérie.* Until we meet again."

He turned and melted into the shadows.

A moment later she heard Percy's voice. "There she is! Raeven are you all right?"

She turned and waved. "I'm fine. Glad to see you." And she walked to meet him.

Seven

"*FILS DE SALOPE!*" BASTIEN FLINCHED AS THE NEEDLE cut through his skin. "Don't I at least get a swig of rum?"

"I used the rum on the wound, Monsieur le Marquis. You are a big, strong captain, no? It is only four little stitches."

And he felt every one of those stitches as the ship's doctor closed the hole made by the ball of El Santo's pistol. Gaston Leveque, the *Shadow*'s doctor, sat back and nodded at his handiwork. "Voilà! Next time you will be more careful, no?"

Bastien dropped down from the table where he'd been sitting, still rubbing his left shoulder. "I think the cure is worse than the ailment," he said in French.

"Eh, *bien*." Gaston raised one shoulder. It was a particularly Gallic gesture, and it stabbed at Bastien's heart. He turned away and gingerly pulled a clean shirt over his head.

"As you know, Monsieur le Marquis, this is not my first profession."

"And in the two decades I've known you, I've

never heard you complain about not having to muck out stables any longer."

"Ah, but I do miss having my feet on land. I grow tired of pitching to and fro." He made rocking motions with his hands, and Bastien nodded absently. He'd heard Gaston's complaints a hundred, no, a thousand, times before. He also knew the old man— for he'd seemed to grow old almost before Bastien's eyes—would never leave him. They'd been together since that horrible summer night so long ago.

"It still troubles you, Monsieur le Marquis." Gaston laid a hand on Bastien's good shoulder. "But you never speak of it."

"No." He shrugged off the hand. He didn't want sympathy right now. He wanted a large jug of rum or three and his bed. "And you never cease calling me *Monsieur le Marquis*, though I've told you more times than I can count to call me Bastien."

"Eh. You will always be Monsieur le Marquis to me."

Bastien reached for the jug of rum on the table and swallowed a healthy portion. "I'm no marquis. Not anymore."

Gaston frowned at the upraised jug. He crossed the infirmary and took two goblets from a shelf on the far side. Taking the jug from Bastien, he filled the goblets, handed one to Bastien and kept the other for himself. "You act very little like a marquis. If your father saw you—"

"My father is dead." Bastien waved a hand to cut off the man. "They're all dead. Even if I wanted to be a *marquis*, it wouldn't matter. The French aristocracy is dead. Let's raise a glass to Madame Guillotine." He gave a mock salute with his mug, but Gaston refused to follow.

"That I cannot toast, Monsieur le Marquis."

Bastien hadn't expected him to. He knew he was being an ass, but he couldn't seem to help himself. He was frustrated that El Santo had gotten away, and Bastien was no closer to locating Jourdain. He was frustrated that he couldn't seem to get the image of Raeven Russell's green eyes out of his mind. And he was frustrated that his shoulder hurt like hell.

He took another swallow of rum.

Still, that was no excuse for taking out his frustrations on Gaston, his oldest and closest friend. The old servant had been with him since the beginning, since he was but a boy in short pants, trying to escape the horror of the revolution and the inevitability of pursuit and death, by signing on with the first captain in Cherbourg who would take him. He'd sailed only once before, the summer before that horrible night, and it had been a pleasure cruise on the Seine.

When he'd signed on as a crewmember under Captain Vargas, Bastien had known nothing of tackle and rigging, bow and stern, port and starboard. He'd started at the bottom and learned quickly. When he made a mistake, he was cuffed, and on occasion, he felt the sting of the lash. It was a shock for a boy who'd been used to commanding those around him.

But he'd always been adventurous. He and his older brother Julien had been sneaking out of their parents' town house and country chateau since Bastien had been old enough to walk. And he'd been in his share of scuffles and fights. He could hold his own.

And he had. So had Gaston.

And he'd never forget the day his captain, Vargas, gave him a compliment rather than a cuff. Over the years, Vargas had come to rely on him, made him his quartermaster, taught him everything he knew about ships and sailing. When Bastien turned seventeen, Vargas gave him the *Shadow*.

It wasn't exactly Vargas's to give. They'd spotted it off the coast of Portugal, its hull low in the water. Bastien led the attack and the boarding party, fighting tooth and nail until they'd subdued the crew and appropriated the silks, spices, wines, and fine tobacco for their own use. As a reward, Vargas gave Bastien the ship. They'd sailed into Malaga, taken on a fresh crew, and he'd begun calling himself Captain Cutlass.

The fanciful name was the only nod to his childhood he allowed. It had been a game he'd played with his twin Armand and their older brother Julien. He was the pirate, Captain Cutlass, and they were, alternately, British or Spanish ship's captains. The British and the Spanish fought valiantly, but Captain Cutlass always won the day.

Now he was Captain Cutlass in truth, and he'd almost forgotten the days of Sébastien Harcourt, marquis de Valère. That had been another life, another person. The boy with the two extraordinary brothers, the beautiful *maman*, and the strong but kind *pére* was no more. Gaston was his only tie to that life.

Bastien raised his goblet to his lips, only to find it empty. He reached for the jug again.

"Why do you drink so much, Monsieur le Marquis?" Gaston asked quietly. "Is it Jourdain? This revenge you seek? Vargas has been dead three years. He knew the risks, no? It was the life he chose. He went down with his ship."

That was true, but Vargas's death at the end of *La Sirena*'s thirty-two guns was not the only reason Bastien sought the Barbary pirate. "Jourdain has stolen from us more times than I like to remember. I want him stopped."

"Eh, *bien*. You steal, he steals. Who is right? Who is wrong? I think it is the revenge."

Bastien swallowed more rum. Little as Bastien wanted to admit it, it was desire to avenge Vargas's death that fueled his single-minded search for Jourdain. He was more like Raeven Russell in that regard than he liked. Just as his cabin girl loved her British captain, he'd loved Vargas. The man had been as much of a father to him as the duc de Valère.

The rum had done its work, and Bastien felt the edge of pain in his shoulder dull. He was warm inside and tired. So tired. "You're the only family I have left, Gaston," he said. He was just drunk enough not to be embarrassed by the sentimentality of the statement.

"And you are my family, Monsieur le Marquis, which is why I tell you to be more careful."

Bastien laughed. "I didn't think the bastard would actually shoot me. I should have let him take the girl, and ran when I had the chance.'

"That does not sound like the man I know. To leave a woman in the clutches of El Santo." He made claws with his hands, and Bastien laughed again. He'd forgotten how good it felt to laugh like this.

"She can take care of herself. El Santo would have

been sorry to ever lay eyes on the little hellion. I know I am."

Gaston raised a brow. "I do not think so. I think you like mademoiselle. I hear she is a rare beauty."

"She's a rare pain in the head." He massaged his temples. "I'd know Jourdain's whereabouts now if not for her." When he would have reached for the jug of rum again, Gaston moved it.

"You will find him, and you will have your revenge. I have no doubt of that, Monsieur le Marquis. And after you destroy *La Sirena*, I think it time you make another search."

Bastien held up a hand. "No. I don't want—"

"I will say it," Gaston said over his protests. "You will search for your brothers and the duchesse. One of them must have escaped the flames that night."

Bastien ground his teeth together. "I don't want to talk about this." He pushed up from the table he'd been leaning against and stumbled for the door. When he would have fallen from drink, fatigue, and pain, Gaston caught him, laid him on one of the cots in the infirmary.

"It is time we spoke of it. It is time you faced your past. You cannot hope to have a future until you have done so."

Bastien shook his head. "There's nothing to face, Gaston. You saw the fire. No one could have escaped that. You saw the papers. My father was executed. Publicly. His head chopped off as the crowds roared."

It sickened him to think of it. His good father. His kind father. The man had a smile for every child, a kind word for every woman, and a helping hand for every man. He was no weakling—a powerful, wealthy duc, he'd been one of the most influential peers in France. But he'd used his power to help those in need, and he'd seen the revolution coming, had warned King Louis of the danger. Had advised him to cut his excesses, to show some restraint.

And this man who had spoken out for the common man, who had tried to help them, this man had been cut down like a common thief at their bloody hands.

"But we only ever saw notice of the duc's death," Gaston said quietly. "I searched every chance I could get for information about the duchesse and your brothers. I found no mention of their executions."

"Because they perished in the fire. I'm the last Harcourt."

"Don't you want to be certain of that, Monsieur le Marquis?"

No, he didn't. As a boy on Vargas's ship, he'd had a favorite fantasy, one he had not even shared with Gaston. In it, his brothers and mother were alive and happy somewhere. He was not an orphan. He was not alone in the world because they would find him and bring him home. Their family would be reunited, and he would be happy again.

But as he grew older, he realized the foolishness of this fantasy. And when Vargas had been killed in the battle with Jourdain, Bastien had faced the facts—everyone he'd ever loved—everyone save Gaston—was dead. It was better for him if he didn't love again. Better if he hardened his heart.

He closed his eyes now, allowed the rum to do its work. He wanted to sink into oblivion, escape the pain—all the pain—for a while. Tomorrow he would begin again, begin the search for Jourdain. And when he found the corsair, he would destroy him.

And after that? He could almost hear Gaston ask the question.

After that, he might just destroy himself.

He groaned, rolled over, and the last image he saw as he fell into a dreamless sleep was Raeven Russell scowling at him.

❧

Raeven scowled at Percy and tried to refrain from grabbing him about the neck and forcibly shaking some sense into him. "You're not listening to me, Percy," she said, her voice deadly calm.

"No, I *am* listening to you, Raeven. That's why I'm saying no."

They were seated at the large dining table in the admiral's cabin. Her father had marched her into his cabin first thing in the morning and ordered her to step foot outside it at her own peril. Then he'd gone to oversee the day's activities, which consisted of painting and repairing the ship and taking on provisions. Raeven would have liked to be on deck, in the sunshine, climbing the rigging or sitting in the crow's nest watching the other ships in the harbor, but she'd seen murder in her father's eyes and decided she'd better do as he said.

This time.

Not to mention, he'd had another coughing fit. She didn't like to think she might have aggravated his illness with her brief disappearance last night.

Certainly the stress of wondering where she'd gone couldn't have helped matters. She hadn't told him or anyone but Percy the truth about what happened. She said she needed a breath of air after seeing Cutlass, had gotten turned around, and ended up in the marketplace. Coincidentally, a fight broke out in the marketplace about that time. But it had been at the other end of the marketplace. She had been perfectly safe the entire time. She'd tripped over a cat who'd run across her path, and that was the reason her dress was torn and dirty. It didn't explain the blood—a point her father made repeatedly—but Raeven stuck to her story.

She didn't think her father believed her, but she thought he believed her enough to let the incident go. He also knew she was capable of taking care of herself, though at times he could be a bit overprotective.

Like this morning.

"I need to get back to my cabin and work on my books," Percy said now. "We've taken on crates of supplies, and I'm impossibly behind on my logs."

"Fine. We'll need a good length of rope, two sharp daggers, and I could use a sword. A rapier would be best." A rapier was light enough for her to wield effectively. It wasn't as effective as her own sword, but she would have it back soon enough. She held up a finger. "And don't say you can't get them. You're the purser. You can get anything."

Percy shook his head. "Are you mad? Cutlass almost killed you last night. Why would you want to get within a hundred feet of him?"

Raeven pushed her cup of coffee aside—it was cold

anyway—and reached across the table to grip Percy's hands. "He didn't almost kill me. He saved me."

Percy shook off her grip. "So now you want to repay him by sneaking aboard his ship and slitting his throat?"

"I'm not going to slit his throat," she said. She'd like to, but she was beginning to accept the fact that she was too squeamish to do it herself. She did not even think she could kill him with a sword in cold blood. For the thousandth time, she wished she had bested him in that tavern in Brest. She could have done it then. She didn't know him. She hadn't kissed his lips, felt his muscular chest push against her breasts, felt his solid legs part her own and press between them…

"I just want my sword back." And perhaps another kiss.

Percy rose, moved toward the door. "You don't even know if he still has it."

"He has it. He said as much."

"Yes, as he was trying to get rid of you. Some people will say anything to get rid of you, Raeven."

She gave him a hurt look. "Fine then, go. I'll get the sword back without your help. I'll figure out who Jourdain is without your help, as well." She rose, went to the cabin door, and opened it.

"And get yourself killed."

"Well, at least you'll be safe. Safe and bored in your cabin."

"Raeven…"

She pointed to the companionway. "Your books are waiting."

He frowned, looked as though he wanted to say something, then left without another word. Raeven slammed the door behind him. She couldn't believe he'd actually left. She couldn't believe he wasn't going to help her.

Or could she? She'd pushed poor Percy too far. He'd never been one for adventure, so the idea of sneaking aboard a pirate ship, infiltrating the captain's cabin, and stealing back her sword was too much for him. He preferred to stay safe and warm on the *Regal*.

Well, she preferred that too. Except she wanted her sword back, and she wanted to know who this Jourdain was and why Cutlass wanted him dead. She wasn't likely to accomplish any of that on the *Regal*. She wasn't about to avenge Timothy's death by sitting and sipping coffee in her father's great cabin.

She put her head down on the mahogany table and let out a long sigh.

She was tired and sore from her activities last night. Even when she'd returned aboard her ship, she hadn't been able to sleep. She'd been too excited.

Liar, she told herself. *You couldn't sleep because you couldn't stop thinking of* him.

And she thought less of how she could destroy him and more about who he was. His enemy, this Jourdain, sparked her interest. He was obviously some sort of Barbary pirate, and equally obviously, Cutlass was searching for him. Wanted him badly enough to go after a dangerous man like El Santo.

Why? What had this Jourdain done to Cutlass?

Somewhere in her tossing and turning, she'd realized Jourdain interested her because he had a personal connection to Cutlass. She wanted to know more about the captain of the *Shadow*.

And as dawn was breaking, she gave up all pretense and admitted to herself she wanted to see Cutlass again. She wanted to kiss him again. She wanted... she wanted to do much more than that.

But she wouldn't. She'd used her father's spyglass to spot the *Shadow*. It was anchored on the other side of the harbor, nearer the open ocean. She supposed pirates often needed to make quick exits.

It was too far to swim from the *Regal*, but she could borrow one of the *Regal*'s longboats, row closer, and swim from there. Only it would be a true test of her strength to row the boat, then swim to the *Shadow*, *then* shimmy up the anchor cable.

She flexed her arm muscles. She was strong. But as Percy had pointed out, she was not as strong as a man, and her plans would exhaust even the most robust sailor. It was then she'd asked Percy to help, and then he'd balked.

She raised her head now and rested it on her wrists. She'd only wanted him to row the longboat...

She sat straighter. She was not going to give up just because Percy wouldn't help. Her father's men were loyal to her. She just had to convince one of them to assist.

But after six hours of trying—her father hadn't really expected her to stay in his cabin, had he?—she was more than discouraged. None of her father's men was willing to help her off the ship. She hadn't even mentioned rowing to the *Shadow*, and still they refused. Apparently, after the incident in Brest, her father had threatened flogging or court-martial to any man who assisted her.

The best offer she'd received was from the ship's bosun, Dickey Pickering. "Show me yer tits, and I'll help you right enough."

"Help me and then I'll show you," she'd countered.

But he'd shaken his head. "I require payment in advance." He'd winked lasciviously, and she'd had to struggle not to vomit. Instead, she'd turned her back and returned to her cabin.

At midnight, she'd gone on deck, taken out the pilfered spyglass, and found the *Shadow*. It boasted few lights, and she wondered what the pirate crew was about. Were they drinking and wenching? Were they sleeping, as most of the crew of the *Regal* was?

She felt someone beside her before she saw him. "Do you still want to go?"

Raeven blinked at Percy. Like she, he was dressed in black trousers and a black shirt. "What are you doing…?"

"I don't know, and I don't want to think about it. But I figure you have a better chance of survival if I help. And you don't even have to show me your…" He indicated her bound breasts.

"Oh, Percy! I *knew* you'd help!" She gave him a quick hug, but he pushed her away.

"This is the last time I help you, Raeven. Everything I've done, I've done for Tim. But even he would have me draw the line somewhere. And he would have punched Pickering for what he said to you."

Raeven laughed. Men had said far worse, but it was sweet of Percy to be so protective of her.

"Agreed. This is the last time I ask for your help, and Timothy would have punched Pickering. Now here's my plan—"

He raised a hand. "No, here's *my* plan. I already bribed a couple of the boys to lower a longboat over the side."

She blinked. "You did?"

"They're waiting now." He took her arm and ushered her across the deck, keeping to the shadows as much as possible. "Once in the water, I'll row you within swimming distance of the *Shadow*. If you make it aboard, I'll wait one hour for you." They were on the port side now, and Raeven saw the boys standing beside the deck rail. Once she and Percy were away, they'd haul the rigging back on board and secure it. "After one hour, I row back and tell your father Cutlass has kidnapped you. I don't have to tell you what will happen then."

"You'll be flogged and court-martialed for helping me."

He shook his head. "That will be later—after your father blows the *Shadow* out of the water."

"I'm not going to allow anything to happen to you, Percy," Raeven assured him. "I'll be on and off in less than an hour. And then I promise the next time we go ashore, I'll buy you an expensive dinner with two—no three—bottles of the best wine."

He gave her a wan smile. "I know you will."

⤜✦⤛

Two hours later, Raeven stood on the deck of the *Shadow*, cold and dripping. She wished she could towel off so she didn't leave a trail of water in her wake, but most likely all but the watch were asleep. And the watch would not be looking for wet footprints on the deck.

She'd climbed up the anchor cable in the bow of

the ship, and now she made her way through the shadows toward the stern, where Cutlass's cabin was located. The *Shadow* was a much smaller vessel than the *Regal*, which meant she'd reach the stern faster. It also meant she had fewer places to hide. But by the time she reached the mizzenmast, she thought she was doing rather well.

Until the bearded corsair stepped in front of her. "Who the hell are you?" he asked in French.

She glanced at his hand and saw the glint of steel. Her heart hitched, and her fingers itched to wrap around her own dagger. "I'm not feeling well," she answered, lowering her voice and keeping her head ducked. She wore a cap and hoped that, in addition to concealing her long hair, it put her face in shadow. "I needed some air."

"You must have needed a swim. I saw you climb up the anchor cable."

She reached for her dagger, but he was too quick. He caught her arm, twisted it behind her back, and marched her forward. "I'm taking you to the captain. He can decide whether we hang you or throw you over the side with a rock tied to your feet. And that's after we sink that boat you rowed in on."

Devil take it! The man had seen everything. She had to think of a way to warn Percy he was in danger. But the corsair was dragging her down a ladderway, his grip rough and punishing. She didn't think Cutlass was going to be amused she'd sneaked aboard his ship. She didn't know him well enough to guess what he'd do—take her prisoner? Send her back to her father? Kiss her?

She shook her head to clear it. Why did she always circle back to kissing him?

She had to think of Percy now. Cutlass would be even less forgiving of the *Regal*'s purser.

So she would have to be certain he never knew about him. In a deliberate move, she tripped and allowed her cap to fall from her head. Her hair was secured on her head, but she shook it free and raised her head to give her captor what she hoped was a feminine look of fear.

"What the…?"

He was distracted long enough for her to stomp on his foot. When he bent over, she kneed him in the groin. He went down on his knees, and she pushed him on his face, shoving her knee in the back of his neck. She had a length of rope secured to her belt in case she needed it, and she used it to quickly tie his hands. She shoved a handkerchief she found in his pocket into his mouth.

The man was too large for her to drag out of the companionway, even if she knew where to hide him. Even now, someone might be coming to investigate the noise of their struggle. So she took his dagger and ran along the companionway. At the first ladderway, she started up, intending to go directly overboard, swim back to Percy, and return to the *Regal*. But she heard voices above and turned back.

For three racing heartbeats, she stood undecided, and then she knew what she would have to do. She knew how she could get her sword and return to Percy safely.

"Fire in the galley!" she screamed. "All hands on deck! Fire in the galley." She shoved her cap back on

her head and continued to call her warning as she ran
for the stern and the great cabin. Men were swarming
up from the lower decks now, and she had to shove
through them. They'd picked up her cry of distress and
paid her no heed as they raced for the bow and the
burning galley. If they wondered why one of their own
raced for the stern, they didn't stop to question him.

A few moments later, the deck was empty and she
recognized the great cabin's door. It would no doubt
be empty. A fire on board was no trifling matter, and
Cutlass would have gone personally to oversee the
efforts to extinguish the galley fire. Still, she only had
a moment before the crew realized there was no fire,
found the bound corsair—if they hadn't already—and
started putting the pieces together.

She reached for the door and found it locked. She'd
picked the lock once before, and quickly extracted
a pin from her wet, tangled hair. She remembered
the lock mechanism and thought she could disable it
within seconds. She inserted the pin and turned right,
then left, then harder left…

The door opened, and she stumbled, all but falling
inside.

She saw black boots that rose to a knee covered in
black trousers. Above that were muscular thighs, slim
hips, and a white shirt, untucked. The sleeves were
rolled up, showing tanned, corded wrists and forearms.
The linen was open at the throat, and she swallowed
at the bronze skin visible in the vee. Above that was a
strong chin, a slash of a mouth, and hard, cobalt eyes.

"Good evening, Miss Russell," Cutlass said. "I've
been expecting you."

Eight

SHE LOOKED LIKE A WET RAT. HER DARK HAIR HUNG IN her eyes and around her shoulders. Her black shirt was too big for her and made her look small and sunken. Somewhere in there was the voluptuous body Bastien had seen at the pasha's ball. But kneeling before him in a puddle of water, she looked very little like the beautiful woman who'd claimed every man's attention when she'd entered the ballroom.

Except the eyes. Those emerald eyes, now wide with surprise and shock, were the same. And even the shocked look was quickly replaced by anger. He almost laughed. What did *she* have to be angry about? The disruption of her plans, no doubt.

He reached out, offered his hand. "Please come in. You must be cold. I'll fetch you a towel."

She didn't move, and he looked up when he heard footsteps in the companionway. "Mr. Ridley," he said before his bosun could speak. "I gather there is no fire."

"No, Cap'n. It were a ruse. You told us to expect one."

The man must have wondered at the urchin on her knees before him, but he didn't even glance down.

"Is the ship secure?"

"Yes, Cap'n. We found Jolivette bound and gagged, but he's unharmed."

Bastien glanced down at his petite cabin girl. Jolivette was easily a foot taller and a stone heavier than she. "Give him a week in the brig for allowing her to get by him." The brig was little more than chaining the man in the hold, but it served well enough.

"Yes, Cap'n. We're bringing her accomplice in now."

Bastien raised his brows. "Accomplice?" He looked down at the girl, but she avoided his eyes. "Chain him in the brig, as well. I'll speak to him in the morning."

"Yes, Cap'n." Ridley nodded and started away then paused. "Mr. Maine goin' to want to give you a report."

"Tell him I'll send for him when I'm ready." Bastien leaned down and hauled his cabin girl up by her wet shoulder. "Right now I want a few moments alone."

"Yes, Cap'n."

Bastien pulled the girl inside his cabin and closed the door. He heard her gasp immediately and didn't have to look to know she was staring at his wall and her sword on display.

"You bastard! You had it here all along."

He gestured to it languidly. "Go ahead and take it."

She blinked, and without waiting for a second offer, crossed the room and snatched it off the wall. She cradled it a moment, like it was an infant, and raised her eyes to meet his. "That's all I wanted. I didn't harm your man or your vessel."

He crossed to his desk where a bottle of wine and two goblets waited. "I wouldn't have allowed you to do so."

She bit her lip. "How did you know I was coming?"

He uncorked the wine and poured it. "There's a towel on the bed. You're dripping on my rug."

She seemed confused, opened her mouth to speak, then closed it and gathered up the towel, pressing it first to her face and hair, then quickly over her body. He watched as she did so, noting the flatness of her chest. She must have bound her breasts again.

When she was through, he held out a goblet. She stared at it as though it might be poisoned. "Would you like to change first? I have an assortment of clothing in the trunk. A few gowns might fit you. But then perhaps you'd rather borrow something of mine. You seem to have a proclivity for dressing as a boy." He gave her legs a long perusal. "Not that I mind."

"I-I'm not going to take off my clothes."

Since she didn't appear likely to take it, he set her wine on the desk. "No? Then why are you here? And don't tell me it's simply to retrieve your sword."

She clamped her mouth closed.

"You could have had another sword made."

She cocked her head to the side. "Why do *you* think I'm here then?"

He shrugged, drank some wine. "Me." He looked pointedly at the large berth.

She laughed. "Oh, really? You have a rather high opinion of yourself."

He sat down behind the desk, lifted his glass to examine the red wine in the candlelight. "You went to a lot of trouble to see me again. Perhaps my arrogance isn't entirely misplaced." He gestured to the untouched glass. "Have some wine."

She shook her head. "You can hardly expect me to sit here drinking wine with you while you put my friend in the brig. I want you to order your men to release him and send him back to the *Regal*."

"No."

"No? You owe me, Cutlass. I saved you the other night."

Now it was his turn to laugh. "*You* saved *me*?" He stood. "You got me shot, mademoiselle. And my shoulder is doing much better, *merci*."

"I didn't ask you to challenge El Santo. You should have run away when you had the chance."

"I know."

"You—" She stopped, obviously not expecting him to agree. "So you would have left me to that barbarian? You really do have no sense of honor."

"I never claimed to. Is that the reason you're drawn to me?"

"I am *not* drawn to you. What you think of as affection is nothing more than a desire to see you dead."

"Ah, that tired story." He stood, brought the goblet to her. "Drink this. You're shivering."

"I told you, I'm not going to sip wine while my friend—"

"He's fine. I'll order my men to see he has a meal and dry clothes. Will that suffice?"

"No. I want to be released. You can't hold me captive. I'm Admiral Russell's daughter. When he finds out I'm on board he'll—"

He put a finger over her lips. "He's not going to find out you're on board. He believes you're fast asleep in your cabin, does he not?"

She didn't have to answer. He could see the truth of it in her eyes.

"And by the time he realizes you're gone, it will be too late."

"What do you mean?"

He grinned, pushed the goblet into her cold hands, and went to the door. "I'm going on deck. Change into something dry while I'm gone. You're still dripping on my carpet."

He opened the door, stepped outside, and shut it on her curse.

❧

Raeven waited exactly two minutes before she went to the door. He'd left it unlocked, and when she opened it, she saw why. He had a guard posted outside. The man was bare-chested but for a long, gold chain. In his hand he held a sharp dagger. He was in the process of cleaning his fingernails with the tip when she opened the door, but he paused to grin at her, showing two gold teeth. Before she shut the door again, she noted he also had a pistol and a cutlass at his belt.

She was definitely in trouble. Percy, too. Oh, why hadn't she listened to him? But now wasn't the time to bemoan her choices. Now was the time for action. She had to figure a way to get her and Percy off this ship.

She paced back and forth, formulating and dismissing half a dozen ideas. Finally, she paused. She was indeed shivering and cold in her wet clothes. She couldn't think when she was last so cold. Or thirsty. Telling herself she was drinking only to ward off the chill, she sipped the wine.

Not surprisingly, it was good wine.

She took another sip then opened the trunk he'd indicated earlier. His clothes were neatly folded and organized, and she thought immediately of her own haphazard trunk. She could never find anything in it because she always pawed through the items and didn't bother to restore the contents to rights.

But Cutlass's shirts and breeches were neatly pressed and folded. She imagined the wardrobe against the wall held his coats and boots. They were probably similarly arranged. Below the neat stack of his clothing peeked something silky and feminine. She tossed his clothing onto the floor, knowing it would annoy him, and pulled out the rose-colored gown. Below it was another in a vibrant shade of blue. And below that a gown in white...

The man obviously did not lack for female companions. But did the women leave naked, or did he buy gowns with the expectation of meeting women who would need them?

She shoved the gowns back into the trunk and reached for one of his shirts. As a rule, she was more comfortable in male dress, and she did not want to draw attention to her femaleness on board the ship. But even as she lifted the fine linen, she realized her mistake. She remembered the warm way Cutlass had looked at her at the pasha's ball. She might have more sway over him dressed in a gown than a baggy shirt.

Ten minutes later, she glanced in the large mirror secured to the far wall. The rose-colored gown was sweet and pretty with long white sleeves and a delicate trim of narrow lace at the hem. But there the sweetness ended. It was made for a woman taller and slimmer than she. The skirts dragged and the bodice was too tight. The neck was a vee and the waist so high it ended just under her breasts. She had no stays or other undergarments with her, and her breasts swelled out of the dress sensuously. She had dug through the trunk in search of a tucking piece and found none. But she had found a pair of simple white slippers that fit and slipped them on. She had been barefoot before, as boots would have slowed her swimming.

Now this last glance in the mirror convinced her she ought to wear Cutlass's clothing after all. One look at her and he would think she meant to seduce him. Even her hair did not help matters. It dried curly and wanton, falling in tousled waves over her shoulders. Her cheeks were red from embarrassment and the earlier exertions of the night. Indeed, she looked like a wench newly climbed from bed.

She was reaching for one of Cutlass's shirts when the cabin door opened and he stepped inside. She whirled to face him, his shirt in front of her chest like a barrier.

He raised a brow. "Having difficulty deciding on your wardrobe?"

She shook her head. "Not at all. If you'd wait outside, I'll be finished in a moment."

He gave her a long perusal then reached over and plucked his shirt from her hands. "I don't think so. You look quite presentable as it is." He reached for the goblet of wine he'd left on the desk. "More than presentable, considering your evening activities. Mr. Williams enlightened me, you see. Don't frown so.

He wanted only to secure your release. He worries for your father's health."

Raeven's stomach roiled as she thought of her poor father waking in the morning and finding her missing again. He would indeed worry, possibly becoming so anxious his health was further compromised. Oh, why hadn't she considered the possibility of capture before?

Because, she told herself, you think you're indestructible. But you're not.

"I assured him both you and he would be sent back to the *Regal* before the night's end."

"That's still several hours away," she pointed out.

He grinned and lifted the goblet to his lips. "Did you poison this while I was away, or is it safe to drink the contents?" He took a long swallow, and she fisted her hands. She wished she'd thought to bring some poison. He would be writhing in agony right now, and she would be the one smiling smugly.

He set the goblet back on the desk and filled it again. He filled hers as well, crossed to the berth, sat, and began removing his boots.

"What are you doing?" she asked.

He dropped one on the floor beside the berth. "What does it look like?"

Undressing. But she didn't want to say it. "Why are you—er, doing that?"

He glanced up at her. "Come now, Raeven. You can stop pretending this"—he gestured to the bed—"isn't what you came for."

"Is that what you think? Well, you're wrong. I came for my sword, and now that I have it, I'd like to leave."

"Fine. But this may be your last opportunity. We're leaving Gibraltar very soon."

She crossed her arms over her chest, watched as his eyes followed the action, then realizing her actions pushed her breasts farther out of the dress, lowered her arms quickly. "And good riddance to you. I'd rather kill you than kiss you."

He nodded, dropped the other boot on the floor, and putting his hands behind his head, lay flat on the berth. Raeven couldn't help but notice it was large enough to comfortably fit two. "If that's what you want, go ahead."

She frowned at him. "What do you mean?"

He indicated the open collar and the bronze skin of his neck. "Go ahead. Slit my throat."

He'd called her bluff, but she wasn't about to admit it. Besides, she was annoyed enough with his arrogance to consider killing him. "And if I slit your throat, then what happens?"

"I'm dead, and you've avenged your murdered lover."

"He was my fiancé." And thinking about him had her reaching for her sword. The hilt felt comfortable in her hands, like an old glove.

"Even worse for me. Go ahead then. Kill me."

She clutched the hilt tighter, thought about plunging the blade through his heart. She could do it, she thought, even as she lifted the sword. She could do it for Timothy. She took a step forward and paused. "And what happens after I kill you? Your men…"

"You didn't worry about your welfare in Brest or the last time you were in this cabin. Why worry now?"

He was right. She didn't care what happened to her. She'd vowed to kill Timothy's murderer, no matter what it took. "But what about Percy—Mr. Williams? He hasn't done anything."

"Fair enough." Cutlass stood, walked to the door, opened it, and signaled to the guard. "Jean, no matter what happens to me tonight, the prisoner, Mr. Williams, is to be freed. Tell Mr. Maine."

"Yes, Captain."

Cutlass closed the door again and walked back to the bed. She found herself admiring his easy gait, the way he managed to swagger even without boots. "How do I know he'll do as you say? How do I know your men won't turn on us once you're gone?"

He gave her a hard look. "Because my men follow my orders whether I'm dead or alive. You can be assured no harm will come to your precious Mr. Williams." He lay back on the bed, adjusted the collar of his shirt so his throat was bare once again, and motioned to her. "Let's get this over with." He tucked his hands behind his head, moving a little stiffly. At first she thought his hesitation was out of fear; then she remembered he'd been shot, and his shoulder most certainly still pained him. And yet, she never would have known he was in any discomfort at all from his actions. He really didn't seem to worry she'd kill him. But she'd show him...

Her heart was thudding in her chest now, and her palms were sweaty. She hefted the sword, and it felt suddenly heavy and slippery against her damp skin. But she held on and walked to the berth. He squinted up at her. "Not with the sword."

She'd been staring at that swath of bronze skin, at the corded muscles of his neck. "What?"

"If you're going to do this, it's personal. Make it personal. Use your dagger."

She had the dagger strapped to her thigh under the thin dress, and she knew it would feel even more familiar in her hand than the sword. She looked at his neck, could almost see the pulse beating steadily there. With one flick of her dagger, she could end that pulse, that life, just as Cutlass had ended Timothy's life.

She reached for the dagger, aware he watched as she lifted her skirt and unsheathed the blade.

"If I'm going to die, at least my last view was pleasant," he drawled.

If he was trying to enrage her, it worked. She clutched the dagger tightly and looked down at him. He didn't blink, didn't flinch as she raised it. She could see her hand waver, see the dagger shake, but she gripped it tighter. She could throw it now. He'd seen her skill and aim. He must have known he was in danger, and yet he didn't move. Didn't try to block her.

She moved closer, rested one knee on the edge of the berth. Through the thin material of the gown, she could feel his heat, feel his comfortable warmth against her cold leg. Gaze never leaving his, she bent and pressed the dagger to his throat. She thought perhaps his pulse jumped, but she couldn't be certain. She waited, dagger ready, hand still shaking but steady enough to do what needed to be done.

And then he turned his head slightly—toward the dagger. He didn't dislodge it, didn't move his hands from where they rested behind his neck, but he turned into the blade. Raeven frowned, certain the sharp tip must cause him some discomfort. He glanced up at her, and she could feel his breath on her wrist. Very slowly, he pressed his lips against her skin.

She gasped, shocked at the feel of his mouth on her and even more at his audacity. She was about to kill him, and he was kissing her.

"What are you doing?"

He nuzzled her wrist with his cheek, and she could feel the prickly stubble on her sensitive skin. A shiver ran up her back, but she battened it down before it could spread farther. She gripped the dagger tighter, tried to muster the effort to dig the blade into his flesh, but it was difficult to think when his warm breath tickled her. It was difficult to think when he touched the tip of his tongue to her pulse—once, twice, no, three times.

"Stop it," she whispered.

"Make me." He lifted his head slightly and kissed the skin above her wrist. She inadvertently pulled the dagger back slightly, not wanting to stab him.

Not wanting to stab him? What was she doing? She was *supposed* to stab him!

"If you're trying to save yourself, it won't work."

"I'm not trying to save myself," he murmured, soft lips pressing against her skin, warm breath tickling her. "I haven't moved my hands. Go ahead and do it. But I deserve one last moment of pleasure."

He slipped back, moved his lips away from her wrist, and she let out a pent-up breath, only to draw it in again as he drew her last and smallest finger into his mouth.

"Stop." But her words were a whisper. The feel of that moist mouth on her finger, the gentle suction as he drew it inside, the rasp of his soft tongue on her skin… she couldn't think. She didn't want to think. Didn't want him to stop.

He released her finger, looked up at her, his eyes smoky and full of sultry promises. "Kiss me, *ma belle*."

"You're trying to trick me." Her voice wavered, shook.

He feigned innocence. At least she thought it was feigned. "Have I moved my hands? Have I dislodged your weapon? Kiss me or kill me. It's your decision."

She was unable to move. His body seemed to burn her wherever they touched. She was too warm. She could feel a trickle of perspiration roll down her back, could feel another meander between her breasts.

"Or perhaps kiss me then kill me," he suggested. "There's time for both."

And still she didn't move, didn't dare.

"You needn't even move the blade to do it," he whispered. "Perhaps I'll die with your lips on mine."

She almost rolled her eyes. "I told you flowery words don't affect me."

"Then what does?" He raised his brows. "You can tell me your secrets. I'll take them to the grave."

"Your—" She paused and swallowed. Her lips felt dry. They tingled where she could imagine his mouth on hers. "Your breath on my skin," she whispered. "Your tongue when it touched me…"

He nodded. "Let me touch you more." But he didn't move his hands, and she knew how he wanted to touch her. She need only lean forward. Indeed, her mouth was already so close to his. On an oath, she bent and touched her lips to his. She didn't move the dagger, kept it pressed firmly against his throat. And he didn't protest, but his tongue darted out and dragged a path of fire across her lips.

She moaned, feeling heat pulse throughout her entire body. The room swayed, and it was more than the gentle lap of the water. It was her mind and her body waging war.

Her body won for the moment, and she crushed her lips to his, taking him completely, mating her tongue with his. He allowed her to control the kiss, to explore his mouth, his tongue, his lips. And then he gently gave all the pleasure back to her, slanting his mouth over hers, showing her how a flick here or the press of his lips there could make her shiver, could make her whole body feel as though it would explode.

At some point, she was aware she'd released the dagger. Her hand was fisted in his hair, pulling his mouth harder against her own, demanding he give her more, take more. And he was responding. One of his hands snaked behind her, wrapped around her back, and drew her body flush against his. Again she was amazed at how warm he was, how solid. And the smell of him—fresh and inviting, like a sandy beach in the morning. She wanted to burrow into his shoulder, his chest, inhale deeply. She wanted to taste his skin to see if he tasted as good as he smelled.

His lips moved from her mouth to her neck, and she arched it to give him better access, glanced up at the mahogany paneling above the berth. And, unbidden, the thought came to her: Timothy's cabin had been fashioned of oak.

She stiffened suddenly and drew away. Cutlass's hands tightened on her for a moment, but only a moment. She looked at his face—his too-handsome pirate face—and could see his resignation.

He released her. "You're thinking of him."

She pushed away so she was once again kneeling on the side of the berth. "This is wrong. I don't know what I was thinking." She began to rise, but he grasped her hand.

"Perhaps you need to stop thinking so much." He looked about the cabin. "Look where all your thinking and planning has landed you."

"In the arms of the enemy."

He raised a brow. "How very dramatic, *ma belle*." He rose on his elbows. "What if I told you I'm not the enemy? What if I suggested we could be friends? We're too alike *not* to be friends."

"We'll never be friends." She spotted the fallen dagger below the pillow near his head and reached for it. But he was too fast and had it in his hands while she groped the sheets. He sat, eyed the dagger, and then her. "So we'll be lovers, but not friends."

"We'll be nothing, pirate. I was wrong to allow you to kiss me, wr—"

He laughed. "*Allow?* Mademoiselle, you kissed me." He touched the tip of her chin with the point of the dagger. "And I think you want to do it again. I think something draws you to me. Whatever you felt for this Bowers, he didn't make you feel the way you feel with me."

She slapped him. Hard. She did it without thinking, angry he dared speak of something so private.

Even angrier because what he said was true. She had cared for Timothy, adored him, loved him. Their love had been perfect in every way but one.

His kisses didn't fire her blood. His caresses didn't inflame her body. She had thought something lacked in her. She had thought she was incapable of passion. It was no matter because she loved Timothy.

But she was *not* incapable of passion.

And she had another realization. She was far weaker than she had ever imagined. Even the thought of Cutlass made her lips tingle, her breasts feel heavy, her cheeks grow warm. He was Timothy's murderer, and she couldn't stay away from him. She wanted to be here in his bed. She'd known it would end this way the first time he'd kissed her.

And he must have known it too.

He put a hand to his cheek briefly where her hand had left a red print. "I must have hit pretty close to the mark to earn that."

"Shut up," she hissed. "Give me my dagger. I'm leaving."

He held out the dagger, tip pointing toward her. "I don't think you're leaving. Neither of us is yet satisfied."

"I'm satisfied I never want to see you again. I have my sword." She spared a brief glance about the cabin. Where had she dropped it? "That was what I came for."

"So you keep telling me." He lowered the dagger so the point was aimed at her heart. "But I think there's more. Perhaps you like the adventure." He touched the dagger to her skin, and she felt the cool, sharp blade at the juncture of her breasts. He pressed lightly, almost tickling her. "Perhaps you enjoy the danger."

He slid the dagger point over the exposed curve of her breasts—first one, then the other. He traced their contours, and God help her, she couldn't stop from shivering.

"*Oui, ma belle*. You like the danger." He slid the dagger back to her cleavage, lowering it until it touched the thin, rose-colored material of the gown. "But more than that, you like this." With a flick of his wrist, he slid the sharp blade down, neatly slicing open the material. It gaped, and she caught it to stop her breasts from spilling out.

"You like"—he used the dagger to coax first one hand then the other away—"me."

The material split open, but he was there to catch her flesh. He leaned forward and pressed his mouth to the valley between her breasts. She could feel the stubble there, and she liked its roughness against the softness of her skin. His lips were cool against her flesh, teasing her until she was warm—warm and writhing against the ministrations of his tongue, his teeth, his so-very-skilled lips.

He took one nipple inside his mouth, twirled it about with his tongue, and she could not stop her head from lolling back. One hand caught her at the waist and held her to him, held her so the sweet torment could continue.

And she didn't want it to stop. She wanted him to rip the dress from her body and take her hard and fast. She wanted him to do it now so she wouldn't have time to think about what she was doing. She didn't want to think about who she was with.

But Cutlass was not so obliging. He moved slowly,

seemingly in no hurry to explore farther than her neck
or her shoulders. Gradually, he peeled away the material of the gown and eased her back on the berth. He
rose over her, and she looked up at him.

A piece of his long, dark hair had fallen over his
forehead, and it enhanced his already roguish look.
His blue eyes were hooded, dark with desire. His
hands were everywhere—on her body, in her hair, his
fingers in her mouth. When he looked at her, she felt
a jolt of need and arched to kiss him.

But he looked away, bending to her breasts again.
She felt the cool blade of the dagger and the whisper
of satin as he slit the dress to her waist. He pressed a
cool, stubbled cheek to the flesh of her belly, and she
moaned. He turned the cheek slightly, pressing his
lips against her. Her hands fisted in his hair, and she
whispered, "Yes."

And then his teeth scraped against flesh, lightly,
teasingly, and she couldn't stop a small laugh. Instantly,
he was on his elbows, staring down at her. "Do that
again, *ma belle*."

She squinted at the decadent angel looking down at
her with undisguised need. "Do what?" she murmured.

"Laugh." He touched a finger to her mouth, and
she could not help but wonder where he'd dropped
her dagger and how quickly she could reach it. "I do
not think I have ever heard you truly laugh."

She smiled, brushed his hair out of his eyes. "I think
you might find more ways to make me laugh."

"*Oui, je suis*—"

The sound of drums had both of them stiffening.
He was the first on his feet, but she was right behind

him, gathering her dress closed and darting her gaze about the cabin for dagger and sword.

"*Aux postes de combat!*" came the shout from somewhere above them. She translated silently. On the *Regal*, the order would have been "beat to quarters," and she would have reported to her father's cabin to assist him with strategy.

"*Branle-bas de combat!*" came the next order, and this time the voice was closer.

"What's going on?" Raeven shouted. Were they under attack? Had her father realized she was on board? Was the whole harbor under some kind of threat? She peered out the bank of windows behind the berth and saw the harbor was still dark. No signs of fire or smoke, no sound of gunshots or cannon fire.

Someone pounded on the door, and Cutlass had it open before the man could rap twice. In the companionway, she could see men rushing to their stations, could hear the scrape of cannons moving into position on the deck above them.

"Report," Cutlass ordered, strapping on a pistol. Raeven recognized the man as Mr. Maine, the *Shadow*'s quartermaster.

He must have recognized her too, because he gave her a brief glance then another before stuttering, "Lookouts have sighted *La Sirena*. She must have hidden in a cove. But she's sailing past the harbor, trying to make a run for it."

"Well, she won't get far." From the wall, Cutlass pulled the weapon that bore his name and secured it about his waist. "What's the weather gage?"

"*La Sirena* has it, sir. But the wind is picking up. We can catch her if we act now."

"Good. Set a course to intercept her." He started out the door, but Raeven caught his arm.

"Release Percy and lower us in one of your longboats. We'll be away in minutes."

"No time," he said, walking away from her.

"There *is* time." She ran after him, one hand securing her dress closed, the other lifting the skirts so she could run. "I must return to my father's ship. If you keep me as prisoner, you'll have the whole of the British navy after you."

"They'll have to catch me first." He strode up a ladderway and onto the gun deck, and Raeven tried to ignore the startled glances of the gunners as she ran by. She tried as well not to notice how efficiently they moved, how quickly they were in place. Why, their timing was as good as or better than the crew's on the *Regal*, and she knew her father drilled the gun crews almost every day.

She followed Cutlass to the poop deck, jumping aside as men rushed to positions. The wind whipped at her dress, threatening to tear it free. She grasped at the bodice with both hands. But aboveboard, she could see her pleas were hopeless. The *Shadow* had caught the wind, the anchor was up, and they were moving out of the harbor. Without any real hope, she followed Cutlass onto the poop deck, saw the helmsman with his hands on the wheel, turning it hard to starboard to catch the wind.

All hope vanishing, she turned to stare back at the dark harbor. If she looked hard enough, she thought she could just make out the main mast of the *Regal*. And as she watched, it grew smaller then faded away.

Nine

SIX HOURS LATER, BASTIEN STORMED INTO HIS CABIN, threw his cutlass down on his berth, and cursed. He didn't know where the fog had come from, didn't know and didn't care. They'd lost *La Sirena*. The brigantine had vanished like some sort of phantom, and they were sailing blind, searching for one tiny fish who could have swum anywhere in this vast sea.

Or could she?

Bastien went to his desk and pulled out the chart he wanted. He put his finger on Gibraltar. They'd been sailing west, following *La Sirena*. He moved his finger westward on the chart. Where could she be headed? Was she…?

With a start, he jerked his head up and stared at his berth. The bedclothes were mussed and a reddish gown thrown over them. He knew he was alone, but he turned in a complete circle anyway. She wasn't there.

He tried to remember the last time he'd seen his petite cabin girl. She'd been arguing with him, telling him to lower a longboat so she and the boy she'd come with could be away.

He'd refused her... That had been on the main deck. Had she followed him to the poop deck? He couldn't remember. Hell, remembering her state of dress—or undress, rather—when the drums had sounded, he hoped not.

He focused on the torn dress again. She'd come back to the cabin, taken off the gown, and then...

He'd find her in the hold, no doubt. She'd be with Mr. Williams. He crossed the room, prepared to order her to be brought to him, but decided to go himself instead.

The brig was located in the hold and was nothing more than several sets of chains fastened to a bulwark. Bastien went down the ladderway, feeling the air chill as he made his way lower. The hold was dark, foul, and infested with rats and other vermin. It was no place for a lady. He lifted a lantern and shone it over the cargo and barrels of water, chains, cables, and spare rigging. An area had been set aside for the prisoners. In one set of chains, fastened to the ship, sat Jolivette, knees drawn to his chest, head down between them. He glanced up once then looked back down dejectedly.

Bastien had half a mind to release him. His petite cabin girl was a crafty one, and he could hardly expect poor Jolivette to keep a hold on her when he himself had yet to do so. Just beyond Jolivette sat the cabin girl herself. The hold was dark, but her eyes must have adjusted by now, and she was already watching him.

He scowled. He didn't want her here, in the dark and cold.

She'd obviously helped herself to one of his trunks.

She wore one of his white linen shirts and a pair of tan breeches with boots. He didn't know where she'd appropriated the boots, as his would have swallowed her feet. Even so, she'd belted his shirt at the waist, which only made it look that much bigger on her.

Across from her and in chains, Mr. Williams sat cross-legged on the floor. Bastien appraised him quickly: scared but trying not to show it, indignant but not for himself... for Raeven. Hopelessly in love with the little hellion.

Bastien's fist clenched, but one look at Raeven's actions toward Williams, and Bastien relaxed. The boy was little more than a puppy to her. She even stroked his arm as though petting him. The two captives had been talking, but now the only sound was the creak of the boards and the muffled shouts of "Look lively now, lads!" from above.

"Am I interrupting?" Bastien would have liked a cigar, but the powder magazines were aft, and he didn't want to risk any sort of spark.

"If I say yes, will you leave?"

He grinned at her. "No. How are you faring, Mr. Williams?"

"As well as can be expected under the circumstances. Raeven—Miss Russell—tells me we've left Gibraltar."

"Indeed, we have."

"And our course, sir?" The *sir* was given in a mocking tone.

Still, it was a good question. In the bilge, water dripped, and he listened to the *plink, plink, plink*.

"I heard the crew talking about *La Sirena*," Raeven said finally. "That's Jourdain's ship, isn't it?"

"And what do you know about Jourdain?" Bastien asked.

"Barbary pirate, your enemy, headed"—she paused, lifted her head—"west, I should think."

"Very good." Now if he only knew precisely where...

"Why are we chasing him?"

"You said yourself. He's my enemy." Bastien was aware Jolivette had raised his head, and Bastien wondered how many of the crew knew why he hated Jourdain. Wondered how many followed him out of loyalty and not because they remembered Vargas.

To her credit, his cabin girl didn't ask any more questions. She merely waited, allowed the plink of the water to grow louder.

"Why do you hate me?" Bastien asked.

"You know why. You killed..." She paused, and he could see her tilt her head, knew she was thinking. "So this Jourdain killed someone you cared for."

He didn't answer, didn't affirm or deny.

"Who?" she asked finally.

"Not a lover, if that's what you're thinking. Or a fiancée," he added, because he'd seen her stiffen and knew she was about to protest. "But someone important to me. So you see, you are not the only one with a vendetta, *chérie*. We have more in common than you realize."

If she disagreed, she didn't voice it. Instead, she turned back to Mr. Williams, and they seemed to exchange some sort of silent signal. Bastien reached for the keys at his belt and unlocked Jolivette's chains. "Report to your station, Jolivette."

The man was instantly on his feet, knuckling a salute. "Yes, Cap'n. I won't let you down again. I won't—"

"I know, Jolivette."

The man knuckled another salute and dashed up the ladderway as easily as he scampered up the rat lines. Bastien moved forward, and when the girl saw his intent, she rose to move out of his way. "Are you releasing him or imprisoning me?"

Bastien chuckled. "I'm not certain yet. Which do you prefer?" He would rather have his fingernails pulled out than lock her down here, but he wasn't prepared to admit as much.

"If he has to be locked up for the duration of this voyage, I want to be, as well."

Bastien leaned forward and whispered in her ear. "Coward."

She stiffened. "I don't know what—"

"Much safer down here than up there"—he pointed toward his cabin—"with me."

He stepped to the lock, inserted the key, and freed the boy from his chains. "Mr. Williams, it's almost noon. Will you join us for some refreshment? I think Salviati, our cook, has something special prepared."

The man looked at Raeven first, and Bastien had the distinct feeling she had all the men on board the *Regal* eating out of her hand. He knew it. There was no other way she could have engineered a plan to escape her ship and infiltrate his with the help of this one boy alone. The men might be loyal to her because she was the admiral's daughter. But more likely, they admired her strength, her skills with dagger and sword, and her cunning.

Her beauty didn't hurt either.

He led them up a ladderway and to his wardroom. In smaller vessels, the captain's cabin and wardroom were often one, but Bastien had wanted a separate space and had a wall erected between the two. His officers had yet to arrive, and he had a few moments alone with his guests. He drew a cigar from a box on the table used for consulting maps, strategizing, and dining, and offered one to Mr. Williams. Williams declined.

He turned to the cabin girl and waved one at her. "Never let it be said I'm not equitable in all things. Cigar, Miss Russell?"

"Thank you, but I don't smoke," she said through clenched teeth.

He raised a brow, studying his trousers and shirt. "Too masculine a pursuit?"

She shook her head, went to one of the windows. "Too disgusting."

With a chuckle, he leaned forward, lit his cigar on a candle and nodded to Williams. "I understand you're the *Regal*'s purser, Mr. Williams."

"Yes… Captain. I've been serving with Admiral Russell in one capacity or another for two years." He stood straight, making it patently obvious he hated being interrogated but was prepared to withstand it if necessary.

"And so you've known Miss Russell for some time." Bastien leaned back in the chair, watched his petite cabin girl stare out the window and pretend not to listen.

"We were friends even before I joined the *Regal*."

"Ah. And does she always cause you this much

trouble?" He saw her shoulders stiffen, but she didn't look at them.

"Not usually this much."

Bastien grinned. "You'll be flogged for certain."

The man nodded. "Flogged and court-martialed. The Admiral's consequences for helping Raeven with any more of her schemes."

Bastien rose, uncorked the wine on the table, and poured three glasses. He handed one to Williams, set one down, and swirled the liquid in the third. "And yet you were not dissuaded."

"Someone would have helped her. I figured she'd be better off with me."

She turned from the window now, scowling. "I wasn't going to show him anything!"

Bastien raised his brows and looked to Williams for an explanation. The man was flushed with what looked to be embarrassment and took a drink of the wine. "The ship's bosun offered to help, but she had to—er—"

"I had to show him my tits. But I wouldn't have."

Bastien laughed, strolled to her, and handed her the glass of wine. She took it without turning away from the window, and he leaned down, whispered in her ear. "You showed me, *ma belle*."

"Much to my regret."

He laughed and went back to the table. "I imagine with those consequences hanging over your head, you're not in much of a hurry to return to the *Regal*."

"You'd be mistaken," Williams said stiffly. "I don't shirk my duty or my punishments. But I wouldn't mind returning with the *Shadow* as our prize."

Bastien laughed again, but from the corner of his eye

he saw his cabin girl turn, glance at Williams, and look thoughtful. So now she was planning a mutiny, was she? He'd like to see how far she'd get. She might have the crew of the *Regal* wrapped around her little finger, but it would take more than spunk and a pretty face to turn the hearts of his crew. Now if she were rich, he might worry. His crew's greed knew no bounds.

"Do you mind if I ask your plans, Captain?" Williams said. He'd been toying with his wine glass, drinking little. He looked pale and tired. Bastien was certain he was wishing he'd never laid eyes on Raeven Russell, much less allowed her to convince him to come along on her latest adventure.

Bastien sat back, put his feet on the table, and stared at the ceiling. "We search out *La Sirena*, destroy her, take the survivors captive, and sail back to Gibraltar. We'll sell Jourdain's men, resupply, and sail on for Spain."

"Bastard," he heard the girl hiss behind him.

Without looking away from the ceiling, he inquired, "To what exactly do you object, mademoiselle?"

"You call yourself a privateer, but you're nothing more than pirates with a piece of paper from Spain. In another month, you'll be attacking English vessels again."

Bastien threw his head back and laughed long and hard. So long, in fact, she came to stand beside him, arms crossed, frown deep. "What is so amusing, pirate?"

Bastien winked at her. "You. You don't care if I sink a vessel, kill hundreds of men or plan to sell the survivors into slavery. You're only concerned I might survive to attack one of your British ships. No worries, *mademoiselle*. England and Spain are friends at the moment. Your ships are safe from me. Much safer than you."

He reached out, snaked an arm about her waist, and drew her close. With a look of alarm, she wriggled and scampered away to stand beside her Mr. Williams. "Do you think he'll be able to protect you, mademoiselle?"

The man stood. "I will do whatever is needed to protect her virtue, Captain. I would rather die than see you molest her."

Bastien nodded solemnly at the boy's grave expression. "Understood, Mr. Williams. I assure you I will not do anything Miss Russell does not agree to. Her virtue, if she has any, is quite safe with me."

That riled up the boy. He stomped to Bastien and stared down at him. "Sir, I'm afraid I cannot allow a slight like that to be said of Miss Russell. I have no choice but to challenge——"

Bastien stood, looked down at the boy. "Say on."

He cleared his throat. "I have no choice but to——"

"Wait!" His cabin girl wormed her way between them. She pushed Bastien, but when he didn't move, she turned her attention to her friend. "Just wait a moment."

"Pistols or swords, Mr. Williams?" Bastien asked.

The boy paled but nodded. "Swords, I think."

❧

Raeven let out a small scream of frustration and rounded on Cutlass. "There will be no pistols *or* swords. He didn't even issue a challenge, and he's not going to."

"Yes, I——"

She rounded on Percy and shoved him into the far corner. "Stubble it! I'm not going to let you fight

Cutlass. I'm responsible for enough of your trouble right now. I won't have your death on my conscience, as well."

He gave her a hurt look. "What makes you so certain I'll lose?"

She made a herculean effort not to roll her eyes. "I've seen him fight, Percy. You are good," she lied, "but he is better. Besides, I don't need you to defend my virtue. I can more than handle Cutlass."

Not that she'd done a very good job of handling him so far. He'd almost had her much-vaunted virtue in his cabin earlier. And, unfortunately, Cutlass was correct in saying there was little left of it. She'd given her maidenhead to Timothy, hadn't seen any reason to wait until the wedding, especially when they were so often apart. She wanted some memory of him to keep her warm on the long nights while she waited for their wedding day.

Now he was dead, and she didn't regret her actions. Everything she'd shared with Timothy had been special. But she certainly didn't want Percy killed defending her nonexistent virginity.

She turned to Cutlass, who was standing across the room, looking slightly amused. He always seemed to look slightly amused. Except when they'd heard the order to beat to quarters. He'd gone deadly serious then.

"There was no challenge issued. Nor will there be. Mr. Williams and I would like to remain on board as your guests. We'll depart at the first port or when we return to Gibraltar, whichever comes first."

Cutlass smoked his cigar, his cobalt eyes appraising her. "Very well. I assume Mr. Williams has some degree of seamanship. He can sleep with the men. I'm certain an extra hammock can be located. But you"—he lifted his wine glass—"you present more of a problem. I can't exactly put you among the men in their hammocks."

"I've slept in hammocks and among the men before. I can do it again."

Cutlass smiled. "No doubt you have, and while I trust my men implicitly, you don't dangle a steak before a starving dog and expect the creature not to at least take a small bite."

She bristled. "Am I the steak in this scenario?"

"Indeed. A rather juicy steak, I might add. And that's why you won't be sleeping among the men."

"Well, I certainly hope you don't think I'll be sleeping with you."

He grinned, and she knew that was exactly what he thought. A brisk knock on the door interrupted them, and he added, "We shall work out the details later."

She recognized the red-haired man who entered first. She didn't understand the pirate hierarchy, but she thought Mr. Maine was something of a first lieutenant. Cutlass called him the quartermaster and nodded to him now. "Mr. Maine. I believe you remember Miss Russell."

She saw his surprise at seeing her in the wardroom flicker across his face a moment before he nodded and smiled. "Miss Russell, a pleasure to see you again." The perfect gentleman, he took her hand, kissed it.

"And this is our ship's bosun, Mr. Ridley."

Raeven took a deep breath as she looked up and then up again at the large black man standing before her. She'd seen men with tattoos before but never one with tattoos on his face. This one had a large swirl made of small dots on his right temple, extending down along his cheek. His right ear boasted a large gold hoop, while his left had three small hoops dangling from it. He grinned at her, his smile broad and white and somewhat less than friendly. He took her hand in his—swallowed it was a more apt description—and she forced her lips into what she hoped was a smile. "Mr. Ridley, was it?" she breathed.

"Dat right. And you is Miss Russell. The troublemaker."

She opened her eyes wide. "Troublemaker? I'm not a troublemaker." Even as she said it, she heard Percy and Cutlass snort. She expected as much from Cutlass, but at least Percy could be loyal!

"Good." Mr. Ridley squeezed her hand. "I doan want no trouble on dis here ship."

She nodded.

"Mr. Ridley generally gets what he wants," Cutlass drawled.

Raeven imagined he did indeed.

"But, Mr. Ridley," Cutlass added. "You should know Miss Russell is accustomed to having her own way, as well. Keep an eye on her, will you?"

"Yes, Cap'n."

Raeven threw Cutlass a hard glare before Mr. Ridley moved away, and a small, elderly Frenchman stood before her. He had a shock of thinning white hair, thin lips, and a weathered face, but his brown eyes were clear and lively. "*Bon soir, mademoiselle. Enchanté.*"

He kissed her fingers with paper-dry lips, and over his bowed head she gave Cutlass a questioning look. The man was obviously too old and feeble to fight.

What use would he serve on a pirate ship, where every man was expected to fight to the death?

Cutlass met her gaze, but his expression gave nothing away. "Our ship's doctor, Monsieur Leveque."

"*Je suis Gaston, mademoiselle. S'il vous plait.*"

She nodded. "Gaston it is then. Please call me Raeven."

His eyebrows rose and he glanced at Cutlass. "Ah, so you are the raven. I wondered why he was speaking of birds in his sleep."

Raeven frowned. "I'm afraid I don't understand."

Cutlass moved between them, taking her arm and leading her to a chair. "Salviati is our cook. Do you speak Portuguese?"

She shook her head. "Very little."

"Then you'll have to make your requests through me, as Salviati speaks only Portuguese."

The other men took their seats now, and Raeven could see there was some uncertainty as to who would sit where. Obviously, she had taken one of their places. She sincerely hoped it was not Mr. Ridley's. But he settled down quickly at the far end of the table, while Cutlass sat at the head, to her left. The ship's doctor sat on his other side, and Mr. Maine sat across from him. That left one chair next to Mr. Ridley, and poor Percy took it, trying very hard not to look too long at the large man.

A moment later, the cook entered, carrying a tray with a steaming platter of… something. She wasn't certain what it was, but it smelled edible. The places were set, and Cutlass served her first then each man in turn. He took what was left for himself, and she was surprised to see how little it was. He was either not hungry or did not care for the offering. He did pour first her then himself more wine. He passed the bottle to Gaston.

The doctor filled his glass and turned to her, saying in heavily accented English, "And so you are named after a bird? Or have I translated incorrectly?"

"No, a raven is a bird, but my name is spelled with an extra E. I was actually named because of the color of my hair. Apparently, when I was born, I had a head full of black hair, and my mother said I was to be named Raeven, but with the extra E so as not to confuse me with the bird. At least that's the story I've been told. I never knew my mother, and I have no idea if it's the truth. But"—she lifted a piece of her matted hair—"I still have the dark hair, so I'm inclined to believe it."

"If you don't mind my asking, Miss Russell," Mr. Maine said quietly, "what happened to your mother?"

Raeven cleared her throat. "I'm told she died several days after my birth. They think it was some sort of complication or infection." She lifted her fork and pressed it into the glop of brown mush on her plate. It was some type of meat… or perhaps a potato?

"I'm sorry."

"Don't be." She looked up. "I mean, thank you, but I never knew her. And had she lived, I imagine I would never have been allowed to sail with my father. As it is, I've been sailing with him since I was four."

"That explains a lot," Cutlass murmured under his breath.

She turned to glare at him but was distracted by Gaston. "Monsieur le Marquis lost his mother, as well," he said. "He was eleven."

She blinked, not expecting such a revelation. The other men at the table were looking down, obviously uncomfortable. "Marquis?" she asked. She had to look past Cutlass to see the doctor, and she could see Cutlass's jaw tighten.

The doctor nodded, spooning some of the brown mush into his mouth. "*Oui*. He is the marquis de Valère. His parents were the duc and duchesse de Valère."

Ah, so he did spread stories of his noble lineage. At least she wanted to believe it was a story. "And did you know the duc and duchesse?" she asked.

"*Assurément*. I——"

"Why don't we speak of something else?" Cutlass interjected.

"Oh, no." Raeven was intrigued now. "You won't tell me why you're after this Jourdain. I think I deserve to know something about you." Even if it was a lie.

She turned back to Gaston. "Are you the duc of something or other?"

He smiled and shook his head. "No, I was their servant. Monsieur le Marquis and I escaped the night of the fire."

"Gaston, enough."

From the looks of the others at the table, Gaston's remarks were revelations to them all. Most had forgotten to eat and were staring at the old man. The food was not very good, but she knew few sailors who didn't eat what was given them.

Gaston shrugged. "He doesn't like me to speak of it, mademoiselle. Would like me to call him Bastien, but he is still the marquis to me."

Raeven felt a prickle run up her spine. Was it

possible this man spoke the truth? He was certainly speaking it as he believed it to be true. And she knew the revolution in France had killed and displaced much of the aristocracy. She glanced at Cutlass. *Could* he be a marquis?

She looked at Gaston again. "Bastien?"

He nodded and indicated the captain. "His name. His real name is Sébastien, but the family always called him Bastien."

She blinked again, amazed at the amount of information she'd gleaned about this man who had been such a mystery only a few short minutes before. "And I suppose Cutlass is not his real surname." She knew it was not, but she was interested to hear what old Gaston would say.

"Cutlass? Oh, no! That was—"

"Mr. Maine," Cutlass—Bastien—interrupted. "Does the fog show any sign of lifting soon?"

"No, Captain. But I expect it will burn off in the morning."

They continued their discussion of winds and weather, a conversation Raeven would have found interesting at any other time, but she could only stare at the captain and wonder how much of what the doctor had said was true. She didn't know if she believed he was a marquis, but why would the old man lie about having been the family's servant?

Sébastien... She studied the pirate. He did look something like a Sébastien. His features were refined, his smile charming, his voice smooth. And yet the way he sat, the leisurely way he smoked, and that intense look on his face when he spoke of Jourdain—that was when she could see Bastien was a better name for him. He was no lily-white aristocrat. She glanced at his hands. She'd felt them on her skin, knew they were roughened from work. Her own were rough as well from furling sails and climbing rat lines.

Interesting. A deposed marquis. She wondered what other secrets he hid. And she worried she might just find out.

Ten

Bastien stood at the taffrail and stared into the gray dawn. The fog hadn't lifted as Mr. Maine expected, and he scowled at Jourdain's shield. The man had the devil's own luck, but one of these days it would fail.

He heard a light footstep behind him, and without turning, said, "Miss Russell, you're up early." He'd given her his cabin last night, as he didn't intend to sleep. Ridley had posted a guard outside the door to make sure she didn't hatch one of her schemes and attempt something like commandeering the ship while his crew slept. Now it was morning, and she must have talked the guard into allowing her on deck.

"I'm not accustomed to lounging in bed," she said, coming to stand beside him. She still wore his white shirt and breeches, but he saw she'd taken a comb to her hair—most likely *his* comb—and it hung in a neat black ribbon the length of her back. "The fog hasn't lifted."

He stared at the grayness.

"Jourdain could be just on the horizon or several hundred miles away," she said, stating the obvious.

"In any case, you've lost him. Perhaps it's best if we turn back."

He glanced at her, arched a brow. "Is that what your father would do? If he had orders to... say... burn, sink, or take a ship—*this* ship, for instance—a prize, would he turn back at the first hindrance?"

Her lips thinned. "No, of course not."

"And you think me any less determined?"

She sighed, and they stood in silence for a long while. He listened to the water slap the sides of the boat, the wind pulling the sails tight, and the creak of the rigging.

"If you don't turn back," she said, "Jourdain will be the least of your worries. My father will find you—fog or not—and when he does, he'll destroy you."

Bastien nodded. He had no doubt the admiral would piece all of the events together once he realized his daughter was missing and the *Shadow* gone, as well. But he had at least a half a day on the *Regal,* and the fog would hinder the man-of-war as it now hindered him. The *Regal* might find them, and he'd deal with that problem when it arose. He seriously doubted the admiral would fire and risk injuring his daughter. There would be negotiations and bargains struck. And then, no matter what the admiral promised him, once he had his daughter back, Bastien would get the hell out of there.

He had a fast ship. He'd outrun the British Navy before. With luck—a *lot* of luck against a 110-gun first-rate ship of the line—he could do it again.

"Bastien."

He looked at her, saw her eyes were wide. "That really is your name."

"I prefer you call me *Cutlass* or *Captain*."

"Not Monsieur le Marquis?"

Her tongue fumbled over the words, pronouncing *marquis* in the English fashion, *marquess*. "Your accent leaves something to be desired," he drawled, changing the subject. "Where did you learn French?"

"Oh, here and—" She paused, and he saw her stiffen then lean forward. Something about the way she moved, the way she... went on alert had his pulse beating.

"What is it?"

She didn't answer at first, and he found himself holding his breath. Listening.

Listening.

"There," she whispered. She'd taken his hand, and hers was warm in his cold one. He didn't think she even realized she was touching him. "Did you hear it?" she whispered again.

He shook his head. "Hear what?"

"Call for the lead, and order silence on deck."

He opened his mouth to tell her he was the one who gave the orders, but again, something in her demeanor had him doing exactly as she said. He turned and motioned to one of the yardmen. "Climb up and tell me what you see. Silence on deck!" he called. "And bring me the lead."

A moment later, a spyglass was thrust into his hands, and he peered through it, searching the fog for some sign of movement. He scanned the wisps of gray once, twice, and saw nothing. Lowering the spyglass, he said, "I don't see—"

And then he heard it.

The faint tinkling of a bell.

It could have been his imagination. But he knew it wasn't. He knew looking at the way Raeven Russell leaned forward, listening with her whole body, that the bell was as real as the oak rail under his hands.

"What do you see…?" He squinted at the yardman on the mizzenmast. It was Jolivette. "What do you see, Jolivette?"

"Fog and clouds, sir. Nothing more. Nothing—wait!"

But Bastien had seen the orange and red burst from the fog bank, as well. "All hands down! Down!" He dove for the deck, taking Raeven with him. He wrapped his arms around her, cushioning her fall and rolling to position his body over hers. His wounded shoulder howled with pain, and his vision grayed for a moment.

Under him, Raeven let out a soft "oof," and then the world around them exploded. He kept his arms around her, and they flew across the poop deck, landing hard against the rail together. Wood splinters showered them, a loose piece of canvas slapped him in the face, and he felt the *Shadow* lurch. More pain to his shoulder, but he bit down and pushed through it. He lurched to his feet.

"*Aux postes de combat!*" Bastien ordered before turning to Mr. Jackson, his carpenter, who was scrambling toward him. "Damage report, Mr. Jackson."

"Right away, Captain."

"Mr. Khan." He turned to his sailing master, who was at the helm. The man's cheek was bleeding, and he looked somewhat dazed.

"Yes, Captain!"

"Turn this ship starboard. We're going to hit them full on."

He could hear the shouts of "topmen aloft," "hard to starboard!" and Mr. Castro's order for his gunners to "be ready now, boys!" All around him, men scrambled to do what they knew best—sail and fight.

And Raeven Russell was right beside him. "I see a brig, thirty-two guns. Is that *La Sirena*?"

He turned and looked off the stern. *Merde.* It was *La Sirena*, and she was gaining on them.

"He must have hidden in the fogbank," Raeven was saying. "And when we passed him, turned to port and fired."

He'd already pieced together what had happened, but he didn't object to hearing her opinion, especially as it mirrored his own.

"He couldn't see, so it was a blind shot, but I'd say he didn't do half bad." She leaned over the rail, watching as one of the *Shadow*'s men climbed down a rope to inspect the rudder. "He's coming up on our starboard side. He'll fire as soon as he's broadside."

Mr. Jackson was beside him a moment later. "Not much damage on deck, Captain. Masts are fine. A few sails torn…"

"Mr. Jackson!" came the voice of the mate hanging over the stern. Bastien and his carpenter ran to peer over the rail. "The rudder is damaged, sirs!"

Bastien turned to look at Khan. "How is the steering?"

The man shook his head. "I haven't much, Captain."

And indeed the ship was not answering. It hadn't turned to starboard, and *La Sirena* was gaining on them. Another five minutes, and she'd be alongside.

"Damn it!" It was up to his gun crews now. He raced down the short ladderway to the main deck, giving the order, "Prepare to repel boarders!" as he went.

The gun crews were at the ready, as he knew they'd be. His master gunner, Felipe Castro, was an experienced sailor and a veteran of the Spanish navy. "We don't have much steering," he told Castro. "It's up to you and your men to do as much damage as you can. If not, we might all be making a visit to the slave auctions at Gibraltar."

It was a very real threat, for if the crew of *La Sirena* boarded them, Jourdain would kill Bastien, but he'd take the men and sell them as slaves. For a fleeting instant, Bastien wondered what would happen to Raeven, and then he shouted, "Stand fast. She's not close enough. Now! On the up-roll…"

The ship rose, and through the gun ports, he could see *La Sirena* coming beside them. He could see Jourdain's men, faces blank, eyes hard, at their cannons.

"Fire!" Mr. Castro ordered, and his own cannons boomed even as *La Sirena* answered. To his right, a cannon and its crew took a direct hit. Men and metal flew back, and Bastien raised his hand involuntarily to shield his face from the flying debris.

The men lay wounded, but he could see the cannon might still fire. *La Sirena* was directly across from them now, but even as he scrambled to take over at the cannon, he was pushed aside by Castro and… his cabin girl?

He watched as Castro blinked at the girl, but she merely ordered, "Help me get this cannon into the gun port. Quick now!"

The two of them pushed the heavy weapon back into position. Bastien couldn't help but notice that Raeven slipped on the blood of one of his men, but she didn't falter, didn't waver. He watched in awe as she covered the air vent then rammed the sponge rod into the barrel as though she had done so a thousand times.

Perhaps she had.

He turned back to his crew, watched as they primed their own weapons. "Ready!" he called. "On my word…"

From the corner of his eye he saw Castro insert the heavy cannon ball into the barrel. Raeven inserted the fuse, prepared to light it…

Bastien studied the sea, watched the roll of the waves… "Fire!"

La Sirena returned fire, and this time the damage was forward. Bastien ran to inspect it, knowing his gun crews would have little opportunity to do much more for the moment. Jourdain's ship was pulling ahead, and without steering, Bastien could do nothing more than he had.

But once on the fo'c'sle, he could see the whole picture. Yes, his foremast was damaged. Yes, several men were down and looked to be mortally wounded. Gaston would have a busy day ahead.

But that was nothing compared to the havoc aboard *La Sirena*. Their main mast was damaged. Badly. It looked as though it might topple at any moment. It was less of a hindrance than his own trouble with the rudder, but he did not think Jourdain knew his rudder was damaged.

As he stood and watched *La Sirena* shear off

starboard, he saw the man he sought. Jourdain stood on deck, hands on hips, head held high—much in the same way Bastien stood.

The two men eyed one another, and Jourdain raised a hand in mock salute. With a curse, Bastien watched as the pirate and his ship sailed away.

⚜

The damage was not as bad as she had initially thought, Raeven decided several hours later. And she knew much of the reason the ship remained so intact was her captain. If she had any doubts before as to his abilities, she did not harbor them now. The way he'd leapt into battle, the way he'd issued orders and raced to the areas where his leadership was needed most had more than impressed her.

She adored her father and thought him an able leader, but she had often thought that he should be more involved when the *Regal* was engaged in battle. He tended to rely on his lieutenants to bring him reports and devised strategy from their suggestions. But she had always wondered how much more effective he might be if he saw for himself the state of the ship.

Now she had glimpsed that type of leadership, and she could not fail to be impressed. Cutlass—Bastien—whatever his name—had saved them only because he had been where the most leadership was needed at the time. Oh, they easily might have lost the battle. If *La Sirena* had noted their damaged rudder, she might have turned, assuming she had enough maneuverability with her damaged mast, and fired again. The *Shadow* would have been little more than a fish in a barrel.

But Cutlass hadn't given *La Sirena* opportunity to think of doing anything but escape. He hadn't shied away from a direct confrontation, ordering his cannons to fire even as she could see *La Sirena*'s men looking at her across the expanse of water between the ships. That had taken guts.

But it had paid off for him. They were now paused, making repairs to the ship's rudder and sails, but they would be after *La Sirena* again before the dawn. She found, as she worked to repair a damaged shroud, she was almost excited about the prospect of another battle. She'd been escorting merchantmen too long, she decided. It was foolish to look forward to an event which very well might kill her. And yet, she always felt a rush when she heard the call to "beat to quarters."

She knew she'd surprised the captain and his master gunner when she'd fired the cannon. But what did the crew expect her to do? Sit and embroider handkerchiefs? No, if they went down, she went with them. The gun deck was where she was needed, and that was where she'd been.

Now she could see some of the men eyeing her with a grudging respect. No one had objected when she'd asked Mr. Jackson, the ship's carpenter, how she might be of assistance. He'd only paused a moment before pointing out the damaged shroud. It was an easy task, but she knew she'd have to earn the men's trust before they gave her anything more substantial to do.

She looked up, frowned, and shook her head. And why should she want to earn the trust of a crew of pirates? They'd kidnapped her and were taking her God knew where.

She should hate them. She *did* hate them.

And yet when Mr. Jackson gave her another task, she set to it with alacrity. It was only when the quarter-master, Maine, found her several hours later, she realized how long she'd been working and how late it was.

"Miss Russell?"

She turned and saw the red-haired man behind her. So strange to see an Englishman, all stiff and formal, aboard a privateer.

"Yes, Mr. Maine?"

"The captain has requested your presence in his cabin, miss. Would you care to accompany me?" Though it was phrased as a question, she knew it was no request. He offered his arm, and she stood, aware her muscles ached and protested.

She rolled her shoulders and tried to work some of the stiffness from her back before nodding to Maine and following him.

"Mr. Maine," she said, walking by his side as they arrowed for the stern and the captain's great cabin. "How did you come to serve under Captain Cutlass? You're obviously a former subject of His Majesty's Royal Navy."

He squinted at her over his shoulder. "That obvious, is it?"

She smiled, noncommittal. From the corner of her eye she spotted Percy working to repair sails damaged by cannon and grape shot. He didn't see her, too engrossed in his conversation. For a moment her heart tightened, but she didn't know if it was because he had made other friends so quickly or because she had not.

"I suppose the easy answer is the pay is better on the *Shadow*. I grew tired of being paid a pittance or nothing at all for my hard work. I have a wife and a child to support."

Raeven blinked and tried not to look shocked. But truth be told, she was shocked. She had never considered pirates might have families.

"Do they live in England? Your wife and…"

"Son. They live somewhere safe," he said.

She waited for him to continue then realized he had said all he would on the subject. Apparently, she could not be trusted with even the name of a city. Did the man think she would run to England at the first opportunity and seek out his family to denounce them as—what? Relatives of pirates? Did he think she wanted his family arrested?

Yes, in fact that was probably exactly what he thought, and who could blame him? She had done nothing but threaten this man's captain and his ship since the first time he'd seen her. If she were in his place, she'd want to protect her family, as well.

He led her down the ladderway to the great cabin, knocked briskly on the door, and at Cutlass's "Come!" opened it for her. She stepped inside, and Maine closed the door behind her, leaving her alone with Cutlass.

He was seated at his desk, his head down. She stepped forward and saw he was studying charts. He had a magnifying glass and was staring at the print it enlarged. He didn't look up or speak, and if her own father had not done the same thing a hundred times, she would have thought Cutlass did not realize she was there.

"You know how to fire a cannon," he said, moving the magnifying glass a fraction of an inch and studying the result.

She nodded, realized he couldn't see, and added, "I do."

"Mr. Jackson tells me you know how to mend a shroud, furl a sail, and swab the decks." He leaned close to the chart and squinted.

"Of course. I've lived almost all my life on a ship. I know how to do everything."

"You're not one to sit idle." Now he looked up at her. "Are you?"

She'd forgotten the effect of his direct gaze on her. She'd forgotten how handsome he was, how effortlessly seductive. His mouth was turned in a sardonic smile, his black hair fell disheveled about his face and shoulders, and his cobalt eyes seemed to disrobe her. He looked every inch the pirate, and why that should make her heart thump in her chest was beyond her. She hated pirates.

He leaned back, drawing her attention to the breadth of his chest and the vee of bronze flesh at his open collar.

She *hated* pirates.

He raised a brow, and she realized he was awaiting an answer to his question. Of course, she couldn't remember the question now. She'd been too busy admiring his impossibly blue eyes to pay much attention. Now she wondered what it would be like to touch her tongue to the bronze skin of his neck. She'd felt his skin on hers before. He was always warm, hard, and a little rough.

"You didn't have to do that today."

"Hmm?" She blinked. "I mean, pardon?"

He smiled. Was it her guilty conscience, or was his smile knowing? "You seem distracted, Miss Russell."

"I'm tired," she said immediately. Then his words registered. "And when did I become Miss Russell?"

"When someone has my respect, I show it."

Now it was her turn to raise her eyebrows. "Is this a new ploy to get me into bed?"

He burst out laughing, making her face heat with embarrassment. "No. Why? Is it working?"

"Of course not." But she was already seduced by him. She had the feeling if he but crooked his little finger, she'd come running.

But *he* didn't know that, she reminded herself. He thought she hated him. And she did. Hate him. Only, she wanted him, too.

He was smiling, probably still thinking about getting her into bed, so she cleared her throat. "What have I done to earn your respect? I did nothing the other members of your crew weren't doing."

"Yes, but you aren't a member of my crew."

Weary of standing before him, of feeling his direct gaze, she moved aside and studied one of the paintings on the wall. "No, but I'm not a member of Jourdain's crew either, and frankly, I like my chances with you better."

"Smart girl."

She glanced over her shoulder, narrowed her eyes at him. "You're certainly full of compliments."

He rose now, moved toward her. "I told you, you earned my respect." He was standing at her side and put his hand on her shoulder. She shrugged it off. "Don't think I did any of it to earn anything from you. I'm in this to save my own neck."

"And see a noose about mine."

She turned back to the painting, not trusting herself to lie convincingly when he was standing so close. She could smell him, the scent of sea and sand and clean air, and she could feel him, the heat of him. He was like a fire burning bright beside her.

"What's this, *ma belle*?" He leaned close, all but burying his face in her hair. "Am I to assume from your uncharacteristic silence you *don't* want to see a noose about my neck?"

She leaned away from him. "Don't do that."

His hand was on her waist, drawing her back. "Do what?"

"Put your face in my hair. My hair smells bad."

"On the contrary, *ma belle*, it smells as it always does."

She looked at him, couldn't help it. Immediately, she regretted the action because she was drawn in by those blue eyes. "What do you mean, 'as it always does'?"

To her surprise, he drew a lock of it through his fingers, put it to his nose, and inhaled deeply. "Like cherries," he said. "Did you know that?"

She shook her head, unable to speak. His hand was still at her waist, and now he turned her to face him, turned her into his arms. It was a small movement really. She was halfway there already. "You're a beautiful woman, Raeven. Desirable. But I'm sure many men have told you so."

She nodded. It didn't feel like arrogance to admit as much to him.

"I've known a lot of beautiful women."

She raised her eyebrows. "If you're trying to seduce me, you're sailing in the wrong direction."

He laughed. She loved how he was always laughing. He did it so lustily, the sound starting in his chest and seeming to reverberate throughout his body. He wrapped a strand of her hair about his finger until she bent her face close to his. "Give me a moment. Now what was I saying?"

She rolled her eyes. "You've known many beautiful women…"

"Ah, yes."

She could feel his breath on her face. He'd been drinking wine again. She could smell its sweetness.

"But I was going to add—before I was interrupted—I've known very few women who impressed me. *You* impress me." His lips were so close to hers, his last words had their mouths brushing together. "When I saw you at that cannon…"

She wasn't certain if he was speaking to her or kissing her. She only knew she was trembling. She wasn't cold. Could one tremble from desire?

"When I saw you, I had half a mind to grab you and take you right there." His hand moved down from her waist and cupped her bottom. She could feel its warmth, its sureness in the way he pulled her body closer to his.

"No, you didn't," she whispered. "*I* saw you. Like any good captain, you were focused on the battle with a single-minded intensity."

He looked into her eyes, and she saw wonder there. "Now it's my turn to ask. Are you trying to seduce me?"

Yes. "No. I recognize leadership when I see it. You had no more thought of bedding me at that moment than you did of eating a roast of mutton."

"Perhaps that's true," he finally conceded. "But the thought came to me shortly thereafter."

He lowered his lips to her ear, nuzzled it enticingly. She began to tremble more violently.

"Raeven, I want you," he whispered. "I've wanted you from the moment I pulled that ugly cap off your head in the tavern in Brest. I want you more now— more than I think I have ever wanted any woman. But if you say no, I'll leave you in peace."

She drew back, gazed into his eyes. There was passion in their depths, but behind it was also control. He meant what he said. This was her last chance.

A small part of her still resisted him, the part of her still loyal to Timothy. Another part of her yielded to… whatever it was between them. She'd wanted Bastien the first time she laid eyes on him. Somehow she'd known, even in her haze of rage, he could give her pleasure no other man ever had.

She opened her mouth to tell him to take her, but the words would not come. There had been only one other man: Timothy. How could she betray his memory by giving her body to this pirate, to Timothy's murderer?

"I see the war within you," Bastien said. At some point in her most private thoughts, he'd become Bastien to her. "Which side is winning?"

"Yours," she said. "But I feel disloyal and… and wanton."

He grinned, and she felt as though she should be

angry he was all but laughing at her. But all she could think of was his smile. It was infectious.

"Well, far be it from me to discourage any wantonness on your part, but I've always thought life was for the living. We can't guess what someone who's gone from us would want. I like to think your fiancé would want you to be happy. But then you knew him, and I didn't."

"Would you want me to be happy if our positions were reversed? Say you had been my fiancé and Timothy killed you. Would you want me to share his bed?"

He laughed. "*Merde*. You have me there. I'd want you to kill him." He touched her nose with a finger then kissed that same spot with his lips. "But there's no reason you can't bed me and then kill me."

She shook her head. "You know I'm never going to kill you."

"I know." He kissed her lightly. "I've known it all along, but I didn't think you'd realized it yet." He kissed her again, and she found her lips, her body, responding without even meaning to.

"What else do you know?" she whispered, wrapping her arms about him and digging her hands into his thick hair.

"You're going to make love to me."

"Have I realized that yet?"

He scooped her into his arms and carried her to the berth. "I think you might have an inkling."

Her head was spinning, and she didn't know if it was because she had forgotten to eat or because he'd scooped her up so quickly. She suspected it was a bit of both and also because her heart was pounding in her chest. He put her down gently, keeping his hand behind her head, so as soon as she touched the pillow, his mouth was on hers and his body was pressed against hers.

She felt herself responding immediately to his warmth, to his touch, to everything he was she shouldn't want.

Pirate. Rogue. Seducer.

She pulled him hard against her, buried her face against his neck and licked the swath of bronze skin she'd been eyeing earlier. She could feel his strong muscles and taste sea salt and something indefinable but definitely *him*, something definitely masculine.

He made a sound low in his throat then pulled back, cupping her face. "Aren't you going to even make a show of protesting?"

She stared up at him and knew this was what fallen angels looked like. "Protesting?" Did he think she could actually refuse him? She ran a finger along the hard planes of his cheeks, down the smooth bridge of his nose.

"*Oui*—protesting. 'No, no, monsieur, we shouldn't,'" he said in a high-pitched voice. "And finally you give in because you are overwhelmed by my caresses."

"I am overwhelmed by your caresses. But I might be more overwhelmed if we were both wearing less clothing."

He laughed, as she'd hoped he would. "I like you more and more," he murmured. She could feel his fingers loosening the belt at her waist. "No pretension.

Now let me see if I can do something about the clothing issue."

A moment later, her belt dropped to the floor, and he pulled her up, taking his shirt over her head. She'd bound her breasts again, but when he reached for the cloth, she pushed his hands away. "I'll do it. You deal with your shirt."

"Gladly, mademoiselle. Any other orders?"

She paused in the act of reaching for the binding cloth. "Oh, am I...?"

"No, no. I'm teasing you. This can be fun, no?"

Fun. She pondered the idea as she unwrapped the long cloth. It had never been fun with Timothy. The few times they'd been alone together had been furtive and rushed. He'd been so intense, so eager to be inside her. They'd not exchanged two words during the act.

But Bastien had not stopped talking and acted as though they had all the time in the world. And she supposed in a sense they did. No one would dare interrupt him. But she wasn't certain she knew how to have fun in the way he meant.

She heard him inhale sharply and glanced at his face. He was staring at her, and his expression made her knees feel weak. She looked down and realized she had but a thin strip of cloth left and she'd be bare to the waist. Slowly, she allowed the cloth to fall away.

He didn't even touch her, but she felt her nipples warm and harden under his hot gaze. She could almost feel his fingers on her, was eager to thrust herself into his hands.

But he was not so eager—or if he was, he was in no hurry. He sat, holding his bunched shirt in one hand, and studied her. She was not particularly modest or prudish, but after a moment, she felt herself grow self-conscious. She made to raise the cloth, and he dropped his shirt and grabbed her wrists. "No, *ma belle*. I'm sorry. I did not see before how perfect you are."

She made a sound of denial and tried to raise her hands, but he held them down. With a slight movement, he pushed her back against the pillows and leaned over her. "You don't believe me?" He kissed her mouth lightly, and she felt the lightest trace of his fingertips on the side of one breast. She arched; heat jolted through her body.

"No, I don't believe you. I'm not perfect."

"Oh, but you are." He bent, cupped one breast, and rubbed his lips against the upthrust nipple. "You're full and heavy." He traced the sides and cupped her underneath as though testing the weight. "Pink and cream." He said this against her nipple, and she bit her lip to stop a moan. "Soft and hard." He took the nipple lightly between his teeth and raked his mouth over her.

Raeven couldn't help but throw her head back. She was on fire. Never had she wanted something so much as she wanted Bastien to divest her of the rest of her clothing and finish what they'd begun.

"Oh, you like that?" he murmured, suckling her, which was an entirely new sensation. "What else do you like?"

"I don't know," she breathed. "But don't stop doing that."

He chuckled against her, his stubble tickling her sensitive skin. "Don't grow shy now, *ma belle*. Tell me what you want."

She met his gaze. "Really. I don't know."

A small flicker of alarm flashed in his eyes. "Don't tell me you are a virgin."

She almost laughed at the worry in his voice. "No, but I fear I am not very experienced. I…" She didn't know what else to say without revealing parts of her life she had shared with only Timothy and which were too personal to tell anyone.

"Ah." He was studying her face, his expression again full of wonder. "Have you ever experienced *la petite mort*?"

She raised her brows. "The little death? What does that mean?"

He grinned. "If you have to ask, you have not had the experience. I think I know what you would like."

She raised her brows. "I'd like you to take off the rest of your clothes."

"All in good time. But once I remove my breeches, I find it hard to think of anything but myself. I want to think about you"—he rubbed her nipple lightly between two fingers—"for a little while longer."

He bent to kiss her, and she arched to give him better access but was disappointed when he bent lower to kiss her abdomen. She thought of pulling his lips back to her nipples but resisted when she felt his fingers on the fastenings of her breeches—his breeches, really. He didn't even need to unfasten them to remove them. They were far too big on her, and he ended up pulling them over her hips and tossing them across the cabin. She watched them land on the floor then looked back, expecting him to rise over her.

But he was kissing her stomach now, and his hands were on her hips. She could easily see where he was going with his explorations, and she tensed, unsure if she should allow him.

He glanced up at her. "I thought you were feeling wanton."

She swallowed. "This might be more than wanton."

"What did you expect?"

She would never have dreamed of what he proposed now, but she had to admit she expected passion. She expected pleasure. She felt his fingers run along her thigh, resting at the juncture of her legs. His gaze was locked on hers as he gently coaxed her legs open and then caressed her lightly but quite effectively. She jumped, and to her shock, pushed harder against him.

He touched his lips to hers, kissed her cheek, kissed her neck—all the while sliding his fingers against her deliciously. "If you like this," he whispered in her ear. "Imagine what my tongue will feel like."

She groaned. She *could* imagine it, but she could not speak of it. Instead, when he lowered his head again, she made no protest and opened willingly for him. At first she kept her eyes on the ceiling above them. His breath on her thighs was warm, but she dared not look at what he was doing. She felt the first light touch of his tongue, and she could not help but stare down at his dark head. His hair spilled over his forehead as he bent to his task. She could not believe she was allowing this, but then he glanced up at her—a wicked gleam in his eyes—and she could believe it. She would probably have allowed him to do anything.

He touched his tongue to her again, and the last of her thoughts fled. She could think of nothing but the mounting pleasure. She'd had a taste of it before, but then the experience had ended, leaving her wanting more. She knew Bastien would not leave her that way.

Unwittingly, she arched her hips against him, and instead of shocking him, he grasped them and pulled her closer. "Come for me, *ma belle*," he whispered against her.

His tongue scraped against her again, and her world exploded.

Eleven

BASTIEN WATCHED *LA PETITE MORT* RIP THROUGH HER and thought how aptly the French metaphor fit the experience. She did look as though she might die. She'd flung her head back, reached up to cup her breasts, and arched hard against him. Now she lay with eyes closed, panting lightly.

He took the moment to study her body. He had not lied when he told her she was perfect. Men had many different tastes when it came to female beauty. He was of the opinion that most women were beautiful in one way or another. He might admire one woman's face, another's legs, a third's bottom. But he could not stop admiring every inch and aspect of Raeven.

Her breasts were exquisite. Like most men, he preferred large breasts, and hers were abundant. He did not know how she had ever hidden them so well. Softly curved, they were almost too large for her small frame, for she had a tiny waist and slim hips. And yet her legs were long and muscled. And her bottom—he would have to turn her over so he could see it in the flesh. But he'd had his hands on it, and he knew it was round and firm.

She opened her eyes and looked at him. The emerald color was not quite as sharp as before. Her irises had turned soft and muted, her pupils large. She gave him a tentative smile. She didn't smile often, and seeing the corners of her mouth turn up now, he couldn't resist kissing her swollen lips.

"Did I please you?" he asked. He knew he had, but he had to ask anyway. He wanted to know what she'd say after her moment of uncharacteristic shyness. But it had been only a moment. Once he'd applied himself, she'd come hard and fast and without reservation. He wanted to please her again. But this time he wanted to be inside her. He wanted to feel her tighten against him, feel those breasts thrust against his chest when she bucked against him.

"Yes," she breathed. Her voice was low and husky, and he didn't think it was possible, but he grew harder. "I don't think 'pleased' is a strong enough word for what I felt."

He looked into her eyes and saw she was completely serious. If he had not already been an arrogant man, he would be one now. "That's only the beginning, *ma belle*." He kissed her lips again. How did she manage to taste like cherries after more than a day at sea? "I can show you more pleasure."

She yawned and stretched. "That's quite all right. I'm ready for a nap now."

One look at his face, and she burst into laughter. "Oh, you should see your expression, pirate." She put a finger under his chin and pretended to close his mouth. It hadn't really been hanging open. At least he didn't think it had. "You're the one who said love-making can be fun, no?" She mimicked his voice and accent, and he gave her a grudging smile.

"I didn't think you had much of a sense of humor," he said.

"I guess you don't know everything about me."

No, he didn't, but he thought he would like to. And if he couldn't know everything, he'd like to know much, much more. He nuzzled her neck. "Why don't we become better acquainted?"

She pushed him back. "Very well. Why don't you remove the rest of your clothes? I feel quite exposed, lying here naked with you still wearing breeches and"—she made a sound of dismay—"you haven't even taken off your boots."

"Would you like to take them off for me?" He took a moment to enjoy the image of her removing his boots, naked, then he stood, removed them himself and stripped off his breeches. He would have climbed right back beside her warm body, but she was staring at him so intently, he glanced down to see what was amiss. Had he been wounded in the fighting? Was he covered in bruises?

He could see nothing remarkable and gave her a questioning look.

"I suppose I've seen naked men before," she said slowly, her gaze roving over him. *Bon Dieu* but he was feeling almost self-conscious at the intensity of her perusal. "But I've never seen anything like you."

Women had complimented him before, but the words had never meant anything to him. He did not know why, but he wanted to please this woman, this Raeven. Perhaps it was because he knew her praise was rarely given.

He gathered her into his arms, pressing his body against her warm, soft flesh.

"Your shoulder," she breathed. "Does it pain you?"

For a moment, he had no idea what she spoke of; then he remembered the wound Gaston sewed closed. "Not when I'm with you." One hand found her rounded hip, and he fit her to him so she was pressing intimately against him.

She gasped and whispered, "You don't waste any time."

"I'm eager for you, *ma belle*. I've been waiting many long months and imagining this moment since I first saw you in that gown."

"Really?" She looked up at him, her emerald eyes full of questions. "Is this how you imagined it would be?"

"It's better." He bent, kissed her mouth, opening her to delve his tongue inside to taste. Her tongue met his eagerly, her body moving against him as he deepened the kiss. He could feel her trembling beneath him as he pressed her legs open farther, felt her moist heat against the tip of his erection.

He moaned. "*Mon Dieu*, but I want you."

"I want you too," she whispered, and that was all the invitation he needed. He slipped inside her, sheathing himself in her heat. He could not have imagined such molten heat or that she would fit him like a glove. He moved inside her, felt her tense, adjust, and finally accept him. He moved again, and she tightened around him.

With gritted teeth, he held himself in check. "Do not do that, *chérie*," he ground out, "Or this will be too quick."

Her response was a moan and to tighten against him again. He would have to go slowly another time, he realized. This first time he was too eager—she was too eager—and so he gave up the soft, slow movements to thrust hard and fast.

Her eyes flew open at his new pace, and a cat's smile crept across her face.

"You like that," he said, driving into her again. But she was too far gone to answer. She gripped his unhurt shoulder then his bicep, and with a cry, her hips rose to meet his. Their bodies thrust and parried, thrust and parried, and finally he sank into her and surrendered to the white oblivion. He'd felt her shuddering release only a second before, and he thanked God, as he didn't think he could have survived her another moment.

Later, when his breathing slowed and he could think again, he rolled away. Normally, he would think of some excuse to go on deck, smoke a cigar, or breathe fresh air. Instead, he gathered her close. She smelled much better than the men on deck and was far warmer than the brisk ocean breezes. At least that's what he told himself as he burrowed his face into her hair and lazily stroked her back.

He didn't doze. He was too aware that Jourdain could return and attack any time. But he also knew *La Sirena* had been damaged in their skirmish. Jourdain would be supervising repairs and making attack plans tonight, just as Bastien was—should be.

"*Merde.*" He set Raeven aside and sat.

Sleepily, she pushed her hair out of her eyes. "What's wrong?"

"Jourdain will come for us in the morning. I need to call my officers, make a plan."

She nodded, the sleepiness leaving her face, and her swollen, rosy lips thinning. He wished he could erase her serious expression, replace it with the satisfied look she'd worn moments before. "I know I'm not one of your officers. I'm an outsider, and on top of all that, I'm a woman. But I'm good with strategy. My father always consults me." She pulled up the bedclothes and tucked them under her arms. "And he always wins."

Bastien stood and pulled on his breeches. "I have no doubt of your abilities, but I think it's better if you wait here. You should get some rest."

She rolled her eyes. "*You're* not going to rest. And even if I wanted rest, how could I? If this ship goes down, I drown along with the rest of the crew. If the ship is taken, you face death, but I'll find death a merciful release."

She was right. If Jourdain took the *Shadow*, she would be fair game for all the men. The captain might claim her first, but when he'd had his fill, the rest of the men would all have a turn.

He shrugged his shirt over his head, his wounded shoulder stiff and protesting. "My men won't accept—"

She jumped to her feet, pulling the bedclothes around her. "Your men are—as you told me before—fiercely loyal to you. If you listen to me, they will."

He bent to pull on a boot.

"You know you have a traitor on board."

He stilled, his hands frozen on the soft leather, his

foot half in and half out. "I don't know what you're talking about." He shoved in his foot and looked about the cabin for the other boot.

"Yes, you do. Someone alerted Jourdain to your position. He didn't fire randomly in that fog bank. He knew you were there."

He saw the other boot and scooped it up. "Perhaps he was simply lucky."

"That's possible," she acknowledged. "And I might even entertain the idea if he hadn't attacked. He didn't have time or enough visibility to identify your ship. If he didn't know it was you, he would have been firing on a ship unknown and unseen. That's foolish, especially with the number of British and American men-of-war patrolling these waters. He might stand a chance against your sloop but not against a man-of-war. No." She shook her head, her hair falling about her shoulders. "He knew it was you. He was sitting in the fog bank waiting for the *Shadow*."

She was right. He'd thought the same thing as soon as Jourdain attacked. The Barbary pirate shouldn't have even expected him to be following, much less been lying in wait. He glanced at her, and she stared at him for a long moment.

"But I'm not saying anything you don't already know, am I?"

"No." But she'd forced him to acknowledge his suspicions. He would have been happier thinking his crew completely loyal.

He would have been happy, but he would also be dead. The traitor had to be found and dealt with. But how to hook a traitor?

He glanced at Raeven again. She narrowed her eyes. "Don't tell me you think *I'm* the traitor."

He didn't, but he decided to play out the idea. "You have more motive than anyone else aboard this ship. You and your Mr. Williams."

"But neither of us had any idea you were going after Jourdain. How could we?"

"You managed to get aboard my ship. You managed to incapacitate my guard. You managed to make it to my cabin and put a dagger to my throat. I think you could manage to find out our plans."

She pulled the bedclothes tighter, hugged herself. "Is that what you think I did?"

He went to the mirror, pulled back his hair, and secured it with a thong.

"Very well, tell me this. If I knew you were going after Jourdain, and I had somehow alerted him so he might surprise and destroy you, why did I sneak on board? Why did I warn you about the attack when we were on deck?"

He watched her in the mirror. She paced when she spoke. Back and forth, back and forth, dragging the sheet with her. She really should have been a barrister.

"Why did I help with the cannons? Wouldn't it have been better for me to…?"

"Enough." He turned. She was so damn logical. "You're not the informant. But I don't know who is. Until I do, it suits my purposes to allow the suspicion to fall on you."

"You think others will assume there's a traitor." Clearly she didn't. The tone in her voice was dubious. "Sailors are a superstitious lot. More likely, they'll consider the incident bad luck. They might chalk it up to having a woman on board."

He gathered maps and charts from his desk. "Some will, yes. But my officers aren't so foolish. If the idea hasn't occurred to them already, it will soon."

"And you plan to name me? I might as well jump ship now. It's better than being forced to walk the plank!"

"Don't jump quite yet. When the suggestion arises, I won't name you, but I won't discount you either. Unless there's a mutiny, you're safe under my protection. For a little while."

"And while I'm the prime suspect, the true traitor thinks he's safe."

"It might be enough to cause him to make a mistake."

"And if he doesn't?"

He looked up at her tone.

"Jourdain is coming back for you," she said. "You don't have time to wait."

He grinned, crossed to her, and took her pointed chin between two fingers. "Let me worry about that. You—if you're so good at strategy—study the copies of charts I've left. Figure out where the hell he's hiding."

She nodded, and he went to the door, opened it, stepped into the companionway. But he turned right back around, surprising her as she leaned over his desk. "And Raeven, I'll be back. Don't bother getting dressed."

&

She did bother to dress. She wasn't some courtesan, paid to lounge about in her dressing robe.

Not that she had a dressing robe. She didn't have

much of anything, so she raided Bastien's trunks once again and donned a black shirt, black breeches, and cinched all in place with a large belt. She wished she could find boots that fit better because the ones she'd borrowed were too large, but she found a pair of woman's slippers among the gowns. They were still too big for her, but she didn't think she'd trip over them as much.

She fully expected a guard at the cabin door, but the companionway was clear. Most of the crew were using the last of the dying daylight to finish repairs to the *Shadow*. At night she imagined Bastien—Cutlass—would order all portholes covered, all lights extinguished. If Jourdain was out there, Bastien wouldn't take any chances the Barbary pirate might spot him. She could imagine the conversations in the wardroom at present. The men were probably drinking and smoking and tossing out idea after idea. She could picture Bastien smoking his own cigar, listening patiently, and making his own plans.

Was the traitor in the wardroom even now, or was he one of the mates? Would he try to help Jourdain again soon or bide his time? It would be easy to "accidentally" leave a porthole uncovered, shine a light on the deck during the watch…

She missed the safety and security of her father's ship. In truth, there were many times she'd been in as much danger on the *Regal* as she was here, but for some reason, she felt more exposed on the *Shadow*. Perhaps because she didn't know the crew here, didn't know the ship's capabilities yet, didn't trust the captain.

But that wasn't quite true. She did trust Bastien.

She'd seen his skills and leadership abilities. She knew he'd protect her. He'd done so in Gibraltar to his own detriment. He was more of a gentleman than he probably wanted to be.

She did trust him with her body. But not with her heart.

And she was afraid their lovemaking had touched something in her heart. Something different than Timothy had touched.

She stood in the companionway and shook her head. Why should she allow Bastien to touch anything inside her? Why couldn't she be like a man—give her body and nothing else? She knew Bastien wasn't thinking about how she'd touched his heart.

The thought made her smile ruefully. And wonder what Bastien *was* thinking. She didn't know him well enough to guess.

But she knew who did.

A few minutes later, she made her way along the companionway until she reached the infirmary. She couldn't have said how she knew which it was. Perhaps she could smell the blood or laudanum.

The door was open, and she peeked inside. Mr. Leveque sat at a table, folding strips of white cloth. The men in his care, there were two, slept on cots. One had a bandage around his head, the other around his arm and leg. She wasn't certain of their injuries and didn't want the details. Even the idea of blood made her stomach protest.

"Can I help you, mademoiselle?"

Happily, she turned her eyes back to Leveque. "I hope I'm not interrupting, doctor."

"Not at all. And you mustn't call me *doctor*. As I told you before, Monsieur le Marquis gave me this position, but I have no qualifications."

She nodded toward his patients. "They seem well enough."

"Eh, well. I knew something about caring for horses. Men are not so very different, and I have been on ships for many years. I have seen almost everything, as I imagine have you."

She nodded. She'd seen injuries so horrible she wished she could erase them from her mind. But she had never tried to deal with the injuries. She had never tried to save a man's life. The most she had done was apply a tourniquet and help the injured soul to the infirmary.

And she hadn't stayed to see the doctor work.

She thought at one point her father hoped she might work as a nurse. When she'd been twelve and her father had been captain of the HMS *Titan*, he'd brought her to the infirmary one day and offered her as an extra pair of hands. She'd done well for several hours: rolling bandages, sorting medicines, cleaning instruments. But later in the day, a man who'd severed his finger in an accident with a coil of rigging stumbled into the infirmary, his injured hand clutched to his breast, blood gushing over his shirt. She'd gone pale and—she was loathe to even remember this now—she'd fainted.

It was the first and last time she'd fainted, and it had been the end of her glorious medical career. For some reason, she could draw blood in battle. Oh, her stomach grew queasy when she saw it, but she did not feel lightheaded. But when not in the throes of musket fire and booming cannons, she could not even think of blood without her head swimming.

"How long have you been sailing?" She eyed the men on the cots. They seemed still enough—unlikely to convulse or begin bleeding out. Gingerly, she stepped farther inside.

"Thirteen years. You?"

"Since I was four, and I'll be twenty this month."

He shook his head, a reaction she had not expected. Most sailors were impressed by her many years at sea. She raised her brows. "You disapprove?"

"You've known nothing else," Mr. Leveque said. "It dismays me." He set the bandages aside.

"I love the sea," she countered.

"That's what he says too." He gestured toward the stern and the captain's cabin. "But he's known little else, either. Jumped on board when he was but eleven. It was the only way to escape the bloodshed. He could do anything now, and he chooses this." The look of disgust on his face indicated he didn't approve of the choice. "Battles, death, risking life and limb." Leveque shook his head again.

"Why do you stay?" she asked.

"How can I leave him, mademoiselle?" He shrugged. "We have no one but each other."

"Surely you have family back in France."

"No." He reached for a pair of wine glasses, but she shook her head. He filled both anyway. "My family was the duc de Valère and his family. I began working for him as little more than a child. I don't know who my parents were, but the duc took me in. He was a good man."

"What happened to him? You said the duchesse is dead. What about the rest of the family?"

"All killed in the revolution. Monsieur le Marquis had two brothers. One was his twin, and both were killed that night. We heard later his father was guillotined."

"I'm sorry." And she was. The violence in France a few years before was unimaginable to her. Whole families denounced and killed. Children even. "How did you and… er, the marquis escape?"

The man looked thoughtful then said, "That is a story for him to tell. It is very personal to him. I may have already said too much."

She nodded. She could respect the old man's decision, but she knew it meant she would probably never know Bastien's story. He seemed unlikely to reveal it to her. "Might I ask one more question? On another topic?"

The doctor inclined his head. "Why are we pursuing Jourdain? Bastien told me it was because the Barbary pirate killed someone he loved."

"His father."

She frowned. "But I thought you said—"

"Not his real father. The man who became his father, Vargas, the captain of *El Cuchillo*. That's the ship that took us on, and the man who taught Monsieur le Marquis all he knows about ships and sailing."

"What happened? Or is it too personal to reveal?"

Leveque shrugged. "The story is widely known." He lifted his glass, sipped, and indicated she should drink also. "Do not make me drink alone, mademoiselle."

Obligingly, she lifted the second glass and drank. The wine was good. From what she had seen on board, the crew of the *Shadow* did not want for what might be considered luxuries aboard the *Regal*.

"Jourdain and Vargas were not partners, but they often worked together for this pasha or that. I don't know the politics of the region, but I know both men became rich."

Raeven frowned. It was no mystery how pirates made their fortunes. They ran blockades and robbed merchant ships. "How did Bastien get his own ship, this one?"

"Vargas and Monsieur le Marquis took it in a raid. He gave it to Monsieur le Marquis as a reward. And that is what caused the rift. Jourdain thought the ship should have been his. He claimed he was instrumental in the fight. Vargas disagreed, and they went their separate ways. Six months later, Jourdain attacked Vargas near Tripoli. He raised the flag for parley, and when he was close enough, blew *El Cuchillo* to splinters."

Raeven bit her lip. "Where was Bastien?"

"We were out at sea, making our own fortunes. But as soon as word reached Monsieur le Marquis, he began searching for Jourdain. But the coward went into hiding. It took money and time, but now we have him where we want him."

Money. Raeven thought about the arms and medicines she'd seen her first time on board the *Shadow*. She'd thought they were meant to fuel a war between Spain and England, and perhaps they would, but now she considered that Bastien might not have been as interested in war as he was in the profit he could make from selling the cargo.

And that made him no less of a pirate.

And for some reason, that status was no longer as unattractive.

Twelve

BASTIEN SURVEYED THE MEN HE'D INVITED TO THE wardroom and wondered who the traitor was. He didn't like this feeling of suspicion. He didn't like feeling as though he had to look behind him every time he stepped into a shadow. But Jourdain had gotten to at least one of his men.

He glanced at each man seated at the table. There was Mr. Jackson, the ship's carpenter. The man was English, built like a bull and with that same animal's sense of humor. He didn't mince words, and he didn't use them frivolously. Beside him sat Mr. Castro, his master gunner. Castro was Spanish and had served with Vargas before Bastien offered him a position on the *Shadow*. Castro had no love for Jourdain. Beside him sat Mr. Khan. Also an Englishman, he was a former naval officer who had no qualms in telling everyone he was after gold and gems. He wanted his share of any prize. Could Jourdain have got to Khan? How much money would it take to sway Khan's loyalties?

He looked at the men standing near the windows, Ridley and Maine. They were the last two men he'd ever suspect of turning traitor. He'd known Alan Maine for years, and the man was as straight as they came. He did his job and did it well. He was well liked and well respected. It was one reason the crew had voted him quartermaster.

Ridley had sailed on the *Shadow* for years, as well, but Bastien knew little about the bosun. Still, Bastien had no reason to suspect Ridley would sell him out to Jourdain. Ridley had always been loyal, always fought hard, usually at Bastien's back.

So if it wasn't Jackson or Castro, Khan, Ridley or Maine, who was it?

Bastien sighed. He was supposed to be listening to a discussion of strategy, but he hadn't heard a word Khan said. And now the man was looking at him as though he wanted direction.

"Let me consult my charts again," Bastien said. "I don't feel confident we know where the bastard is hiding."

He rose and headed back to his cabin. His statements in the wardroom had been no exaggeration. He had no confidence he knew where Jourdain hid. He wondered if Raeven had any ideas.

And then he wondered why he was relying on her. She was smart, but she wasn't omniscient. She couldn't know where Jourdain lurked. And yet, he wanted her opinion. He found he valued her opinion.

He strode into his cabin, surprised to find it empty. Not only that, but she'd left the bedclothes strewn about the floor. Some cabin girl she would have made. He thought about going to his desk, studying his maps and charts, but he knew he wouldn't be able to concentrate without her. He'd wonder where she was, what she was doing—he eyed the bedclothes on the floor—what she was wearing.

He stood at his desk and tried to imagine where she might have gone. If he were a woman... no, if he were *Raeven*, where would he go?

He smiled and started for the infirmary.

Five minutes later he found her, sharing a glass of wine with Gaston. The two looked as though they were old friends. And before Gaston, who was facing the doorway, saw him, he heard the word *Jourdain*.

"So you've got that story out of him," Bastien said and had the satisfaction of seeing Raeven jump. He'd surprised her and had the feeling it didn't happen very often. "Anything else?"

"If you're concerned the good doctor has told me anything about who you are or where you came from, never fear," she said with a smile. He noted she'd pulled her hair back from her face and secured it with a ribbon. Where had she found a ribbon? She was wearing a pair of his black breeches and a black shirt. A belt held it all in place, but the garments were ridiculously big on her.

Still, she looked pretty. And tempting.

"I wasn't concerned," he said. "Gaston will never talk. He can withstand even the worst tortures."

"*Oui*, Monsieur le Marquis. But I have entertained this lady with other stories." He smiled at Raeven. "Come again when you have time."

"I will." She rose and turned to Bastien. "What is it?"

"Why do you assume I've come with a purpose?"

"You don't strike me as the kind of man who does

anything without a purpose. And I know you've just come from the wardroom."

He nodded. "Very well. I wanted to go over the charts and maps with you. Have you had time to peruse them?"

She gave him a look that told him the question itself was absurd. They returned to his cabin in silence, and she went straight to his desk, sorted the maps, and pointed to the one she wanted. "Here," she said without preamble.

Bastien leaned close, studying the map of an area somewhat west.

"Do you see these shoals? He'll want to stay away from those, keep in open water. But he's close enough to land, as well, in case he needs to drop anchor and complete further repairs."

"And he might think to box me in. The *Shadow*'s main strength is her speed and agility. If we have land on one side, we lose maneuverability."

Raeven nodded. "He has more cannon, and he's bigger, sturdier. You can outrun him, but he has the advantage if you stand and fight."

"But not if we surprise him. Not if—" He glanced at her suddenly.

"What is it? Did you think of something?"

"No. I've just realized I've come farther in planning my strategy with you than I did all those hours in the wardroom."

She shrugged. "I told you I could be of service." She bent to the map again. "Look here. If you want to surprise him, I suggest you come along this way. It will take an extra day, but he won't expect it."

Bastien studied the route, frowned. "Will he wait that long? I don't want to lose him."

"It's a risk. He has a prime position, so I think he'll wait. If not, you still have the advantage of surprise. Of course"—she took a seat in his chair—"all the surprise in the world will come to naught if your traitor sabotages you. Have you found his identity yet?"

He'd watched her study his maps, sit in his chair, and now she leaned back and questioned him as to his own ship and his own crew. For a moment, he felt as though he were a mate again, reporting to his captain. "You look quite comfortable. Can I get you anything? Wine? Cigar?"

"Oh." She stood. "I'm sorry. I didn't think—"

"I don't mind." Much. He didn't mind much. "I'm not used to it. No one else on this ship would dare take my seat."

"Old habit. I used to sit in my father's chair and do schoolwork."

Her words lit an old memory in his mind. He remembered sitting in his father's library, his feet dangling from the chair, looking at a book that seemed so big it must hold all the knowledge in the world.

"Should I assume, from your silence, you haven't discovered the traitor's identity?"

She didn't miss anything, did she? He sat in his own chair, not because he wanted a seat but because he wanted to remind himself it was his. *He* was the captain of this vessel. "Not yet. But I will. Soon." He studied the map again, thought about the plan they'd made. It might just work. He knew from Mr. Jackson the repairs were almost finished. They'd continue throughout the night and could sail at first light.

He rose, went to the door, then stopped and looked back at her. "I'm going to tell Mr. Khan to set a course. When I return, I want to find you naked and in the berth."

She raised a brow. "Is that an order?"

"Take it as you like it."

He shut the door and started up the ladderway. He'd done no more than step foot on deck when Percy Williams stepped in front of him. Bastien halted. He had little choice, as the man stood directly in front of him. "Mr. Williams."

"Captain." Williams didn't move.

"Now that the pleasantries are over, might you move to one side or the other?"

"You're bedding her, aren't you?" Williams asked. Even in the twilight, Bastien could see the man's face turn red. Embarrassment or anger?

Embarrassment, Bastien decided. "That's hardly your concern, Mr. Williams. I assure you, I've done nothing against Miss Russell's wishes."

"Good." He didn't speak, didn't move, either.

Bastien sighed. "Was there something more you wished to say, Mr. Williams?"

"Captain Bowers was a friend of mine."

"I see." Bastien sighed. Apparently, Bowers had been a popular man. "I'm sorry for your loss. But I'll tell you what I told Raeven, I didn't attack the *Valor*. She pursued us, probably looking to press my crew. Nor did I kill Captain Bowers. Not with my own hands, anyway. We didn't board their vessel. It was a quick skirmish, bloody and damaging, mostly to the *Valor*. I'm not sorry we won. If we'd lost, my men would be virtual slaves on the *Valor*, I'd be dead or imprisoned, and my ship would be another of the navy's prizes. I will say I never intended to kill the ship's captain, but he attacked in a storm—foolish choice—and he suffered the consequence."

"I understand. One day Raeven may, as well. She loved him, and he loved her."

Bastien nodded. "I suppose it adds insult to injury to have me—Bowers's murderer—in her bed."

"Actually, no."

Bastien raised a brow.

"I respect you, sir, and you're a good match for her. Tim would have wanted her to be happy. And, as unlikely as it seems, you make her happy."

Bastien let out a bark of laughter. "I fail to see that, Mr. Williams. She seems most intent on killing me."

"Yes, before she met you. But after Brest, all she could do was talk about you. Mostly about killing you, it's true," he conceded, "but she admires your talent with the sword."

Bastien tried not to show his surprise.

"One thing you should know about Raeven, sir," Williams said. He looked around him, obviously making sure she wouldn't overhear.

"She's in my cabin," Bastien told him. "You're safe."

Williams laughed. "You only *think* she's in your cabin. Who knows where she really is?"

Bastien gave a grudging nod. She was particularly slippery when it came to staying where he'd put her. "You were saying, Mr. Williams?"

"She's soft, sir."

Bastien frowned. "I'm well aware of certain soft features she possesses."

Williams went red again. "No, I meant, she's not as hard as she pretends. On the inside, she's vulnerable. She lost her mother and now her fiancé. Her father is ill. She may well lose him, and that leaves only me. I suppose I'm asking you to be gentle with her—when you put her aside."

"What makes you think I'll put her aside?" Of course he would set her aside. He had no intention of marrying the woman. But he was curious.

Williams shook his head. "I-I just assumed—"

"I'll be gentle. I'm sure, given enough time, she'll be the one to leave me."

Williams nodded. "Thank you."

"May I speak to my sailing master now, Mr. Williams?"

"Oh!" He moved quickly out of the way. "Of course. I'm sorry."

Bastien moved past him and headed for the helm and Mr. Jackson. He couldn't stop the conversation replaying in his mind. Williams hadn't told him anything he didn't know, but it did make him think— he and Raeven were not so different after all. They'd both lost people they loved.

Did that make it impossible for them to love again?

Perhaps. He knew he would never risk his heart. Not for her, not for any one. So perhaps they were doomed to—as Mr. Williams put it—set each other aside.

But Bastien swore they'd enjoy one another to the hilt until then.

❧

Raeven didn't undress. She wasn't quite ready to behave so wantonly. She supposed Bastien was used to seductresses, but she was the daughter of a sailor. She knew how to set, reef, and furl a sail. She knew how to load, prime, and fire a cannon.

She didn't know how to seduce a man, and she wasn't going to make a fool of herself by trying.

Still, she thought as she stood in front of his mirror, she could make some effort to try and look more presentable. There was little she could improve about her clothes. He had told her to take them off, so there was no reason to don one of the gowns. It would only look as though she was trying too hard.

Her face was her face. Even if she had face paints, she wouldn't have known how to use them. Similarly, she could do nothing about her body. She didn't have any undergarments to lift or shape her, and besides, he'd seemed to like her body fine as it was.

But her hair. There she could make an effort.

She'd never liked her hair. It was thick and heavy, not curly and not straight. She'd tried cutting it short, but after her father had recovered from his apoplectic fit, he'd told her she looked like a boy.

An unattractive boy.

She'd had to admit he was right. Her face was too round or too square—too something. The long, dark hair softened her features, and the longer her hair, the less it curled up and stuck out.

Like it was now.

She looked into the mirror and sighed. She used Bastien's comb to try and tame the puffy mess into something pretty and stylish, but either her hair was recalcitrant or she had no talent with hair styling. Perhaps if she tried securing it up…

"I'm only going to take it down again."

She jumped and whirled. Bastien stood inside the cabin. The door was closed behind him, and she had no idea how long he'd been standing there. Her instincts must be failing her because she hadn't even heard him come in.

"I-I was trying…" She couldn't think of the words. He was too handsome, and the way he was looking at her seared her body, rendering her temporarily unable to think. Devil take it, she could barely stand. She wanted to dissolve into a puddle on the floor.

He crossed to her, lifted a hand to her cheek, and carefully undid all her hard work, loosening her hair so it fell in a cascade down her back. With both hands he fanned it out then leaned in and inhaled deeply. He gave her a roguish smile. "Still smells like cherries."

"No, it doesn't. It smells like salt water and—"

"Shh." He put a finger to her lips. "Just now, were you trying to make yourself beautiful for me?"

She felt heat and color flood her face. "No."

"You don't have to. I already think you're the most beautiful woman in the world."

More heat and color flooded her face. "I told you foolish flattery doesn't impress me."

"It's not flattery. It's the truth. Look into my eyes." He took her chin between two fingers and forced her to look into his eyes. "Do you see the truth there?"

She did see the truth, and it stunned her. How could he possibly think *her* the most beautiful woman in the world? She was far from it, especially dressed in baggy men's clothing and feeling as though she were half asleep on her feet.

"But do you know how you could be more beautiful?"

She was about to shake her head; instead, she frowned. "Take off my clothes?"

He grinned. "How did you know?" His fingers hooked around the belt she wore and tugged her to him. He loosened the belt, and she heard it drop with a clink on the floor. "I would have thought you"—he took her shirttail in one hand while he undid the buttons at her throat with the other—"would be able to follow orders."

"I'm not one of your crew," she said as he drew the shirt over her head. She wasn't wearing anything beneath and had to fight the urge to cover her breasts.

"Much to my regret." He looked as though he might cup her breasts, but his hands moved to the breeches and slid them easily over her hips. She wasn't wearing anything beneath the breeches either. "You'd be the most valuable crew member I had—in here or on deck."

She stood naked now—feeling vulnerable and hardly like the most beautiful woman in the world—but then he reached out and caressed her cheek. He leaned close, kissed her lips tenderly, and suddenly she felt beautiful again. His hands brushed over her. They traced her shoulders, molded to her arms, slid down to her waist, cradled her hips, skimmed over her bottom... and stayed.

"Mmm," he said into her neck. "Turn around."

"You can't kiss me if I turn around."

"Oh, no? Try and see."

He turned her, and his hands came around her waist, pulled her bottom hard against his erection. She felt the tickle of her hair as he moved it away from her neck, then the softness of his lips as he nuzzled her. Meanwhile, his hands were free to roam. They circled her waist before moving to test the weight of her breasts. Finally, his fingers found her nipples. He teased them until they strained and peaked, until she was practically thrusting them into his hands. She could hear her breathing, heavy and hard, but she didn't start moaning until one hand slid between her legs.

He teased her there, sliding fingers in and out and around, all the time flicking her nipple with two fingers and tracing his tongue along her earlobe. She shivered and cried out, wanted to turn into him, make him sink himself into her.

But he had other ideas. When she tried to turn, he shook his head, bent her over the bed. The fingers between her legs never stilled, but she heard him rustle with his clothing then felt his flesh against her bottom. He parted her legs with his own—kicked them apart—and she felt him warm and solid at her entrance. He slid into her, his fingers still working their magic as he thrust inside her.

Her body didn't know which way to move. She wanted him deeper inside her and wanted his fingers to move faster. She bucked and writhed, and he continued the sweet torture.

Finally he cupped her, pressed and thrust hard into her at the same time. With a shout, she exploded, rearing back and arching. He caught her, tumbled with her onto the berth, and rolled her into his arms. Before she could think, could breathe, he was kissing her again. Her senses were overwhelmed, her body on fire. She didn't think it could burn any brighter, but the harder he kissed her, the more he stroked her, the more she wanted him again.

He pulled her on top of him so she was straddling him, and it took no persuasion on his part for her to take him inside again. She needed relief. Again.

She reared back as his hands cupped her hips, held her locked against him. He moved with her, and just before her world went white again, she felt his release.

Before she fell into a deep, dreamless sleep, she heard his breathing change as he fell asleep beside her. She smiled and thought, thank God. She was beginning to think he wasn't human.

She awoke sometime later. She wasn't certain how much time had passed, as the cabin was still dark. But she was cold, and she fumbled for the bedclothes, pulled them around her. She blinked, looked around the darkness. Bastien was dressing, slowly and quietly, but deliberately. She watched him don a plain white shirt.

"No lace?" she murmured.

He turned to grin at her. "A battle is no time for a fashion statement."

She sat. "Have they spotted *La Sirena*?"

"No, but we're getting close. Dress and come on deck. I could use a good pair of eyes and ears."

She blinked, more flattered by the plain words than all the compliments about her beauty hours before. She didn't even think he realized how much his simple trust in her affected her. She felt strong and powerful, as though she could have single-handedly defeated Bonaparte. Her heart swelled, and she felt… beautiful.

When she didn't rise immediately, he turned back to her. "What is it?"

"Nothing," she said. But she felt her heart constrict in a way she had never felt before—not even with Timothy.

Thirteen

THIS WAS IT, BASTIEN THOUGHT. THIS WAS HIS LAST chance. He would destroy Jourdain or be destroyed. The cat-and-mouse games would end today.

He stood on the bow of the ship and trained the spyglass back and forth over the horizon. Jourdain was out there. He could feel the man's presence in the prickle on the back of his neck. It was an hour before dawn, and Bastien had ordered the *Shadow* silent and dark. Now he could hear the creak of the ship's bow as it plowed through the water, the slap of the wind through the sails, and the hitch in the breathing of the woman who stood beside him.

He lowered the spyglass and turned to Raeven. She was peering through a second glass, but she held it steady and sure, no longer sweeping it across the water.

"You've found him," Bastien murmured low and close to her ear. He knew even the smallest sounds could travel across the open water. He smelled the faintest scent of cherries before she lowered the glass and turned to him.

"There," she whispered. "Three points off the starboard bow. I think I see a light."

Bastien nodded and lifted his spyglass. If anyone but Raeven had reported seeing a light, Bastien would have been skeptical. Jourdain was no fool. Surely, he'd ordered his men to maintain silence and darkness as a precaution.

But there were always mistakes. One mistake could cost a captain a battle. One traitor could mean destruction for all aboard. Bastien hoped the bastard, whoever he was, showed himself today. He'd send both Jourdain and his traitor to the bottom of the ocean.

He gripped the spyglass tighter and stared long and hard at the flickering light. The ship and the water moved, hiding the light then teasing him with a quick glimpse. He lowered the spyglass, looked at Mr. Maine behind him. Maine's lips were tight, his jaw clenched. Probably unhappy at having to give up his glass to Raeven. "Order Mr. Khan to maintain course, and make sure the men are at battle stations. *Silently.* I want the element of surprise as long as possible."

"Yes, Captain." He moved quickly to carry out the orders, and Bastien turned back to the ocean before him. He had Jourdain now. At the end of the day, one of them would be dead.

"Raeven," he whispered. She'd been looking after Mr. Maine, and Bastien could see he'd startled her out of some reverie.

"Don't tell me to go to your cabin," she said immediately. It unnerved him how she could read his thoughts at times. "I won't sit and hide while men fight and die around me. I can fight too."

He'd seen that on the gun deck, and he was short gunners. But firing a cannon was hard, exhausting work. Even with the best of intentions, she wouldn't be able to maintain the strength and stamina to fire as quickly and effectively as he needed. But he had to find a job for her to do. A safe—*safer*—task. He could not have said why, but he wanted to protect her more than he cared about protecting himself. Of course, logically he knew if he was killed, she would fare no better. But the woman had defied logic more times than he could count. He wouldn't be surprised if she singlehandedly destroyed Jourdain and took over *La Sirena*.

But she had to survive to do so.

"How are you at sharpshooting?"

She blinked, surprised. "I'm a fair shot. I'm better with a sword and dagger."

"I'll expect you to have my back when we board *La Sirena*." He'd been joking, but she nodded soberly.

"You'll need someone to cover your back. I'll go to your cabin now and retrieve my sword. Do I see Mr. Castro about a rifle?"

Bastien grinned. "Can you manage a rifle? You might do better with a pistol. I still have one of my Samuel Brunn flintlocks secured in my desk."

"I know. I've seen them."

They were in a locked drawer then locked again inside a hand-carved wooden box. He was the only one with the key, and he carried it on his person at all times.

Of course she had seen the pistols.

"Not that you need this." He handed her the key. When she took it, their hands brushed, and even with his mind and body tense with anticipation of the battle, he stiffened at the flash of heat unleashed when they touched. "I'll see you after the battle."

She grinned. "You'll see me in the thick of it." On tiptoes, she kissed his cheek. "For luck."

And then she was gone, and he was standing among his men, most of whom were trying to pretend they hadn't witnessed the last exchange. Bastien raised the spyglass again, feeling for the cutlass hanging at his side, the pistol tucked into his waistband.

He was ready.

⁂

Raeven was ready. She had the second of Bastien's beautifully engraved and embellished pistols in her pocket, her dagger strapped to her thigh, and her sword hanging at her hip. The weight of it was comforting. She'd missed it. She was making her way to the mizzenmast. She'd position herself there and hopefully take out some of *La Sirena's* topmen. Fewer men manning his sails meant it would be harder to maneuver the ship away from Bastien's advances.

She turned as she made her way across the deck and spotted him standing on the poop deck. Her heart lurched as she saw the first gray fingers of dawn behind him. In another hour they'd be visible to *La Sirena*. But right now, they were cloaked and had the essential element of surprise. Her heart pumped fast and not just from the anticipation of the battle.

Bastien stood with solid legs braced apart, black boots firmly set on deck. His black breeches were tight, and she saw the glint of steel at his hip. His hands rested surely on his hips just below his white shirt, which was open at the neck. His face was grim, his jaw set. His cobalt eyes burned as they looked out over the ocean, and his long brown hair had been caught back by the wind.

Her heart felt as though a fierce wind had caught it, turned it, and tumbled it around. She didn't know when it had happened or how, but she was in love with Bastien…

Devil take it! She didn't even know his real surname. How could she be in love with a man when she didn't even know his full name? It was another sign she'd gone mad. But then hadn't she been mad the first time she'd seen him? Hadn't she fallen in love with him the first time they'd crossed swords? It was only now, when she knew she might not see him again, she could admit to herself the true depth of her feelings.

What was she going to do? She couldn't tell him. Even if they won the day, it didn't mean their relationship changed. They were enemies. He was a pirate, and she was the daughter of a British admiral— an admiral who was probably hot on his heels at this moment. He'd have another battle on his hands very soon if he didn't rid himself of her. And a sloop against a man-of-war stood no chance. Bastien might try to outrun her father, but in the end, the *Regal* would catch him.

No, falling in love with Bastien would not save him. Leaving him and finding some way to convince her father not to pursue him would do the pirate more of a service than giving her heart ever would.

Besides, he didn't love her. She thought he felt something for her, perhaps even something more than he'd felt for other women. She knew he respected her experience on ships, valued her judgment, trusted her with his ship and his men. That should be enough for her. It was more than she'd receive from most men.

But a tiny part of her heart wanted his love too. Even though they could never be together, she wanted to hear him say the words: *I love you, Raeven.*

She heard the sound of alarm bells across the water, the call to beat to quarters, and knew they'd been spotted. Knew, too, her silly reverie was over. She hurried toward the bow and almost toppled over when Maine all but jumped on top of her.

"I'm sorry!" Maine grabbed her arm and steadied her. He carried a lantern, and it bumped hard against her arm.

"I didn't see you there, Miss Russell," Maine said.

She stared at the lantern, stared at Maine, and then looked across the water.

"That's quite all right," she stuttered. She had her balance back now, and she withdrew her arm from his hand. The air around them shattered as the first volley of cannon fire exploded from *La Sirena*. They were too far out of range, and Jourdain was wasting ammunition, but the sound of it was terrifying.

"I need to get to my station."

She nodded as he hurried away, but she didn't load her pistol. Instead, she watched Maine. What was the quartermaster doing with a lantern when the ship had been ordered to maintain silence and darkness? And why was the man on the bow? Even on a pirate ship, where positions and duties varied from those on a naval vessel, she could see no reason for the second-in-command to stand uselessly on the bow. And where was the watch?

She stared up the foremast as a foretopman scurried across the deck and, brushing past her, began to climb aloft. She frowned at him. She had no authority, but it didn't stop her. "You there!"

He looked down at her. "Yes, ma'am."

"Why are you just now reporting to your station? Where are the other foretopmen?"

She thought he might ignore her, tell her to be about her own duties—perhaps adding some surly remark about how her duties were on her back—but she must have sounded dictatorial enough that he answered.

"Mr. Maine sent us to Mr. Castro to help the gunners. Captain's orders. I've never fired a cannon before, and Mr. Castro sent me back. I think the other boys are coming back, as well."

Another boom from Jourdain's cannons, and she saw the youth jump. *La Sirena* was out of range, but the *Shadow* was closing the gap. Mr. Castro, no fool, was standing fast until his guns could hit the target.

"Get aloft," she ordered the boy, "and check those sails. Make sure all is ready."

"Yes, ma'am."

She considered going up with him to supervise, but she saw the other foretopmen stream back on deck and scamper up the rigging. Now she should ready her pistol and get in position, but she couldn't get Mr. Maine out of her head.

Her head had screamed a warning this morning

when Bastien had given the quartermaster orders. Something on his face hadn't looked... right. She'd watched him go, and the unbidden thought had been: *He's the traitor.*

She had no proof. She had no reason other than intuition to suspect him. But she trusted her intuition. It was when she didn't listen to it she found herself in trouble. And so instead of preparing to fire on *La Sirena*, she stared at the bow then up the foremast.

With no one on watch, Maine had been alone. Free to do as he would. Free to open the lantern, briefly shine a light, and give the *Shadow*'s position away. "Bloody traitor," she hissed.

The cannons boomed again—this time the shot coming from the *Shadow*—and the whole vessel shook. Everyone paused to observe the damage to *La Sirena*. One cannonball crashed into the deck, causing minimal damage, while another tore through a sail.

The battle was on now.

La Sirena returned fire, grazing the *Shadow*'s bow and causing Raeven to stumble. The two ships were turning, coming alongside one another, moving into firing position. It would be several more moments before the most effective shots would be fired, and she could do the most good by taking out some of *La Sirena*'s crew. She started toward the rail only to find herself grabbed from behind and thrust hard on deck.

For a moment, she wondered if the ship had been struck again, but she hadn't heard the boom or smelled the gunpowder. She looked up and saw Maine staring down at her.

"You couldn't leave well enough alone, could

you?" he yelled over the sounds of the coming battle. "You couldn't stay in his cabin—where you belong."

She rose up on her elbows and was alarmed when her head swam. Maine seemed to shimmer in front of her. "And I know what you did. You're the traitor."

"No one will ever believe that." He reached for her, but she had her dagger in her hand and ready to throw. She'd end Bastien's problem right here and now. But before she could loose the weapon, she heard someone yell, and a boot came down on her wrist.

She cried out in pain as it ground down, forcing her to release the dagger. She looked up, saw one of the foretopmen had come to Maine's aid. She exchanged a quick glance with the quartermaster, who gave her a victorious smile. He looked at the foretopman, concern in his features. "She attacked me for no reason. I think we have a traitor in our midst, Cooper. Take her to the hold and chain her there until after the battle."

"Yes, sir!" He grabbed her under the arms and pulled her to her feet. She stumbled and was pushed toward the ladderway.

"No!" She fought, tried to reach Maine, but Cooper grabbed her injured wrist, and she buckled from the pain. She was shoved down the ladderway. "Wait. Cooper, is that your name? Wait. It's Maine. He's the traitor. He gave our position away. I was trying to help."

"We don't need yer kind of help. Now shut yer hole, or I'll shut it fer you."

She knew when she'd lost. She shut her mouth and cradled her wrist close until he chained her in the hold and left her. Above, she could hear the sounds of men's feet on the boards, the scrape of the cannons moving into position, the sound of orders. Cooper could follow orders, but he didn't think for himself. She was still armed with her sword and Bastien's pistol. Of course, with her injured wrist, neither was very useful to her, but they were better than nothing.

And she had still had her hairpins. She wasn't going to spend the battle locked down here.

⁂

Bastien stood on deck as the two ships slid alongside one another. Across the space dividing them, he spotted El Santo, and beside him, Jourdain.

Jourdain had not changed. He stood tall in his brightly colored clothing. Bastien remembered that about the man—he preferred bright colors. Now he wore lose brown pants of some sort, a vivid green tunic, and a red vest. His head was bald, and the rising sun glinted off the oiled skin. Bastien couldn't see the earrings glinting from his lobes or the rings adorning his fingers, but he knew they were there.

The two men locked eyes, and Jourdain raised his hand in a salute. Bastien saluted back then stood tall as the brig's cannons fired, and his ship shook under his feet. Wood flew around him, and he heard the tearing of canvas as the grapeshot tore through his sails.

One for Jourdain.

"Mr. Jackson, damage report!" he ordered.

And then his cannons fired. Mr. Castro was deadly

as hell, and Bastien watched as men and wood scattered and shattered on the decks of *La Sirena*. A few of their guns took a hit, as did a portion of their hull. The sails had barely been touched, and there were still far too many topmen handling them. Where was Raeven and her sharpshooting?

Jackson charged up to him. "The ship's holding, sir, but we were missing men on the foremast. They're climbing back up now."

Bastien stared at him. Why the hell weren't his men in position? "Where is Maine? I want this ship running smoothly. I need maneuverability, Mr. Jackson."

"You'll have it, sir!" And he was gone again.

His cannons fired again, and he saw a large chunk of *La Sirena*'s main mast torn away. "Get grappling hooks and"—*La Sirena*'s cannons answered back, and he lifted a hand to shield his face from the spray of what he hoped was wood—"weapons!" he continued. "And prepare to board!"

❧

Raeven swore as she dropped another hairpin. It was bad enough trying to pick a lock with the ship shaking beneath her feet, but doing so with her left hand was all but impossible.

She fumbled in her hair for another, knowing she'd never find any of those she'd lost in the darkness. But she was running out of hairpins. She'd used only a few this morning to keep the hair out of her face. For a moment, she couldn't find one at all, and her belly clenched, but finally she touched glorious metal and pulled the last one out.

"Raeven?" a tenuous voice called.

"Percy? Percy!" she all but screamed it. "I'm here."

He had a lantern with him, and she welcomed the light as he stepped into view. A rat scurried away, and Raeven tried not to shudder. "Here. Shine that over here," she ordered as she fumbled with the lock on her manacled wrist again. Now that she could see, she'd make quick work of it, even with her left hand.

"What's going on? Why are you chained here?"

"Maine," she said through teeth clenched in concentration. The lock was being difficult, and she couldn't finesse her movements as she would have liked. "He's the traitor. He had me brought in here. Will probably be back later to finish me off. Damn!" She felt hot tears sting her eyes as she dropped the hairpin. "Can you shine that light down here?" She dropped to her knees and felt for the hairpin. "I need to get out. Warn Bastien."

She heard a clank and looked up. Percy was holding a set of keys, selected one, and coming forward, inserted it into her manacles. "I came prepared."

"Oh, Percy!" She stumbled out. "I could kiss you."

"I'll settle for your pistol. I don't have a weapon, and we're about to board *La Sirena*."

"We're boarding?" She handed him the pistol and started for the ladderway. "Is it going that well?"

He pushed in front of her. "Let me go first."

She wanted to roll her eyes. Percy was always the gentleman. "Cutlass is a genius. He's all but put a hole through the brig. Now it's just the down and dirty part."

The chaotic part, he should have said. And what

better time for Maine to kill Bastien, if that was his plan, than in the midst of the madness? Regardless, she had to warn him. She had to—

Just as Percy reached the lower deck's ladderway, Maine stepped out. Raeven saw his pistol even before she saw his face. "No!"

The blast of sound filled the cramped space, and Percy flew backward, his blood spattering her shirt and neck. She didn't have time to go to him before she saw Maine look to his weapon again. Ignoring the pain in her wrist, she drew her sword and slashed at him. He jumped back, fumbled, and dropped the pistol. When he looked up at her, his eyes burned with hatred. He gestured to Percy. "That should have been you." He drew his own sword.

"You'll wish it were you," she said, circling him. "I'm going to carve you up."

He laughed. "You can hardly hold that thing."

"I don't need to hold it." Their blades clashed, and she could feel the burn in her wrist as she held steady. "I just need to stab it through you."

He thrust and she parried, almost losing her footing on something slippery.

Blood. Percy's blood. The bile rose in her throat, and she wanted to look, needed to look at her friend, but she didn't allow her eyes to stray from Maine. She could tell from his movements and his thrusts he was no match for her, but she was not at her best. He would take any opening she gave him.

"Why did you do it?" she asked, ducking when he slashed at her. She spun and thrust, cutting his arm and drawing blood.

He swore and came at her. But he was angry, and she easily evaded.

"Money? Power?"

"Money, if you must know." He struck, and she sidestepped, feeling the whoosh of the blade tickle the skin of her throat. He grinned at her. "I told you. I have a wife. A son."

"And Cutlass doesn't give you your share of the profits?" She feigned left, moved right, and sliced across his midsection, opening a gash. She couldn't tell how bad it was, but his face paled visibly, and his movements slowed.

She risked a glance at Percy. He was lying on his side, one leg drawn up and his hand clutched to his abdomen. His eyes were open and filled with pain.

There was blood. Everywhere blood.

She pulled her gaze away, tried to plan her next move, not act out of anger and fear for her friend.

"Cutlass is obsessed with finding Jourdain. Passed up too many opportunities for profit." He thrust, and she easily parried, though her wrist twinged in protest. "I thought, he wants Jourdain, I'll give him the corsair!"

He thrust again, but it was weak. Still, her wrist was aching and she knew she couldn't last much longer. "I'm sorry to ruin your plans."

"Oh, you haven't ruined them, sweetheart. This is far from over."

"That's where you're wrong." She thrust, ducked right, and brought her sword up, stabbing him in the side. She felt the blade go through flesh and hit bone, saw Maine's look of shock before he crumpled, and she pulled out her sword, allowing his blood to drip on the wooden deck planks.

She kicked Maine's sword out of his reach, sheathed her own, and turned.

"Oh, Percy. No…"

❦

Bastien stood on the port side of *Shadow* and threw his grappling hook. Much of his crew followed while others fired pistols at Jourdain's men to give the boarding party cover. Bastien wondered if Raeven had hit any of Jourdain's crew. He hadn't seen her since early morning, and though he knew he shouldn't concern himself with her, she was constantly in the back of his mind.

Half a dozen times, he'd wanted to leave what he was doing and search for her. But he was the captain. He couldn't leave his command to chase after his paramour. Besides, she'd more than proven she could take care of herself. She had probably fared better in the battle than he, as he now had several cuts Gaston would need to stitch later.

She was fine, he told himself as his grappling hook caught *La Sirena*'s rigging. But he had a niggling feeling something wasn't right. As soon as the battle was won, he would find her, hold her, see for himself she was well. Right now, he had little choice but to swing from the *Shadow* to *La Sirena*. He landed with a thud and immediately drew his sword as several of Jourdain's men charged him.

He cut one down and turned to the second when he saw Jourdain step onto the deck. "Wait! He's mine."

Good, Bastien thought. He would finally have his revenge. The two crews moved aside to give them space, but the fighting continued around them. Bastien caught sight of Jolivette, Castro, Jackson, and Ridley cutting a swath through the Barbary corsairs with cutlasses and pistols.

He had a moment to wonder at Maine's absence and a moment to look for El Santo, but he saw neither. No sign of Raeven either. He wasn't sure if her absence was good or bad.

Jourdain lifted his cutlass then tossed it aside. Bastien raised a brow. He still held his sword.

"You want to kill me, Cutlass?" Jourdain asked, his English heavily accented. "You want to avenge the death of Vargas? Then fight me like a real man. With these." He held up his fists in a challenge.

Bastien was no fool. Jourdain had a good fifty pounds on him. Bastien was strong and knew how to throw a punch, but he was better at evading fists than using his own. Still, the challenge had been given, and he could hardly resist bloodying Vargas's killer with his own hands.

Bastien sheathed his sword and raised his fists. The two men circled each other, and Bastien looked for weaknesses. He didn't see any. He moved in, only to watch Jourdain block access. They circled again, and Jourdain smiled. "One of us will have to move first."

"You're right—" And without warning, he struck Jourdain square in the face.

Jourdain turned his head at the last moment, making it only a glancing blow, and when he turned back, he had murder in his eyes. Bastien took a step back and didn't see the hard left jab.

But he felt it. His neck snapped back, and his jaw exploded with pain. He doubled over and charged Jourdain, ramming him in the abdomen. Even when Bastien used the full force of his weight, Jourdain barely moved. He rained blows down on Bastien's head and shoulders, and Bastien endured the pain while continuing to push Jourdain back. Together they crashed into a mast. Bastien felt the thud reverberate through Jourdain's thick body, and he skirted away. Jourdain went after him, and a quick jab of his foot had the Barbary pirate sprawled across the deck.

Bastien got in a kick and would have got in another except he'd pressed his luck. Jourdain grabbed his ankle, and Bastien lost his balance, landing hard on his injured shoulder. He lay still for a moment, willing the black swimming before his eyes to fade, and then Jourdain's leering grin came into focus a moment before his fist connected with Bastien's eye.

"*Merde*." Bastien tried to roll away, but Jourdain had him straddled. He punched him again, and Bastien tasted blood. Jourdain was still leering when Bastien wrapped his hands around the pirate's neck and squeezed. Jourdain locked his hands over Bastien's and the two were at stalemate until Bastien managed to roll over and push Jourdain away.

He rose shakily to his feet, keeping an eye on the equally shaky Jourdain. The two circled each other, hurt now and weary. Around them, the battle between the two ships' crews continued. Bastien couldn't tell which side was winning, but he could feel *La Sirena* listing to starboard. The ship was sinking.

He hoped to hell Maine was preparing to separate

the two vessels. He didn't want the *Shadow* dragged down with *La Sirena*.

Jourdain must have felt the change in his ship, known it was sinking. Known he was doomed. He reached into his boot and pulled out a dagger. Without blinking, Bastien reached for his sword—and found his side bare.

He looked down to see his sword and sheath were missing. He had a moment to scan the deck and locate it sliding away from him.

Then Jourdain attacked.

&

Raeven struggled with Percy's weight. He had always seemed so thin and scrawny, but now that she'd half carried and dragged him to the infirmary, she would have sworn he weighed as much as two men.

As expected, the men of the *Shadow* packed the infirmary. The companionway outside was already lined with sand to minimize slips from all the blood. Raeven tried not to look at the blood or the wounded men. She dragged Percy past the men lying in the companionway, and when her way was blocked and she could go no farther, she called for Gaston.

"Mr. Leveque!"

No answer, and she wasn't even certain he'd heard her over the moans and cries of the men, not to mention the sounds of battle above them.

"Mr. Leveque! Please help me!" She had Percy under the arms, and she slumped now, resting her forehead on top of his white-blond hair.

"Mademoiselle?"

She looked up and said a prayer of thanks.

"Are you injured?"

"No."

He gave her a look that said otherwise, but she shook her head. She had no time for her injuries. "It's my friend Percy. He's been shot. Can you help?"

She could see him take in the throngs of waiting men, but he said, "*Oui*, of course. Here, I will help you bring him in."

Together they managed to lift Percy onto a table, and the doctor tore open his shirt. It was then Raeven saw the true extent of the damage. Percy had been shot in the chest, and she saw blood. Too much blood. It oozed and bubbled from the wound, making a dark crimson river down his chest. His chest still rose and fell, but his breathing labored. She felt weak and faint, but she gripped the table tightly and said through gritted teeth, "What can I do to help?"

She looked up and met the gaze of the doctor. His eyes told her all.

There was no help for Percy.

"Please," she whispered. "Please. You have to do something."

Leveque nodded and brought her a canteen of rum. "Here. Give him this. He is thirsty, no? And the rum will dull some of the pain." She reached under Percy's neck, supporting his head, and eased the canteen to his lips. His eyes fluttered for a moment, but he did not drink. The rum sluiced over his chin to pool around his neck.

"Percy," she leaned close and whispered. "Please drink, Percy. Please." She held the canteen to his mouth again, but he didn't open his lips.

"Percy." She was sobbing now. "Percy, you have to drink. Please, please." She laid her head on his shoulder, feeling the tears wet her cheeks and tumble down her chin. And she didn't care if anyone saw. If she looked weak.

This was her fault. If Percy died—no, she knew he would die—and it was her fault. She had brought him here. She had done this to him.

"Percy, I'm so sorry. I'm so, so sorry." She wept, and her whole body shook with sobs. She lifted her head when she felt something brush against the hair at her neck. She thought it might be Leveque, but he was tending another man. She looked up and saw Percy's eyes half open.

"Grand adventure," he wheezed. She could hear the fluid in his lungs. Could hear the rattle of the blood in his throat.

"Oh, Percy." She gripped his hand then remembered the canteen. "Here, drink."

But he shook his head. "Not your fault. I made my own ch-choices." He closed his eyes.

"Percy." She gripped his hand and shook it firmly. "You have to fight. You can't give up. I still have to buy you that dinner and those two bottles of wine."

"Three bottles," he murmured.

She almost laughed. "Yes—as many as you want. Hold on, please. I need you, Percy."

His eyes fluttered open then closed again. "You don't n-need me." His breathing hitched, stopped, and after a long moment his chest rose once more. "Him." He looked heavenward, and she knew he meant Bastien.

"Percy." She gripped his hand, held it tightly. She didn't know what to say, what to do. If she could have willed him to live, she would have done so. "I *do* need you. I do."

He smiled, but it was sad and wistful. "Lo… you." He breathed out, and she pressed his hand to her lips, kissed it, waited for his chest to rise again.

It never did.

Fourteen

BASTIEN DUCKED, BARELY AVOIDING THE SLASH OF Jourdain's cutlass. He felt the blade cut the air near his neck, and his skin tingled in response. Bastien risked a glance at the deck and his sword. It had caught on a bulwark. Two men were fighting nearby, but Bastien thought he could snatch it. He backed toward the sword as Jourdain closed in. The Barbary pirate grinned. "You will never reach it. I'll have your head on a platter."

"Are there platters at the bottom of the sea? Your ship is sinking."

"Perhaps. Perhaps it can be repaired." He thrust, and Bastien skirted left. He almost tangled feet with one of his own men fighting the pirates. The two exchanged a look, and Bastien moved back, closer to his sword.

"But your ship will be nothing but splinters when El Santo is finished."

What the hell was Jourdain talking about now? Bastien was almost within reach of his sword. The ship was tilting, and he could see the sword balanced precariously. One more lurch of the vessel, and it would slide far, far out of reach.

He reached for the sword, and Jourdain attacked. Bastien raised an arm to ward off the blow and was rewarded with cutting pain as the cutlass sliced through skin. The ship had moved, and Jourdain had managed only a surface cut. But Bastien's fingers closed on his sword just as it slid loose of the bulwark. In one motion, Bastien unsheathed the sword, swung around, and connected with Jourdain's cutlass.

Jourdain still had the advantage. The cutlass was short and better suited for fighting in close quarters, but Bastien could make adjustments.

"You won't be smiling long, my friend," Jourdain said as their swords connected.

"Once I slit your throat, I'll never stop smiling." But Bastien felt a prickle on his neck. Jourdain knew something. What had he said? Something about splinters?

He skirted around two men fighting near them and connected with Jourdain's cutlass again. "What are you babbling about, Jourdain? My ship isn't the one sinking."

Jourdain only smiled. "Boom."

Merde. Bastien glanced at the *Shadow.* Jourdain's men weren't swarming over the sides. The decks were clear but for the reserves he had left on board. And on *La Sirena*, his own men seemed to be winning the battle.

But it took only one. One man to light a fuse near the powder magazines, and the whole ship would blow.

El Santo. Where the hell was El Santo?

And Raeven. Was she still on the *Shadow?* He had to get her off. He had to stop El Santo.

Jourdain thrust again, and Bastien parried. He doubled his efforts, meeting Jourdain blow for blow, but he couldn't get a clear opening at the Barbary pirate. In frustration, he struck again—and made no progress.

&cx&

Raeven stood at the bottom of the ladderway and tried to compose herself. She had to stop weeping. Tears wouldn't save Percy, and they wouldn't save Bastien.

Maine was dead. The traitor gone. But she could hear the battle raging above. Who was winning?

She still had Bastien's pistol and her sword. Percy had said Bastien was boarding *La Sirena*. Perhaps she could help the boarding party. She started up the ladderway just as a set of boots started down. She moved aside, prepared to allow the crewman to go about his work. Until she saw the man's face.

He hadn't seen her there. She stood in shadow to hide her teary face, and El Santo didn't see her when he glanced down. He smiled, jumped down the last few steps and started down the ladderway to the hold.

Raeven stood in the darkness and watched him go, momentarily confused. What was he doing on the *Shadow*? Percy had said Bastien boarded *La Sirena*. Shouldn't Jourdain's second-in-command be fighting at his side?

Of course. Unless... unless he had another mission.

With a gasp, she raced after the Spaniard. He was headed aft and toward the powder magazines in the hold. It didn't take much thought to piece together his orders. "El Santo!" she cried.

She saw the shock course through his body at the sound of his name. Slowly, he turned, pistol raised. But she was ready. She ducked behind a bulkhead and winced when the wood splintered beside her cheek.

She fumbled with Bastien's pistol, but it was dark, and her hands were shaking. She glanced up and saw El Santo bearing down on her just as the pistol slipped from her fingers.

❧

Bastien had almost killed Jourdain half a dozen times, but the pirate had the luck of the devil. He had the feeling Jourdain was biding his time, stalling Bastien until El Santo could complete his task.

Bastien attacked again, and Jourdain spun out of reach. *Merde*! He didn't have time to play with the pirate. He spotted Castro and yelled, "Get back to the *Shadow*! Get to the powder before El Santo can blow us to heaven."

"Yes, Captain!" Castro moved to obey, but his way was blocked by a burly pirate, and he was forced to raise his cutlass and defend himself. Bastien swore again and slashed ineffectively at Jourdain. Jourdain smiled and mouthed, "Boom."

Bastien knew he had two choices: stay and fight Jourdain or return and save his ship. He glanced at Jourdain, imagined how much he wanted to destroy the man, avenge Vargas. But *La Sirena* was sinking. That was vengeance enough.

With a yell, he made his decision. He slashed and cut, forcing Jourdain back, then turned and ran for the railing. He sheathed his sword and grabbed one of the ropes attached to a grappling hook. He swung one-handed across both ships, landed a little unsteadily, and yanked the rope free. Dropping it on deck, he unsheathed his sword and raced for the lower decks.

He almost tumbled down the first ladderway then regained his balance and proceeded more carefully down the second. He could hear the clash of metal before he saw the adversaries.

And for some reason, it didn't surprise him to see Raeven Russell outside the powder room, sword raised against El Santo.

He almost breathed a sigh of relief. Then he saw El Santo stoop and lift something—Bastien's other Samuel Brunn pistol.

"Devil take it!" Raeven swore and attacked. But El Santo parried, throwing her off balance. She stumbled and fell, and El Santo cocked the hammer. Too late he saw Bastien.

"This is for Gibraltar," Bastien said and fired.

El Santo stared at him with a shocked expression then crumpled to the ground, a hole in the center of his forehead.

Bastien glanced at Raeven, saw her scowling. "I could have taken him."

With a laugh, he gathered her into his arms. "Of course you could." He rotated his sore shoulder. "But I owed him that."

She frowned. "I suppose."

She swiped at the tears on her face. "What is it?" If he'd been holding any other woman, he would have assumed the stress of the battle caused the tears, but he knew Raeven. Battle would not shake her.

"I found your traitor," she said.

He stiffened. "Who? Maine?" He wanted her to deny it, to name someone else.

"How did you know?"

Bastien closed his eyes briefly. "I didn't see him during the battle. He's usually right beside me."

She nodded. "He gave away our position just before dawn. Shone a light."

"On the bow? That's why the topmen weren't at their stations."

"I caught him, and he blamed me, had me chained in the hold."

"And yet somehow you're not in chains."

"Percy came for me." Her voice hitched, and he pulled her close. He didn't need her to go on now. He knew Williams was dead.

Her voice was thick as she continued. "We were hurrying up the ladderway, and Maine was waiting. He shot Percy. He thought…" She swallowed and took a shuddering breath. "He thought Percy was me."

"I'm sorry." Bastien resisted the urge to pull her closer, hold her tighter. He'd almost lost her.

"Me too." She swiped at her nose. "Not that sorry will fix anything. Make anything right."

"Where's Maine now?"

"Dead. On the lower deck. I put my sword through his side. He said he did it for money. You were too obsessed with finding Jourdain, passed up too many opportunities for profit."

"*Fils de salope.*" Bastien felt rage bubble inside him, rage and a nausea that reminded him of the seasickness he'd felt the first time he'd sailed. He'd trusted Maine, liked the man. Why hadn't Alan come to him? How could he have gone to Jourdain? The betrayal cut deeply. Bastien thought he could have forgiven Alan anything but betraying him to Jourdain. "Bastard," he said now. "If he wasn't dead, I'd kill him myself."

"What about Jourdain?"

Bastien gritted his teeth. "I had to leave him. But his ship is done." He pulled her to her feet. "Let's go watch *La Sirena* sink."

On the main deck, his crew was streaming back across. Someone—Ridley, Bastien thought as he glanced around—had ordered everyone back. *La Sirena* listed badly, and the crew of the *Shadow* was working to separate the two vessels. On board *La Sirena*, Jourdain shouted orders, and men scrambled to make repairs. But Bastien could see it would not be enough.

The ship was doomed.

And he would be certain of its demise. But the victory gave him little pleasure that moment. He wanted Maine by his side as much as he imagined Raeven wanted her Percy. Bastien had sailed on *La Sirena* years ago. It was fine ship, proud and elegant as it dipped, kissing the rising water.

Bastien turned away and clenched his jaw, clenched his resolve. "Mr. Ridley!"

The bosun grinned at him. "Cap'n! Looks like we done it."

"Yes, sir. You're quartermaster now—at least until we have a vote. Get this ship out of here. Mr. Khan!" The sailing master had just swung back across. "I want to be in firing position. We'll put a few more holes in her." He nodded to *La Sirena*. "Help her along to hell. Castro, gun crews to their stations!"

"Yes, Captain!"

He stood and watched as Ridley ordered the topmen to their work, watched as lines were cut, men scrambled up ratlines, and sails were furled or loosed to catch the wind. He watched it all with Raeven by his side.

And when his cannons blasted another round at the floundering *La Sirena*, he saluted Jourdain, smiled as the corsair stood on the poop deck while his ship sank around him.

≈

"How does revenge taste?" Raeven asked several hours later. She was pleasantly naked and wrapped in Bastien's arms. Well, she wasn't completely naked. Both of them wore bandages, and she had strict orders from Gaston to keep her bound wrist still. Both had orders to rest. And they *were* resting.

Now.

"Sweet." He kissed her neck. "Mmm. A little like cherries."

She laughed. "Was it what you hoped? I'll have to live vicariously, as it doesn't appear I'll ever have my revenge."

He grinned. "You don't have to kill me. What if you made me miserable every day for the rest of my life? That would be a kind of revenge, no?"

She felt her heart hitch for a moment. What was he saying? He wanted her with him every day of his life?

No. He was just being charming again. Pretty words

with no substance behind them. She pretended to consider his offer. "It's an idea. Do I make you miserable?"

He nuzzled her breast. "Extremely."

But as much as she enjoyed the way he was touching her, she moved away. "I think I made Percy miserable," she said, sitting and pulling one of his shirts over her head. "He didn't want to go on my adventures—as he called them. He wanted to do his duty on the *Regal*." She pushed back the tears threatening to spill over. "And now he'll never do his duty again."

Bastien put his arms around her and pulled her against his chest. "I'm sorry. But it's not your fault."

She shook her head. "It is. He wouldn't have even been here—"

"He was a man, and he made his own choices, Raeven." He murmured the words into her hair, and she closed her eyes.

"I know, but—he said he loved me. Those were his last words. I never even knew." She disentangled herself and stood, pacing. "Or did I? Maybe I knew all along and used his love to get what I wanted from him."

Bastien shook his head, and she paused in her pacing.

"I've known women like that, Raeven. You're not like that. You may have used him, yes, but it was unintentional."

"Still." She shook her head. "His death is my fault. He was always telling me to think of others, not only myself. But I never listened. I was so selfish. I *am* so selfish."

Bastien cocked a brow. "You weren't acting very selfish a few moments ago. When you—"

She waved a hand. "That's not what I mean. I

put others in danger. Even you. Right now, you're in danger."

"And I do fear for my life, *ma belle*."

She sighed. "Will you be serious? I'm speaking of my father. He must be searching for you now. And when he finds you—"

"*If* he finds me, I'll return his daughter and sail away. I have no quarrel with the *Regal*."

Her chest felt tight. Would he really send her back so easily? Did not even a small part of him wish her to stay? She cleared her throat, not trusting her voice. "Do you think it will be so simple? Do you think he will thank you and allow you to go?"

"I've outrun a man-of-war before. I'll do it again. But"—he stood, walked to a chair, and lifted his breeches. She couldn't help but admire his nakedness. His legs were long and lean. His body muscled and hard from life onboard ship. He pulled on the breeches, turned to her, and she averted her eyes—"I don't intend to sit about waiting for your father to come at us with guns blazing."

She nodded. "What do you intend?"

"I thought I might put you ashore. Somewhere you can contact your father. Perhaps England."

She blinked. "England?"

"You have family there, no?"

"Yes, but…" She blinked again. "You can't sail to England."

"Why not? I have a letter of marque from Spain. We're not enemies. At present."

"B-but you're a pirate, and now you've undoubtedly been accused of kidnapping the daughter of one of His Majesty's admirals. If you manage to make it to England, you'll never leave again."

He lifted a shirt, inspected it for wrinkles. "What other options do we have? As you mentioned, your father is no doubt pursuing us, so I can't turn and sail back to Gibraltar. And I've always wanted to see England. Surely there are secret coves and harbors where I could drop anchor. Surely the daughter of an admiral knows some of these."

She watched him don the shirt and considered. She did not want to leave at all, but neither could she stay. Her father would come after them, and she would not be responsible for another person's death, even if that person was Captain Cutlass.

And Bastien was right. Her father would hunt them down. That hunt might be suspended if he were to find his daughter safe in England. She wouldn't be able to stop the admiral from going after Bastien, but she might delay him. Give Bastien time to get away.

And why exactly did she want to help a pirate escape the British Navy?

She sighed. Because she loved the pirate, damn it.

Bastien was watching her. "What does that sigh mean?"

"It means I'm going to help you."

His grin was quick and cocky. "Was there ever any doubt?"

She ignored him. "But I still think England is too much of a risk. Why not sail somewhere neutral? Why not France? I can contact my father from—"

But he was shaking his head. "No. Not France."

"Why? We met in France."

"And that's the last time I'll ever set foot on that godforsaken soil; I will never return to France."

She sat on the bed and watched him pull his hair roughly into a thong. "Because of what happened to your family?"

"I don't want to talk about that." His eyes stayed steadily on the mirror.

"Why?"

"Because I don't like to remember."

"But it might help you to talk about it. It might—"

He rounded on her. "Do I ask you to talk about Bowers?"

She bit her lip. "No." But what she did not add was she did not need to talk about Timothy. She loved Bastien now. She would always love Timothy, but that love was different than this one. Not less, just different.

"Then do not ask me to talk about my family. There is nothing to say. They are all dead."

"Are you certain?"

He scowled. "You sound like Gaston, and I don't discuss the matter with him, either."

She rose. She could see the hurt in him. "Bastien." She laid a hand on his shoulder, but he pushed it away.

"I have duties," he said and walked away. She watched the door close behind him, sat on the berth, and wished she could talk to Percy.

❧

Ridley stood at the helm, looking every bit the pirate with his white shirt blowing in the breeze and the gold hoops in his ears. Bastien stood beside him and stared at the ocean, stared at the spot where *La Sirena* had made her last stand. Now she was gone, rotting at the bottom of the ocean, her captain with her. And good riddance. On the *Shadow*, repairs went on around him as the men prepared to set a new course. Bastien knew Mr. Khan was waiting for that course. He could see several of the men looking at him from time to time, waiting for him to inform them of their next adventure.

This wasn't life on a navy vessel. He might suggest a course and his men object. They never had, and Bastien didn't expect they would now—not with their pockets full of booty from *La Sirena*. But this was not a dictatorship, and he owed the men some explanation of what was next.

But for the first time in his career, Bastien didn't know what was next. He didn't know what he wanted to do, where he wanted to go. He no longer cared about seeking fortune and adventure. He had done that with great success.

He no longer cared about revenge. The man he hated was at the bottom of the sea.

What was left?

"What is left?" a familiar voice said from beside him.

Bastien turned to see Gaston. His clothes were stained with blood, his eyes shadowed and weary. "Am I intruding, Monsieur le Marquis?"

"No." But Bastien hadn't realized he'd spoken aloud. He raked a hand through his wind-tangled hair.

"You've had adventures, made and lost fortunes, and now you've had your revenge. Eh, *bien*. Is that all you want?" Gaston gestured to the endless blue ocean, churning and rolling as it had for an eternity, as it had before Bastien was born and as it would long after he was gone. "The sea doesn't love you."

"Love." Bastien shook his head, but he thought of Raeven, the hurt in her emerald eyes when he left her. She was the kind of woman he could love. He thought he might even be half in love with her already.

"You're thinking you can't have her—Mademoiselle Russell."

"I can't. I'd have to fight her father, fight the whole of the British Navy. And even if I was willing to do that…"

He couldn't risk his heart again. He didn't want to, and he suspected neither could she. They'd both loved and lost, and he was not willing to lose again.

"And even if you were willing?" Gaston prompted.

"I'd lose her." Resourceful as she might be, she was also far too adventurous. "*Merde*. If she outlives me, I'll eat my boot."

Gaston nodded. "She will die one day. You've faced your death many times, Monsieur le Marquis, and never shied away."

"I'm not afraid of death."

"Are you so afraid of life? You have a chance at love. You have a chance to *live*. Are you so much the coward you will not even take the chance?"

He thought of his family, his twin, Armand, and his older brother, Julien. Gaston had said he'd never found any record of their deaths. But Bastien had seen the chateau burn. He knew they'd died inside.

But he should have died inside, also. He lit a cigar, stared vacantly through the smoke.

He would have died if he hadn't been out playing

adventurer that night. He would have died if he hadn't used the secret passage to sneak out. He'd only intended to head down to the creek and see if he could catch a frog or two. His nanny, Madame St. Cyr, would not allow him to play with frogs… or spiders or snails or anything remotely interesting. He disliked the country, vastly preferred the exciting city, even at the age of eleven. But if he was forced to live in the country, the least Madame St. Cyr could do was allow him a pet snake. So he'd thought to sneak out and catch a frog or snake, take it back to his room, and perhaps surprise Armand with the creature in his bed.

He remembered looking back at the chateau as he'd made his way toward the nearby creek. He'd seen the light in Armand's room still burned. His brother was probably reading, and if Madame St. Cyr caught him, he'd be in big trouble. He couldn't see his brother Julien's room from that vantage point, but he suspected Julien was fast asleep. Julien usually followed the rules. Madame St. Cyr always said, "Sébastien, why can't you be more like your brother, Julien?"

He'd been on his way back from a successful foray at the creek, two plump frogs in his pockets, when he'd seen the torches and heard the singing. He'd hidden in the trees, waited to see what would happen, and had been shocked when the peasants set the chateau on fire. He'd run straight into Gaston, who'd been coming from the stables, and Gaston had pushed him back into the trees.

"Not that way, Monsieur le Marquis!" Gaston had been out of breath, his eyes frantic with panic. "If they catch you, they will kill you."

"But *ma mère* and my brothers! I must go and help them." He fought Gaston, but the groom held him fast.

"They will have to help themselves. You and I will escape, and we will find them later, no? We will all be reunited later."

"No!" Bastien struggled, but Gaston pulled him away, hid him in the trees, and when one of the horses from the stables came upon them, Gaston and he rode for a city far from Paris. On the way, Bastien realized the situation in France was far more serious than he had known. His parents had told them there was some trouble with the lower classes, but he had not understood they wanted him and his family dead.

Gaston told him they would need to leave France in order to survive. He'd promised they'd return when order was restored, and find the rest of Bastien's family. And so they'd traveled to Cherbourg, and Bastien found himself standing before Captain Vargas.

And here Bastien stood now. He looked at his old friend. "Have I ever told you I'm grateful for what you did that night? I'm grateful you saved me."

"Are you?" Gaston gave him a hard look. "I sometimes think you wish you had died with them."

Bastien flicked ash into the water. It was true. There were days he wished he'd gone back, even if it meant he would be dead now. "I felt like a coward for running," he said. "I *feel* like a coward for leaving them."

"Then perhaps it is time you stop running. You were a boy then. Now you are a man. Perhaps it is time you seek the truth of what had happened that night. Perhaps it is time you stop looking for ways to die and start looking for how you can live." Gaston shrugged. "Eh, *bien*. You know what is best, Monsieur le Marquis." He moved away, and Bastien stared after him. The old man moved stiffly, hunched over. It would not be long before he, too, was gone, and Bastien would be truly alone.

So perhaps the old servant was right. Bastien wanted to know what happened to his family—even if it meant the death of his favorite fantasy. Even if it meant he found out, without doubt, he was the last Valère.

He smelled cherries even before he saw her, and when he turned, she was standing tentatively behind him.

Perhaps the time had come to start living.

He studied her, knew she was probably waiting for him to order her below decks. Instead, he signaled Ridley. "Mr. Ridley, inform Mr. Khan and the crew I'd like to set a course for France. I have business there." He saw Raeven's eyebrows wing upward, but she didn't speak.

"Yes, Cap'n. Doan mind telling you some of the men not goin to like dat."

"Tell them they're free to disembark in Brest, find another ship. There'll be ships aplenty in those waters right now, taking advantage of the truce."

"Yes, Cap'n."

Bastien turned to Raeven. "Would you like to join me for a meal?"

Her brows winged up yet again, but she nodded. "I'd like that."

"Good." He took her hand. "I have a story to tell you."

Fifteen

"I DON'T KNOW WHAT THIS IS," RAEVEN TOLD BASTIEN an hour later, "but it's delicious."

Bastien nodded, sipped more of his champagne. She suspected he'd saved it to celebrate the defeat of Jourdain and had probably imagined sharing it with his quartermaster, Maine. She would never buy that dinner and wine for Percy. The celebration and victory were bittersweet for both of them. She looked about the wardroom. It seemed empty with only the two of them.

But at least the food was delicious. It was some sort of fish, spiced and seasoned in a way the cook on board the *Regal* would never have managed. Salviati, the *Shadow*'s cook, might not be much on presentation, but he more than made up for it with taste. She forked up another bite, noted Bastien was not eating.

"I think there are crepes for dessert," he told her.

She smiled. "How very French. Speaking of France…" The subject had to be raised at some point. "What changed your mind?"

His sipped the champagne again. "I said I had a story."

She laid down her fork, reluctantly, and reached across the table to take his hand. "I'd like to hear it."

He poured more champagne for both of them. "I am a marquis. Actually, I might be a duc. I might be the duc of Valère."

Raeven nodded. She didn't doubt his claims, not anymore. Anyone could look at him and see noble blood flowed through his veins. She, on the other hand, was a sailor's daughter through and through. Nothing special. "Valère." She tapped her finger to her chin. "That name sounds familiar."

"Gaston mentioned it to you, I'm sure. We're an old family—we were an old family. Now I'm all that's left."

She felt his hand tremble slightly and squeezed it tightly. "What happened?"

He told her. He told her about his kind father, a man who was gentle and giving. A father very different from her own, but someone she could see loving. She wished she might have met him. He told her about his mother—how beautiful she'd been, how playful, and how strict. "She never let us get away with anything," he added. "Somehow, she always knew what we were up to."

She smiled sadly, wondering what her own mother would have been like. In the portrait her father kept in his cabin, she looked gentle. She looked like the kind of woman who would have pulled Raeven onto her lap and kissed away all her hurts. As it was, no one had ever done that for her. She'd never been neglected, but she'd never felt cherished. She watched the tender way Bastien twined his fingers with hers, thought of the way he held her at night when he thought she was asleep, the endearments he whispered to her. He had never told her he loved her, but he made her feel cherished.

"And then there was Julien." Bastien smiled, and she could see the little boy in him, see the admiration he held for his older brother. "He was always so serious, so dedicated to his studies. He was a little duc from the day he was born. I wasn't the best student—too distracted thinking about all the fun things I could be doing to pay attention to our tutors."

She laughed because she'd been the same way. The hours she'd spent in her father's cabin with tutors had seemed like months when the sun was out and the wind blowing. She would have rather swabbed the decks than be forced to learn Latin and Greek, which was probably why her grasp of the classics was so poor.

"But Julien always helped me with my studies. He had infinite patience. I didn't realize it at the time, but I can see I must have been a trial to him."

"You're a twin," Raeven said. "What about your twin brother?"

Bastien laughed. "We looked exactly alike, but otherwise we couldn't have been more different. Armand was quiet and serious. He actually liked to read and preferred to stay indoors rather than run around and play. I remember him with his nose in a book. He was the tutors' favorite. He spoke four languages by the time he was ten and had read all of Homer—in the original Greek."

Raeven blinked. She hadn't even read Homer in

English. In fact, she wasn't certain if he was the one who had written about Aeneas or Helen of Troy. She always got them confused.

"It sounds like Julien was something of a cross between you and Armand."

Bastien nodded. "Exactly so." He was speaking in French now, and she didn't know if he realized he'd switched. He sounded comfortable speaking in French, but the more he reminisced, the more she heard the aristocrat in his voice. Sitting across from her—his shirt open at the throat, his hair long and carelessly pulled back—he looked every inch the pirate rogue. But in his straight nose, the high cheekbones, the arch of his brows, she saw the aristocrat. She saw the marquis.

"Julien and I would play pirate, but Armand never wanted to cross swords—fallen tree limbs, in actuality—with us. He'd rather read about pirates than play like one."

"And now you no longer play pirate. Tell me your play pirate name wasn't Captain Cutlass."

He gave her a quick grin, and she groaned and rolled her eyes. But when she looked back at him, his eyes were unfocused, and she could tell he was far, far away. "When I was a child, sleeping in a hammock on the gun deck and feeling homesick—more homesick than I can express because I had no home to go back to—I used to pretend they were still alive. I used to dream they'd escaped and were waiting for me."

She felt her throat close up and hot tears sting her eyes. She would not let them fall. He would not want her tears, but she stood and went to him, put her arms around him. He pulled her onto his lap and cradled her as though she were the homesick child.

"Maybe they did escape, Bastien. Gaston thinks there's a chance."

Bastien shook his head. "I saw the chateau burn." His voice rumbled in his chest where her ear pressed against his heart. "No one could have survived that."

"Did you see your father pulled out? You know he did not burn. Did you see him carted away to Paris?"

"No." And she could hear the sliver of hope in his voice.

"What if others escaped without you seeing? Perhaps your brother Julien, or Armand…"

She felt him stiffen and prepared for him to set her aside, but he continued to hold her. She looked up at him.

"I'll go back and make inquiries, and I'll put this to rest," he said, his gaze meeting hers. "The only question is what to do with you."

She twined her arms around his neck. "I'm going with you, of course." She said it as though it were fact, but she knew it was nothing of the sort. And to her horror, she felt fear well up inside. Fear of losing him. What was wrong with her? Was she turning into a lovesick ninny?

She drew her arms down, but he pulled them back. "I'd like that, Raeven, but what about your father?"

Yes, what about her father? Was she leaving the admiral to take up with Captain Cutlass? And if she was, could she live with herself if her decision resulted in the destruction of the *Shadow* and its captain?

"He'll come after us—you, I mean. He'll try to destroy you."

"I can outrun him. The question is, do you want me to?"

He was looking into her eyes, and she could feel her heart pound at the intensity of his gaze. "What are you saying?" she asked.

"Raeven, don't play games." He spoke in English now, his voice chiding and his accent surprisingly light.

"I need you to say it," she whispered.

He traced a finger down her cheek, kissed her nose. "I want you to stay with me. I want you to be my wife."

She hadn't anticipated the last, and a tremor of shock tore through her. He laughed. "You didn't expect that."

"No. I—why? Because I can fire a cannon?"

He laughed again, and she wished he would stop, because she suspected he was laughing at her. "Among other things. I can always use another gunner."

"I see." She tried to wriggle out of his embrace, but he pulled her close.

"And because you're beautiful and intelligent and almost as good as I am with a sword."

"Almost!" She fought to escape his arms, but he laughed and held on. "I'll fight you right now, and then we'll see who's better."

"You can challenge me back in our cabin," he whispered in her ear.

The *our* was not lost on her, but her back was still up. How like a man to think he was always better at swordplay. Still, if he continued to nuzzle her ear in that way, she might be willing to put the discussion on hold.

"Why do I want you as my wife?" His hand slid over her back, cupped her bottom. "I wanted you in my bed the first time I saw you."

She waved a hand at him. "Yes, yes. You told me—when you pulled the cap off my head. But you said something about marriage."

"Did I?"

She pushed away from him. "Never mind." She struggled to rise, and when she did, she watched in horror and fascination as he dropped to one knee before her. "What are you *doing*?"

"Proposing." He took her hand and she tried to snatch it away, but he held on tightly. "Mademoiselle Russell, I hope I am not too bold, but would you allow me the honor of asking for your hand in marriage?"

It was a formal proposal, one she might receive from any gentleman of the *ton*, but he grinned the whole time as though making a mockery of it. She didn't quite know what to think. Was he serious?

She feared, for all his melodramatics, he was deadly serious.

"I..." she began and didn't know what to say. Finally, she settled on, "Why?"

"I believe I made a promise to myself in the marketplace in Gibraltar," he said, still on one knee, still holding her hand. "I realized I'd met my match, and I'd better marry you before you killed me."

"I was never going to kill you. Not after Brest, at any rate."

"And why is that?" His grin was cocky, and she almost didn't tell him.

"Because I wanted you to kiss me too badly. You couldn't very well kiss me if I slit your throat."

"Not to mention, you're afraid of blood."

"I am not!"

He laughed. "Raeven, the floor is hard, and my knee is starting to ache. Will you give me an answer, *ma belle*, or do I have to kneel here forever?"

She wanted to say yes. She opened her mouth to do so, but the words stuck in her throat. How could she agree? How could she become the wife of a pirate? The wife of Captain Cutlass? The wife of the man who'd killed Timothy?

And how could she not? He wasn't Captain Cutlass anymore. He was Bastien, and little as she liked to admit it, she loved him.

Did he love her? He hadn't said so…

"I…"

His jaw tightened, and he began to rise. "If you need time to think about it—"

"No." She sank down beside him, joined both of her hands with his. "But before I agree, I need to know what happened. I need to hear it from you. The truth."

"Are you ready for the truth?"

He knew exactly what she was talking about. She had known he would, had known he would understand without her having to explain. "I thought I knew the truth. One of the men from the *Valor* told me the story. But I'm willing to hear your version now. I want to know what happened."

Bastien nodded, squeezed her hands. "We were off the coast of Greece, and our holds were full of cargo."

"Stolen from other ships, I'm certain."

He flashed her a quick grin. "Not British ships, *ma belle*."

"You're incorrigible."

"I think you like that about me." He put a hand on her waist, and her whole body tingled. "But as I was saying, we were low in the water, and I think the *Valor* must have thought we'd be... what is the term you English use? Easy pickings?"

She nodded. She could see the *Shadow* in her mind, see it as Timothy might have—an easy target. Except he didn't know Bastien.

"I could see the *Valor* was not fully manned. I think your Captain Bowers saw an opportunity to press sailors and take a prize. I did not approach him."

She looked away. The story she had heard had been very different. Bastien clenched her waist. "Why would I, Raeven? A British ship-of-the-line? There's no profit in that for me or my men."

"Perhaps you wanted the glory." The words were out even before she could think. And she regretted them immediately.

"You know me better than that."

She looked at him, looked at his face, so familiar to her now. "I do."

Bastien wasn't seeking glory. She didn't imagine he ever had. But Timothy... he had needed to prove himself if he hoped to advance in the ranks of the navy. The glory would have been his. "Go on," she whispered. "Tell me the rest."

"The *Valor* went straight for us. If we hadn't been so laden with cargo, I would have turned and run. I wasn't looking for a battle. But when he came for us, I didn't shy away. I don't need to tell you, if he'd won, I'd be dead and my men part of the British Navy—whether they liked it or not."

She didn't agree with the British practice of impressment. She knew ships needed to be manned, but taking a man against his will seemed wrong. And when her father had impressed sailors, they usually caused more trouble than they were worth. And still it was a sort of slavery. She could see why the men of the *Shadow* would fight it. What man, or woman, wouldn't want to be in control of his own destiny?

"I think he expected me to run," Bastien continued, "but I turned and came alongside him. The weather was stormy, the seas rough, and he had to close his lower gun ports. We closed with him amidships. I fired my guns, and he his. But as I said, he was undermanned and cocky. I'm sorry, but there it is."

She nodded. Timothy could be cocky. He was a good sailor, but he had always enjoyed easy victories.

"Still, we took a beating. Damage to the bowsprit, the sails, a few of our guns taken out. But we kept them spitting, and we had the weather gage. He couldn't maneuver as quickly. When the tide turned against him, he couldn't get away, and we damn near blew him out of the water." He tightened his grip on her waist, and she looked up at him. She realized she'd been staring at the floor, envisioning the battle, picturing it in her mind.

"I could have sunk him, but I didn't. *Merde.* I didn't need the whole of the British Navy after me. I spanked him and limped away to lick my wounds, which were fortunately few. I didn't intend to kill Bowers. One of the men told me later he'd seen the captain go down, and the next time we were in port, I heard he'd died. It wasn't my intention to kill him, but neither do I apologize." He released her now and stood. She sunk down onto her heels. He'd been holding her up, and she felt weak.

"He asked for a fight, and I gave him one."

She nodded, stared at the oak floors beneath her. It wasn't the story she'd been told, but considering that story had been related by a sailor from the *Valor*—the losing ship—she could see why it had been altered. No one would want to highlight mistakes the lost Captain Bowers had made. Especially not to his grieving fiancée. Much better to paint him as a hero and Cutlass as a villain.

But perhaps no one was hero or villain. Perhaps both men had done what their natures dictated. Bastien emerged the victor.

"You loved him." Bastien was turned away from her, staring out the dark windows at the endless ocean. "For that I'm sorry—sorry I killed someone you loved."

Her head jerked up, and she stared at his back. The tenor of his voice, the way he said it—she wanted to tell him she loved him. She wanted to tell him no one, not Timothy, no man had ever touched her, body or soul, as he had. But he had not said he loved her…

She rose, went to him, and wrapped her arms around him. He was solid, his body warm and hard against hers. She pressed her cheek to his back, inhaled, and smelled sea salt and tobacco.

"Yes," she whispered. "I'll marry you."

She felt him stiffen, realized he was surprised. He hadn't expected her to agree. But when he turned to take her in his arms, his face showed nothing but confidence. "We'll marry in France."

"Brest?" she said with a raised brow. "It would be appropriate."

"Brest then. I've already told Mr. Khan to set a course. We'll sail directly. If the winds are favorable, we should reach the harbor in a few weeks."

"If my father doesn't find us first."

He looked at her long and hard. "And if he does? What then?"

She knew what he was asking, knew he wanted to know whom she would choose. But she didn't know the answer. If it came to a battle between the two men, the two ships, she could not bear to lose either.

So instead of answering, she wrapped a hand around his hair and tugged his face to hers. The kiss was hard and meant to distract. She felt his initial resistance, felt it melt away as his arms came around her.

❧

It was enough, Bastien told himself as he buried his face in Raeven's long, dark hair. Having her with him now, holding her, feeling her warm body press eagerly against his. It was enough for now.

Her loyalties were divided. Understandably so. But what she did not realize, or perhaps did not want to acknowledge, was at some point she would have to make a choice between father and husband. Between navy admiral and privateer. Between duty and love.

Or at least passion. There was love between them, though neither wanted to acknowledge it. He suspected she feared the fragile emotion as much as he did. What neither feared was passion, and that bloomed effortlessly between them.

She had kissed him, long and hard, but he quickly wrested control from her. She didn't give it easily. She grasped his hands and tugged his shirt over his chest, kissing his chest and licking her way to the waistband of his breeches.

Just when things were about to get interesting, he pulled her up, yanked her own shirt over her head. Rather, it was his shirt, and he was disappointed to see she'd bound her breasts. She reached for his waistband, but he captured her wrists in one of his hands and reached for her bindings with the other. "I want you naked," he growled.

"I want you naked first," she countered. She tried to snatch her hands away, but he held fast, grasped the knot of her bindings with his free hands, and yanked it loose. He spun her around, and the fabric fell away. When it fell to the floor, he took her in his arms again. Her warm, soft flesh pressed against his bare chest.

She looked over her shoulder toward the door. "Perhaps we should lock it."

"There's no lock," he murmured, taking one of her rosy nipples in his mouth. *Bon Dieu*, he loved the taste of her. He could not seem to get enough.

"Mmm…" She arched her back, offered the other breast. "But what if the crew should… oh, yes… I mean, the crew… if they…"

"It's a small ship, Raeven," he murmured against her, cupping her now and tasting her. "I think the men know what's going on, and if they value their lives, they won't interrupt. Now wriggle your hips so I can slide these breeches off." His hands slid down the curve of her bare hips. "Why don't you wear a dress once in a while? Then I could just toss you on the table and lift your skirts."

"That's too easy." She stepped out of the breeches, gloriously naked before him. "But you can still toss me on the table."

He lifted her without a word and did just that. With the swipe of a hand, he cleared the dishes away—Salviati would have something to say about that, but Bastien would worry about it later—and set her down. She sat up, reached for his breeches, but he pushed her back on her elbows, took a long moment to enjoy the sight of her, then kissed her.

Every inch of her.

He knew her body now, knew what she enjoyed—what made her laugh, what made her moan, what made her buck and claw and cry out. And when he was finished, he did it all again. But somehow she managed to take control long enough to divest him of his boots and breeches. And when she touched him, he couldn't stop a growl of pleasure. She clamped her legs around his waist, and he sank into her warmth.

He had intended to take her hard and fast, but once inside her, he slowed, savored and enjoyed. In couplings with other women, he had always sought release—not that he didn't make sure they enjoyed the experience, but he made love because he enjoyed the end result.

But with Raeven, time seemed to stand still. It wasn't simply about his release or hers. It was about them, together, the connection between bodies and—he looked into her eyes—hearts. She felt it too. She hadn't been a virgin with him, and he wondered if it was as different for her as it was for him.

"Mon coeur," he whispered as he moved inside her. *"Mon amour."* He'd never said those words before, barely realized he was saying them now. But at that moment, at every moment since the first time he'd held her, she'd been his heart. His love. How could he not love her? She fit him. It was as though she'd been made for him, and he for her.

"Bastien," she whispered against his neck and arched against him. And he could contain himself no longer. With a groan, he went over the edge, holding her tightly, taking her with him.

Sixteen

HE GATHERED HER INTO HIS ARMS, HELD HER TIGHTLY, and Raeven wished they'd waited until they were back in his—their—cabin so she could lie against him, rest her head on his chest and listen to his heart.

That's what he'd called her. *My heart. My love.* Had he realized he'd said those things, or did he say them to every woman?

No, he'd never said them to her before. He'd called her many pretty endearments in French and English and even Spanish, but he'd never called her his love.

She took a deep breath, bolstering her courage. If she didn't tell him now, it might be days before she gathered her courage again. And who knew if they had that much time. She'd never expected to lose Percy or Timothy. "Bastien," she began, hating the way his name stuck in her throat. She sounded like such a *girl*.

"Hmm?" He'd pulled her into his lap and was rubbing his hands along her bare back, keeping her warm. In a moment, he'd put her down, suggest they dress, and her chance would be lost. She needed to say it now, while his face was buried in her neck and she didn't have to look him directly in the eye.

Lord, she was such a coward.

"Bastien, I–I wanted to tell you… I mean, I wanted you to know…" She could feel him smiling. Irritating man! "I think I…" No. That was no way to say it. She should sound confident. Sure. He hadn't said, *I think you're my heart.*

"I'm listening." He pulled away, looked into her eyes.

Damn it! Now she was going to have to say it while he was looking at her. She felt heat creep into her cheeks. She took another deep breath and made herself say it. "I love you." She stood up, paced away from him. "There. I said it."

He didn't answer right away, and she risked a glance over her shoulder. He was smiling. But then she was walking around naked. Of course he was smiling.

"Come here, *mon coeur.*"

She felt the tightening in her heart ease. She hadn't misheard him then. She went to him, happy when his arms came around her. He kissed her neck. "Raeven—"

"Cap'n!"

She recognized Ridley's voice outside the cabin door. Bastien stiffened immediately, released her, and reached for his breeches. "What is it, Mr. Ridley?"

"We spotted something. Want you to come take a look."

She hastily pulled on his shirt as he strode to the door and yanked it open. She was half naked, but to his credit, Ridley's eyes never wavered from his captain's face.

"Why haven't we beat to quarters?"

Now Ridley's eyes strayed, just for a moment, to lock with hers. "Oh, God," she breathed. She bent, fumbled with the breeches and pulled them on. Her hands were shaking, her body was shaking, and her heart was pounding so hard she thought the whole ship could hear it.

"Are you certain?" Bastien asked. "It's the *Regal*?"

"I doan know the ship well. Can't tell from this distance. But it be a British man-of-war. Dat much I knows."

"I'll go look," Raeven said, pushing past Bastien. "I'll know instantly."

Ridley moved out of the way, and she rushed up the nearest ladderway, stumbled her way to the poop deck. Mr. Khan was there, and without a word, he handed her the lead.

She put it to her eye, scanned the horizon, and her breath hitched in her throat. With shaking hands, she lowered the spyglass. Bastien took it from her. She hadn't even heard him come up behind her.

He didn't say a word, but she knew he recognized the vessel as the *Regal*. It was still miles away and would take a day, possibly more, to catch them. The *Shadow* was fast and sleek, and the wind was in their favor. But that would not matter. It might take weeks, it might take years, but her father was nothing if not dogged. Now he had found them, he would pursue them to the ends of the earth or the ends of time—whichever came first.

Bastien was looking at her, the question in his eyes clear. What did she want him to do?

She bit her lip, knew they could continue running.

They could run for months or years. But eventually her father would catch them. Eventually Bastien would tire of running, turn and fight, and she might be holding his hand in the infirmary when he took his last breath.

She looked at Mr. Khan, at Ridley, at the other men. She did not want to be responsible for their deaths. She did not want to see them in Mr. Leveque's infirmary, their blood staining the sand on the floor.

She looked at Bastien, and she wanted to wrap her arms around him, close her eyes, and pretend the *Regal* was still some distant problem they might encounter. But even as she met his gaze, their plans for a wedding in Brest, the search for his family, their life together began to sink to the bottom of the ocean floor.

His cobalt eyes were steady, the question burning in them.

"Signal them," she said, coldly, decisively. "When he's close enough, I'll make sure he sees me. He won't fire if he sees me."

Bastien held up a hand, and the men stepped back. He took Raeven's arm, steered her to the taffrail. "We can run. I've outrun a man-of-war before. I have the wind, so with a little luck…"

She shook her head. "And how long will you run? Weeks? Months? Years? He won't stop, Bastien. He'll keep coming after you—after us. Think of your men. How long will they tolerate running from a man-of-war when they could hand me over and resume more profitable ventures? Give it one week, maybe two, and you're looking at a mutiny."

He looked away, but she knew he agreed with her.

She wished she wasn't right this time. She wished they might have made it to Brest.

"When my father catches us, I won't go aboard without conditions. For my safe passage, I'll make him promise to let you and your ship go."

Bastien gave a bark of laughter. "And do you think once you're aboard he'll keep his word?"

"Yes. He's a man of his word. If he makes a promise, he'll do it. He may not like it, and he may come after you another time, but..." She looked down. "I'll try to dissuade him. I'll protect you."

Bastien's finger notched her chin up, and she looked into his eyes. He was smiling. "I can take care of myself. You, on the other hand..." He shook his head. "I don't want to let you go."

Her breath caught in her lungs. For a long moment, she couldn't breathe, couldn't think, couldn't do anything but stand on the deck of the ship with him.

The pain in her chest intensified until she had to all but close her eyes against it. She wished with all of her being, with everything she was, she had more time with Bastien. Another day, another week. She would take another moment if that was all she'd been given. She wanted to curse her father for finding them so quickly, but she knew he searched only out of love.

She was in love, too, and the temptation to flee her father was strong. But the little time she and Bastien would gain together was not worth the consequences. She thought of Percy, and she knew for once she couldn't be selfish.

"Maybe we'll meet again." Her voice sounded weak, breathy.

He nodded, but she could see he wasn't convinced. "This is what you want?" He gestured to the *Regal*, just a distant speck on the horizon at the moment but growing larger.

"Signal them," she said.

He turned away from her, all formality and business now. "Mr. Khan, set a course to intercept the HMS *Regal*. Jack"—he gestured to one of the deckhands— "run up the colors. Mr. Ridley, when we're close enough, hoist the signal for parley. Miss Russell will make herself visible on deck. Hands to your stations and beat to quarters. I want you ready for battle." He glanced at Raeven. "I've dealt with the British Navy before. I'm sure your father's a man of his word, but I don't want to take chances."

Raeven knew it would be several hours yet before the *Regal* reached them. She spent the time in Bastien's cabin, mostly pacing but also rehearsing the words she would say to her father. She had to ensure he would allow the *Shadow* to go on her way, and she was not at all certain she could do so.

Half a dozen times, she heard a sound and turned to the door, expecting to see Bastien saunter in. She wanted him to come, wanted him to take her in his arms one last time, kiss her and touch her until she was too dizzy to think of anything but the feel of him pressed against her.

But he didn't come, and as the hours ticked by, she knew he would not.

Finally, she went on deck. She still wore Bastien's breeches and shirt, but she'd left her hair down, made sure it would whip in the wind. She stood on the bow, watching as the *Regal* drew closer. Her father approached cautiously, even after she saw Mr. Ridley himself hoist the signal for parley.

She stood tall, holding her head up as the *Regal* drew nearer. She could not see her father or make out anyone on the decks, but she knew their spyglasses were trained on the *Shadow*. She knew they could see her.

"Now's the time we all hold our breath," Bastien said beside her.

She glanced at him, trying to memorize his features. At some point, he'd found time to change clothing. He knew how to dress the part of the pirate. He wore shiny black boots up to his knees, tight black breeches, a cutlass at his waist, a pistol tucked in his waistband, and a stark white shirt dripping with lace and open at the throat. His long black hair had been pulled back in a simple queue, and the style accented his strong cheekbones, straight, proud nose, generous mouth, and the impossible blue of his eyes. Hard eyes now, all business as he watched the *Regal*'s approach. "Close with him amidships," he ordered. "Gunners be ready."

"He's not going to fire with me standing in plain view," she said and hoped she was right.

Of course she was right, but she held her breath, seeing the *Regal*'s gun ports were open and the men at their stations. All was ready on the *Shadow* as well.

One wrong word, one wrong move, and the whole situation would explode.

Finally, the two ships came alongside one another. Raeven couldn't stop a smile when she saw her father on the deck. She moved to the quarterdeck so she might be opposite him. The admiral didn't smile back at her, and even at this distance, she could see he looked older, tired.

She raised a hand, and he nodded. But his eyes were cold as they looked past her and studied Captain Cutlass.

"Your flag indicates you want to parley," he called. "If this is some trick to lure me close so you can attack, I'll warn you we are fully armed and ready."

"It's no trick, Father," Raeven called before Bastien could answer. "The *Shadow* wants a peaceful exchange of words and terms."

Her father didn't blink. "Terms for what?" he yelled back.

"My return."

The admiral shook his head. "No terms. Send her over now, and we'll consider not killing the whole lot of you."

"I can't do that, Admiral," Bastien said, his voice carrying across the two ships. "If you want her back, you'll have to negotiate. Otherwise, she stays with me." He wrapped an arm about her waist and pulled her possessively against him. Raeven knew it was no affectionate gesture but a move calculated to anger her father.

It worked. The admiral's face turned as red as the horizon at sunset, and he whirled to converse with his lieutenants. After several minutes of discussion, the admiral stomped back and called, "Cutlass, you and one of your crew have my permission to board the *Regal*. You will not be harmed and are guaranteed safe passage back."

Bastien still had his arm about Raeven, and she felt

the anger course through him. "Thinks I'm that much of a fool, does he?" he muttered in French. "I don't think so," he called. "Your ship has more guns, more men, more firepower. I might have outrun you, but the time for that is past. *You* and one of your lieutenants have permission to come aboard the *Shadow*. I guarantee you safe passage back."

The Admiral scowled. "And if I refuse?"

Bastien shrugged as though it mattered not to him. But he stroked Raeven's hair possessively. "She's your daughter."

Another conversation between the admiral and his lieutenants ensued, and finally he called, "Agreed. Have your men throw down a ladder."

Raeven watched as the men went about their tasks, and her father and his first lieutenant moved away from the deck rail to converse. On board the *Regal*, the men began to lower her father's gig. She turned to Bastien. "I want to be included in the discussions."

His eyes never left his crew members. "Of course you do."

She put her hands on her hips. "Are you going to argue with me?"

"No." He raised a hand, and Ridley stepped forward. "Take her to my cabin. Lock the door and post a man outside. Then ready the ward—"

"What?" Raeven screamed. "You do not honestly propose to lock me up while you and my father discuss *my* future. You cannot honestly believe—let me go!" Ridley had her about the waist and was pulling her toward the nearest ladderway. "I'm not going to be locked up! Cutlass! *Bastien*, you bastard!"

Ridley lifted her, hoisted her over his shoulder, and lumbered down the ladderway. Once they were below deck, she stopped fighting. She knew she wasn't going to win, and Ridley was simply following orders.

"You can put me down," she ordered. "I won't fight."

Ridley did so, but he kept one hand firmly on her arm. Raeven balled her fists and seethed. How like a man to pretend to listen to her advice, pretend to respect her opinion, and when the crucial moment came, send her away.

They reached the captain's cabin, and Ridley deposited her inside, closed the door, and locked it. A few moments later, she heard him speaking to the guard outside. There were plenty of windows in the cabin, but all faced the stern, and the two boats were floating side by side. Still, she stared out at the blue sky and the churning waters and wondered whether her father had come on board and what was being discussed in the wardroom.

She still wore Bastien's shirt and breeches, and she wondered now if she should return them and don one of the dresses in his trunks. After all, this would be the last time she would see him for some time, possibly ever. She knew they had talked about meeting again, but those were only words. Once he sailed away, he would find other adventures, other women. She hoped one of those adventures was locating his family.

She supposed she could find other adventures and other men, as well, but she knew she wouldn't. She knew no man would ever measure up to Bastien, no adventure would ever compare to those they had shared, simply because no adventure would have the excitement of sharing the risks with him.

Now that she was alone, she could admit she was well and truly in love with him. She wished she had told him more of her feelings. She wished she hadn't stuttered and stumbled. She'd been afraid he wouldn't reciprocate. Yes, he'd spoken endearments during their lovemaking, but did he really mean she was his heart and his love? Those might have been just words.

She wished she knew for certain. If he didn't love her, at least their parting would be easier.

She glanced at herself in the mirror and decided against changing clothes. In a very short time, these garments would be all she had left of Bastien. And he certainly had plenty of replacements.

She paced back and forth, impatient, playing dozens of potential conversations over in her head, before she finally heard the sound of boots in the companionway outside.

Bastien! She turned to the door and tried not to look too eager.

The door swung open, and her father stood in it. She supposed her face must have fallen, because he scowled. "Don't look so pleased to see me, Raeven."

"Father!" Though she'd been expecting Bastien, she was happy to see her father. She hugged him fiercely, noting with some alarm he seemed thinner and frailer than before. He hugged her back, but his voice was gruff when he said, "You're coming with me. Now."

She nodded. She had expected this, only she thought Bastien would bring her the news. There would be no private farewell for them, she realized as she followed her father into the companionway. She would see him on the deck of the ship, and that would be all.

"Did you come to terms?" she asked her father.

"Yes. And don't ask what they were. One of the conditions was you were not to know the terms."

Raeven frowned. "That seems unusual. Why wouldn't you want me to know the terms?"

He glanced back at her as they started up a ladderway. "Why do you assume it was my condition?"

Raeven felt her heart kick slightly. Just what had Bastien negotiated? "Surely you agreed not to destroy this ship," Raeven said.

"This ship will leave my sight unscathed," her father commented as they stepped on deck. "Much to my regret. But if I ever see her again—*ever*—I'll blow her out of the water and use her hull for toothpicks."

She reached out, put a hand on his arm. "I wasn't hurt, Father. I was treated well."

He glanced back at her, shook his head. "Don't think I don't know what went on here. I may be an old man, but I'm no fool."

"I didn't mean to imply—"

He held up a hand. "We'll discuss it on board the *Regal*. You'll be confined to quarters, so I imagine you'll have plenty of time to unburden yourself and make all of your apologies."

She smiled because it was exactly the sort of thing she would have done in the past. But this time she didn't feel the need to apologize. She was twenty years old and no child. Her actions might have been careless in that they caused worry to her father, but she didn't regret them.

Except for the part she'd played in Percy's death. That she regretted more than she could ever express. And as they neared the ladder, she felt tears prick her eyes. The purser wouldn't be returning with them. He had been given a burial at sea along with the other casualties of the battle with Jourdain. He would never see the *Regal* or English soil again.

As they neared the spot where Mr. Carter, her father's second lieutenant, waited, she scanned the group of men, hoping to spot Bastien. To her surprise, he wasn't among them. To her further surprise, most of the men were scowling at her. Ridley had his arms crossed over his massive chest and his mouth turned down in a frown. Mr. Castro was glaring at her, and even Gaston—whom she rarely saw outside of the infirmary—was on deck and frowning at her. Raeven did not think she had been any of the men's favorite person, but she had thought most of them bore her no ill will.

But judging by their looks now, she would have sworn if she wasn't leaving this instant, they might throw her into the sea as food for the sharks. Where was Bastien? And what exactly were the terms he'd negotiated?

Her father took her arm. "Let's go."

She nodded, scanned the ship one last time. Was Bastien really not going to see her off? She hadn't expected any grand gestures, but was a wave or a simple *good-bye* too much to ask?

Her father began to shuffle her toward the side. She would have to climb down the rope ladder and take her father's gig back to the *Regal*. But she wanted a last glimpse of the pirate. "Where is…?"

"Let's go, Raeven," her father ordered, his tone one of unquestioned authority. She knew she was out of time, but she couldn't leave like this. She couldn't leave without seeing him one last time.

"Bastien!" she screamed, her voice echoing over the vast blue seas. "Bastien!" She scanned the deck but saw only the stern faces of the *Shadow's* men.

"Where is he?" she demanded. "Bastien, you bastard! I don't care what my father told you. Show yourself!" Nothing. No movement. No sign of Bastien.

"Raeven!" Her father gripped her arm and pulled her hard against his side. "You're making a scene."

"I don't care. Let me go!" She struggled, but it was futile.

"He's not coming out," her father hissed in her ear. "You're wasting your time. Now come quietly, or I'll have you dragged across."

She met her father's eyes and saw he meant every word. She was breathing heavily, but now she caught the breath and fought for control. She'd made a fool of herself already. Did she really want to be dragged unceremoniously aboard her father's ship?

With a shaky nod, she stepped onto the rope ladder and began the descent. Her father and Mr. Carter followed. Once they were back on the *Regal* and her emotions were under control, she angled for the deck rail. She had thought she would stand and watch as the two ships raised sails once again and went their own ways. She might have caught a glimpse of Bastien, but as soon as she stepped on the

Regal's deck, the ship's first lieutenant took her arm and escorted her to her cabin.

It was locked behind her, and when she picked the lock and opened the door, she saw a guard was posted. It seemed no matter which ship she was aboard, she was going to be locked away.

So as the men worked above, she sat on her rumpled berth and stared at her cabin. It seemed years had passed since she had last sat here, last paced the small space. Unlike Bastien's cabin, hers looked as though a hurricane had torn through it. Clothes were thrown over the trunk, and others peeked out of the sides. She never quite managed to fold everything so the garments would be contained and free of wrinkles. On her small desk, maps and charts were strewn about, pen and ink lay where she'd left them—the ink staining a paper she'd begun to make notes on—and one of the three pictures she'd hung on the walls was crooked. All of the pictures were of ships and the sea, and she wondered now why she didn't have any of land.

Bastien had paintings of fields and flowers and houses.

She pushed thoughts of him aside, went to her desk, and slid open the drawer. Inside, buried under more maps, several books, and a hairbrush, was a dark frame containing a miniature of Timothy. She stared at the picture, at the man she had loved so much. He looked youthful in the portrait, though at six and twenty, he had been seven years her elder when he died. But it had never felt as though he were older or wiser. She suspected Bastien to be closer to her age—she guessed he was at most five and twenty—but he seemed more experienced in every way.

She supposed he was; she supposed Timothy possessed more life experience than she, as well, but she'd never felt so when she'd been with him. Not like when she'd been with Bastien.

And why, exactly, was she thinking of Bastien anyway?

She heard the scrape of rigging, felt the *Regal* begin to catch the wind, and knew the two ships were parting. Bastien was gone… or would be within the hour. She should stop thinking of him.

And she should definitely not compare him to Timothy, though looking at the portrait again, she saw there was little to compare. Timothy had been fair with light brown hair, doe brown eyes, and a round face. He was handsome but not striking. His gazes had never taken her breath away, the way one look from Bastien's cobalt eyes could.

Bastien is gone. She shook her head, willing her mind to put him away as easily as she placed Timothy's picture back in the drawer and closed it tightly.

Ten days passed, during which Raeven was largely confined to her quarters. For once, she didn't mind the confinement. She wanted to be alone. Her father came every day to visit her, and after the first three days, had stopped lecturing and scolding. Raeven didn't have the fire to argue with him, and she supposed he grew tired of berating her when she did not fight back. There had been times she wanted to argue with him, justify her actions, but now that she'd spent time away from him, she saw how ill he'd become. His cough was worse, and he'd lost weight. He told her they were bound for England again, and she was grateful. A few months on land, eating good food and resting, seemed just the thing for her father's ailing health.

And then one night she couldn't sleep. She tossed and turned in her berth, unwanted memories of Bastien plaguing her dreams. Finally she rose, dressed, and opened the door to her cabin. She expected to see the guard posted there, but no one stood outside. The deserted companionway invited her, and without a backward glance, she stepped outside and within moments made her way on deck.

The wind blew strong and cool, and she stood in the shadows and allowed it to slap her face and toss back her hair. The salt spray of the ocean splashed her arms and face, and she closed her eyes and tried to banish unwanted dreams and memories.

"What d'ye think will 'appen to the poor bastard once 'e arrives in London town?"

Raeven turned at the sound of the voices. She'd known she was not alone on deck. It was late, but the men of the watch were on duty. Undoubtedly, some of them had seen her, but she did not think they would rush to tell her father if she only stood and looked at the water. Still, she'd kept in the shadows, and these two seamen must not have seen her. She had no intention of making her presence known. She turned back to the rail and leaned her elbows on it.

"'E'll be 'anged sure as my name is Tom Skippy. Tried and 'anged. I'd pay a farthing to see it."

"They say 'e ain't said a word since being brought on board. Just sits in the brig, like 'e's some sort of fancy gentleman."

Raeven's breath caught in her throat, and she had

to stop a gasp from escaping. As far as she knew, there were no prisoners in the brig. When had one been brought on board? They'd had no interaction with other ships since they'd left the *Shadow*.

"Some say 'e's a fancy gentleman," the first seaman said. "But I say 'e's a pirate, and 'e should be 'anged for his crimes."

"No." She gripped the rail tighter then pushed back and ran for a companionway that would take her all the way to the lowest deck and the brig. She scurried down the steps, feeling her way past decks dark and crammed with men sleeping in dozens of hammocks. She didn't need a lantern. She knew the ship as well as she knew her own body. She could find her way blindfolded.

It's not him. It's not him. It can't *be him.*

When she reached the orlop deck, the smells of rotting wood, vinegar, and oakum assaulted her nostrils. They were familiar scents, almost comforting. She arrowed straight for the brig and was met by a large sailor, who stood blocking her path. Beyond him she could see the small cells. The *Regal* had three. She stared hard at the dark cells, her heart pounding in her throat.

"Your father said you might run down here," the sailor said, grabbing her arm when she tried to push past him. Raeven shook him off and glanced at him long enough to place his face and name. Everyone called him Rummy because he could drink any man under the table, and his beverage of choice was—what else?—rum.

"Let go of me, Rummy. I'm going back there."

But he blocked her way and grasped her by the arms. Fury bloomed in Raeven. "Get your hands off me, and get out of my way," she hissed.

"I can't do that, Raeven."

She glared at him, and he cleared his throat. "Miss Russell. The admiral said you weren't allowed down here. Go back to your cabin."

She stood ramrod straight and gave him a hard, direct look. "If you don't get your hands off me, I swear by all that's holy, I'll cut them off and feed them to the sharks."

Rummy took his hands off her.

"Good." She nodded to the cells behind him. "Now get out of my way."

But he shook his head. "I can't, Miss Russell. Your father—"

She held up a hand. "I don't care what my father said. Move, or I'll move you."

He grinned. He was easily two feet taller than she and weighed three times what she did. "How are you going to do that?"

In one smooth movement, she extracted the dagger from her boot and pressed against his throat. "This is how. Now move."

But the stubborn man didn't budge. "You wouldn't do that to me, Miss Russell. I'm only following orders."

She bit her lip. "You're right. I don't want to kill you." She pulled the dagger from his throat and swung it considerably lower.

Rummy emitted a high-pitched squeal.

"But I'm not opposed to maiming you."

Their gazes met, and she let him see she meant it.

"You know I'll do it," she whispered. "Run. Go get my father, if you must, but get out of my way."

He nodded and began to edge away from the cells. "Slowly now," she cautioned. "You don't want my hand to slip."

He stepped carefully away from her, and when there was enough distance between his body and the dagger, he turned and went straight for the ladderway. Raeven knew he would probably fetch her father, but she didn't care. She turned and stepped into the brig.

The first cell was empty.

The second cell was empty.

And Bastien stood, arms crossed over his chest, brow cocked, in the third cell.

Seventeen

SHE LOOKED AS BEAUTIFUL AS HE REMEMBERED. PERHAPS more beautiful, standing there, hands on her hips, hair falling brazenly over her shoulders and tumbling over her breasts, chin notched high, green eyes blazing.

Bastien couldn't stop smiling.

Bastien had told Russell his daughter would realize he was a prisoner, but Raeven's father had assured Bastien he'd keep his presence on the ship a secret and Raeven away from the brig.

"Ten days," Bastien said. "I thought you'd find me sooner."

Her mouth—that lovely ripe-cherry mouth—worked silently. "You thought... you thought..."

He leaned a shoulder against the cell bars. "You'd better speak quickly. Your friend—what was his name? Rummy? Unfortunate sobriquet. Rummy will be back momentarily, and he'll bring your father."

She moved to the cell, wrapped her hands around the bars. "What are you doing here?"

He lifted his brows. "Don't you know?"

She gave him a bewildered look, and he shook

his head. "Come now, Raeven. I thought you more intelligent than this."

"You're not here for me." She said it almost as a challenge, as though she wanted him to argue with her. He didn't. He watched her face and could almost see her consider and discard one idea then the next.

"Your ship." Her gaze met his. "You traded yourself to save it. Bastien…" She reached for his hand, and he gave it to her. "I told you my father wouldn't fire on the *Shadow* with me on board."

"No, he wouldn't have fired while you were on board, but once you'd been taken aboard the *Regal*, he would have blown us out of the water."

"Not if he gave his word. You could have used me for leverage. You could have—"

"Your faith in your father is touching, Raeven, but your father is also an admiral. If he left the *Shadow* with nothing to show for it and not a shot fired, what would he tell his superiors in England? He couldn't fire because he gave his word to a pirate? Come now. You're not that naïve."

"And so you agreed to go as his prisoner in order to save your ship. I should have realized before. I should have known you would have to do this."

"It wouldn't have changed anything." It wouldn't have meant he could keep the *Shadow*. He could either sit in the brig of the *Regal* or sit on the bottom of the ocean floor. There had been no choice, really. He'd given the ship to Ridley, and after they hanged him in London, he'd promised to haunt Ridley if the man didn't take good care of her. "I have nothing to lose," Bastien told Raeven now. "No wife, no children, no family."

She gripped his hand tighter. "You don't know that. You were going to search for your brothers."

"It wasn't meant to be."

She shook her head. "Will you really give up so easily? Will you really go so gently to your death?"

He was facing death. Certain death. He'd persuaded Russell to take him prisoner instead of hanging him from the *Regal*'s yardarm. Russell was canny enough to realize the glory he'd receive when he brought the much-vaunted Captain Cutlass to London to face trial and punishment. It was a risk, though. Pirates were known for their tricks and deceptions. The admiral had made sure Bastien was locked up tightly and had no interaction with the crew—less chance he'd be able to sway any of Russell's men or cause a mutiny. Less chance he'd be able to persuade one of them to help him escape once on land.

But Bastien sure as hell would not go to his hanging without a fight, even if he had little hope he'd be able to escape. The British Navy didn't make a habit of losing prisoners. "I have a few tricks yet."

"Perhaps I can help you. Perhaps—"

"No." He all but crushed her hand in his. "This is no game. If you're implicated in aiding my escape, you'll be imprisoned as well. I don't want anything to happen to you."

"What a touching sentiment," a voice said from behind her. "Coming from a rogue. I hope you don't believe that drivel, Raeven."

Bastien met the admiral's eyes, squeezed Raeven's hand a last time, and released her. But she didn't step away from his cell. Instead, she stood in front of

Bastien, as though she were shielding him. Bastien shook his head. He really should have married the girl while he had the chance.

"Father, I demand an explanation. Why is Bastien imprisoned on the *Regal*? He's done nothing wrong."

Her father's brows shot up. "Nothing wrong? Is this the man you wanted to hunt down for the death of Captain Bowers? Is this the man you urged me to pursue because you were certain he carried arms for Spain? He's a pirate and a rogue. He's responsible for the death of Percy Williams. And now you dare defend him to me?"

"I'm responsible for Percy's death, not Bastien. Percy went aboard the *Shadow* with me only because I pushed and cajoled him."

"Be that as it may. If nothing else, the man has the crime of piracy on his shoulders. He's attacked British ships, stolen British cargo, killed British sailors. And I'm not going to allow those misdeeds to go unpunished because you're smitten with him. Now, go back to your cabin. If you're found down here again, the prisoner will receive fifty lashes."

She balked. "Father!"

But he'd turned his back and was headed for the ladderway. Raeven started to go after him then turned back to Bastien. "I'll speak to him. I'll try and help."

Bastien nodded, knowing she'd not budge the man an inch. "If I don't see you again…" he began, uncertain how he would even finish the sentiment.

"You will. I promise. I'll find a way to help you."

He cocked a brow. "I could do without the fifty lashes."

She gave him a quick scowl. "Have some faith." And then she was gone.

Bastien smiled. He had nothing but faith in her. Too bad in the British Navy she'd finally met a foe she couldn't best.

~∽~

Raeven argued most of the way back to England for Bastien's release, but her father would not listen. As soon as she broached the topic of Captain Cutlass, he cut her off and turned his back. On one of the last occasions she tried to reason with him, she caught him in his cabin. "Father."

"Do not start, Raeven," he said, not even bothering to look up from the charts on his desk.

She plopped in the chair across from him. "I have never seen you so unwilling to hear me out. What are you afraid of? That I might convince you Bastien is a good man?"

He glanced up and back down. "I *would* like to be convinced he's a good man, Raeven. Tell me. What is so good about him?"

Raeven opened her mouth, but her father cut her off. "Is it all the times he's attacked British ships or those under our protection?"

"No, but—"

"Was he good when he killed Captain Bowers?"

"No, but that wasn't his—"

"Or did he become good when he sailed away with my daughter and returned her to me thoroughly debauched and now arguing for the bastard's life?" The admiral stood, red-faced, and glared at her.

Raeven was wise enough not to answer. She still worried for his health and did not want him too upset.

"If your mother could see you now…" He trailed off.

Raeven waited, but it appeared he would not speak again. "If she could see me now?" she prompted quietly.

He shook his head, took his handkerchief, and coughed into it.

"What would she say, Father? What would she do? Would she not be happy to see that I'm in love? Would she not want to save the man I care for?" She lifted a hand when her father would have spoken. "Very well. He's not a good man. He's a privateer, and he's not what you wanted for me. But he doesn't deserve to die. If you let him live—"

"How?" The admiral placed his hands on his hips. "How can he live? He's wanted by the Crown. When we dock, he'll be sent to Newgate, tried, and hanged for his crimes. I can't change that. I don't *want* to change that."

"You could help him escape."

He glared at her. "I'm going to pretend I didn't hear that traitorous statement."

"Father—"

"No. No more! Forget him, Raeven. You'll find another man. I know you will. I have dreams for you too." For the first time she saw a flicker of pain in his eyes. "When I retire, I want to take my grandsons fishing. I want to see you happily settled."

"As do I."

"And I do not want to hear another word about Cutlass."

"Please, if you'd just listen to me."

"Not another word." He coughed, waved a hand. "Get out! Go back to your cabin and leave me in peace."

Hurt and dejected, Raeven obeyed.

She was not allowed to return to the brig to visit Bastien, and for the remainder of the voyage, she had only one brief glimpse of him. She happened to be on deck at the same time he was brought up for air. She was quickly dragged back to her cabin, but not before she was able to see he was well and healthy. He looked paler than she remembered, but he was not suffering.

At least she had that comfort.

Because she was no longer trusted, she spent hours alone in her cabin. Day after day, she tried to think of ways to save Bastien, but she knew even if she could help him escape the ship, he'd not be a free man. He'd be a wanted man with a price on his head. It would be next to impossible for him to escape the country by ship, as every captain would be on the lookout for him. She had no money, and if Bastien had untold riches hidden somewhere, she did not think they would be accessible in London.

And every one of her schemes would require funds. Who had funds? The aristocracy, of course. But she did not know any of the *ton*. She was a sailor's daughter.

Bastien's family was of the aristocracy. Perhaps if she could travel to France and find them, they might give her money to help Bastien.

A few days later, she spotted Mr. Wimberley on deck. Fitzwilliam Wimberley was fourteen and the third son of a marquess. He was the closest thing to the aristocracy she knew, and she stopped him as he passed her.

"Yes, Miss Russell?" He had the clipped, formal accent of the aristocracy, and even at fourteen, looked as though he'd be more at home in a musicale than inspecting the rigging on a mast.

"Mr. Wimberley, I wondered if we might have a word in private?"

His brows shot up in surprise. She couldn't blame him. This was probably only the third time she'd ever spoken to him. "I think the wardroom is empty this time of day. Do you have a moment?"

"Yes, Miss Russell." He indicated she should lead the way, and she did so, her thoughts churning as she walked. When they'd settled in the wardroom, Raeven seated across from him, she said, "Your father is an aristocrat, correct?"

Now his brows knotted together. "He's the Marquess of Huntleigh," he said slowly. "Is that what you wanted to speak about? My father?"

"No. But I wondered if, because of your upbringing, you might be familiar with another aristocratic family."

He nodded. "I know my Debrett's as well as anyone, I suppose."

"It's a French family. The name is Harcourt, but the title is the duc of Valère."

"Duc *de* Valère. Yes, I know of the duc. He made an interesting marriage shortly before I signed on to the *Regal*. I remember my mother speaking of it."

Raeven stared at him in open-mouthed astonishment. "The duc is alive and in England? I was given to think he'd been guillotined."

"Oh, I beg your pardon, Miss Russell. The duc *was* guillotined. This is his oldest son. I believe his given name is Jacques or—"

"Julien," she offered slowly. Julien Harcourt, Bastien's

oldest brother, was alive and well—and apparently married—in England. Her head was spinning.

"Yes, that's right. I didn't pay much attention to the discussion. Marriages and engagements don't interest me much, but the duc is quite wealthy and has investments in shipping, so when I heard his name, I listened briefly."

"Mr. Wimberley, do you think when we arrive in London you might be able to take me to the duc de Valère? Introduce me?" She noted she was clenching her hands together, and gently eased her fingers flat on the table.

"I don't see how that's possible, Miss Russell. I don't know the duc, and my own family will be expecting me. They promised to send a coach to drive me to my father's country estate. My sister and my older brothers will be there to welcome me."

Raeven's hopes plummeted, but she kept a brave face. "Of course, you should spend time with your family. But perhaps you could tell me how to discover where the duc lives."

"I expect with the blunt he possesses, he resides in either Grosvernor or Berkeley Square. But that's easy enough to ascertain. I might ask our coachman before I depart for the country."

She reached across the table and grasped his hand. "Oh, would you, Mr. Wimberley? I'd be so appreciative."

His face colored, and she realized he probably wasn't used to women holding his hand. She hadn't meant to fluster him, and she released his hand.

"Miss Russell, do you mind if I ask why you want to meet the duc de Valère?"

"I don't mind if you ask," she said, rising, "if you don't mind my not answering." She winked at him and watched him blush again. "Good day, Mr. Wimberley. I'll find you when we dock."

Raeven went straight to the bow and stared at the vast blue ocean before her. The wind was strong today, the clouds in the cerulean sky billowy white, and the ship moved through the water at a fast clip. Raeven's heart pounded, and she grasped the oak railing to calm herself. Oh how she wanted to rush down to the brig and give Bastien the good news. His brother was alive! More of his family might be alive! All this time they had been living in England. Perhaps they had been searching for him. When she imagined Bastien's happiness at this news, it took all of her willpower to stay on deck.

It would hardly be good news if the reward for hearing it was fifty lashes.

If the weather held, she knew they would reach England in less than a week. They would sail up the Thames into London, and Bastien would immediately be taken from the docks to Newgate. He'd be tried at the Old Bailey and hung at Tyburn.

Unless she saved him. Unless she found the man who could save him, the duc de Valère.

It was next to impossible for Bastien to escape from the brig, and even if he did, there was nowhere to hide on the ship. But once they reached the shore, escape was another matter entirely. And he might not even have to hide long if she could quickly find the duc, his brother. A powerful man like the duc could surely find ways and means to, if not exonerate Bastien, see him safely out of the country.

And when Bastien left the country, she would go with him. Unless... unless he stayed. What would she do then? She was no aristocrat. She would never be accepted by the *ton*.

She shook her head, unwilling to think of that possibility now. Right now she had to save Bastien. That was all that mattered.

Raeven stared at the open sea and formulated a plan.

❧

Bastien knew when they'd reached the Thames because he could smell it. Even in the dank, musty brig at the bottom of the *Regal*, the stench of the Thames permeated. He'd never been in London, never sailed up the Thames. He would have liked to see it, but he supposed there were many things he'd like to have seen before he had his neck stretched at the end of an English rope.

Not that he'd given up. He had nothing but time to formulate an escape plan. He would implement it when they docked, but as he didn't know the ship and didn't know the city, he had little hope he'd be successful.

But his main worry was for Raeven. If he knew his cabin girl, she wouldn't be content to allow him to handle things on his own. She'd want to meddle, to save him, and that would only ensure her own death. Aiding and abetting a criminal were serious charges.

And that was why when, on the night he felt the *Regal* dock, he was not surprised when Rummy handed him a note.

Bastien took it with a sigh.

"I think we both know who that's from," Rummy said, eyeing the note as though it were a snake. "If you're caught with it, I didn't give it to you."

"I found it in my coat," Bastien said, rubbing the parchment between two fingers. Rummy and he had struck up a sort of friendship, as prisoner and jailor often do. Bastien liked the man, but he was not sorry to leave the brig and Rummy behind, even if it meant the prospect of another jail.

"Are you going to read it?" Rummy asked. "She went to some trouble to get it to me. Threatened me, too. She's a wild one."

"That she is," Bastien agreed. He looked at the note and back at Rummy. "You know it's an escape plan."

"Well, it ain't a poem professing her undying love. Not if I know Raeven Russell."

Bastien sighed again and broke the seal on the paper. The handwriting was the same he remembered from the note in his chamber pot all those months ago. It seemed years now since they'd shared that first kiss, and he'd thought to punish her by making her his cabin girl.

The note was short and simple: *Look under the seat.*

There was only a small bench in his cell, and Bastien went to it now and peered underneath. Nothing but dirt and mouse droppings.

"What's it say?" Rummy asked.

Bastien shrugged. There was no harm in telling the man. "Look under the seat." Bastien indicated the bench. "Nothing there."

Rummy scratched his chin. "She might mean another seat. You'll be taken to Newgate in a carriage—not a fancy one, but it'll have seats. Maybe she means those seats."

She undoubtedly did. "Do you think if I asked you to tell her not to risk it, she'd abandon whatever plan she's concocted?"

"No. I'll tell her if you want, but I'll probably get punched in the jaw for my efforts."

"Far be it from me to be the cause of a scratch on your pretty face, Mr. Rummy." Bastien sat on the bench and stretched out his legs. Rummy was still watching him. "How much time do I have?" Bastien asked.

Rummy shrugged. "Hour. Maybe two. You'll watch out for her, won't you?"

"I'll protect her with my life," Bastien promised. "But you and I both know that may not be enough."

Three hours passed before two armed British soldiers marched into the brig. They were escorted by the admiral, who oversaw Bastien's removal from the cell. One was short and blond, the other tall, obscenely thin, and dark. The blond soldier held up shackles, but Bastien spread his hands in entreaty. "Gentleman, those won't be necessary. I am unarmed. I promise to go quietly."

The soldiers exchanged glances. "We're supposed to shackle prisoners," the dark one said.

Bastien shrugged and held out his hands. "If you must."

The blond shackled him and led him up the ladderways until he was standing on deck. It was full dark, and that was a surprise. A glance at the sky told him it was close to midnight. Docks always stunk, and the London docks were no different. He was careful not to take a deep breath, careful not to look for Raeven, either. He didn't expect she would be standing about on deck, watching him being led away, as some of the ship's crew was doing. He wished she were.

He was led down the gangplank to an old, sturdy carriage. Its curtains were drawn, and a coachman armed with a blunderbuss stood beside the open door. It appeared as though Bastien would be traveling alone. When he reached the conveyance, he looked at the soldiers. "Need I be shackled while inside?"

"You might as well get used to it," the thin, dark soldier muttered.

"Then give me one last taste of freedom." Bastien held out his hands.

The blond soldier nodded. "All right. One last taste, but if you try anything…" He unlocked the shackles and pushed Bastien into the carriage. Bastien settled on the poorly sprung seat, crossed his arms, and looked bored. He waited until the soldiers mounted their horses and the coachman hoisted himself into the box before he parted the curtains for a quick look. The soldiers were in position, one in front and one behind, but there was no other escort. No sign of Raeven either.

He heard the coachman call out to the horses and he reached under the thin squab covering the seat. His fingers touched metal and, slowly, he withdrew a pistol. A quick glance told him it was primed and ready to be fired.

"Thank you, Raeven," he muttered. "Now stay the hell out of danger."

Bastien sat quietly for several minutes, listening to the sounds of the city, waiting for the carriage to turn into a quiet street. After a time, he could tell they had left the docks behind, but despite the late hour, the city was busy. He heard voices and the sounds of other carriages passing. Still, he bided his time.

Finally, the carriage turned again, and the noise dimmed. Bastien gripped the pistol he'd hidden under his coat and took a deep breath.

"Halt!" a voice called. "Stand, or we'll blow your heads off."

Bastien heard the soldiers swear and the horses protest loudly before he heard the first shot from a pistol. He couldn't tell if it came from the soldiers, the coachman, or one of the attackers, and he didn't wait to find out. The carriage was still moving, and he had to get out before it stopped and the soldiers could secure him. He aimed both feet at the carriage door, kicked, and watched it slam open. He rolled onto the floor, his head landing near the doorway, and he saw the ground rush by.

Another shot sounded, and someone screamed. Bastien still had the pistol in his hand, and he rolled to his belly and peered into the dark night. The short, blond soldier was riding up beside the carriage. Bastien aimed, fired, and watched the man go down. Another horse approached, and Bastien prepared to throw the used pistol at him when he saw the ribbon of ebony hair down the rider's back.

"*Merde*. Get back!" he yelled. "You're going to be shot."

"The coachman is down," she called back. "I need to get control of the horses."

Another shot rang out, and she ducked. The look

on her face when she rose up again told him it had been close.

"You take care of him," she ordered. "I'll slow the horses." And she rode forward.

Bastien wanted to ask just how she expected him to protect her and dispatch the dark soldier, when the carriage careened wildly, and he almost tumbled out. He caught the edge of the door but lost the pistol. He watched it bounce on the road and tumble away. With a curse, he levered himself up and crawled across the carriage to peer out of the curtains on the other side. The dark soldier was right beside the conveyance and gaining ground. He had his musket aimed for what, Bastien imagined, was Raeven's head. With a roar, Bastien slammed the door open, hitting the soldier's horse and startling the beast so it veered off course. The thin man tried to control the beast as it knocked over a cart sitting beside a building. Bastien now saw they were in a narrow lane, but he glanced ahead and noted the lane opened into a larger street. There were other carriages about, and if he could stall the soldier or knock him off the horse, Bastien and Raeven might disappear in the crowds.

When Bastien looked again, the dark soldier had the horse back under control and was gaining on the carriage. Bastien kept one hand on the door and crouched. As the soldier neared, he sprang, He didn't know what he'd intended, perhaps some acrobatic maneuver whereby he knocked the soldier from the horse and seated the beast himself.

But he landed on the animal long enough to grab the soldier's boot before he slid down and was dragged along the road. He held on just until the carriage wheels were no longer a threat, and then he released the soldier and tumbled onto the hard lane. As soon as he came to a stop, he raised his head and watched the carriage speed away. The thin soldier was fighting to seat his horse once again, and Raeven was fighting to slow the carriage's horses.

With a sigh, Bastien stood up and raced after them.

❧

Raeven had one of the horses by the reins, and she was pulling with everything she had. But there were four of the beasts, and even though the one she held was considering slowing, the other three were not so obliging.

"Devil take you!" she yelled, turning when she spotted movement behind her. She frowned. Hadn't she told Bastien to deal with that soldier? And then her heart thudded. What if the soldier had dealt with Bastien?

She chanced a look over her shoulder and saw a man lying on the road. "Bastien!" But she had no time for concern. She had to get rid of the soldier before she could go back to Bastien. A glance ahead told her she was about to enter a busy street. But if she could maneuver the carriage into cutting off the soldier before she did so, she might be rid of him long enough to go back and collect Bastien.

She measured the distance to the street and decided she had about two minutes. She released the horse's reins and began screaming at the beast. She pushed her own horse closer to the animal and cursed her poor horsemanship. She was just as likely to tumble from her beast as she was to encourage the carriage horses to veer right. She screamed again and waved her arms as she saw the soldier come up on the other side of the carriage. He was almost level with her.

Another glance forward, and she saw she had about thirty seconds left. She kicked her mount hard, jerked his reins, and brought him closer to the carriage horses. The one beside her shied, screamed, and veered away.

Yes!

The others began to follow the lead horse, but to be certain, she screamed again and pushed her mount as close as she dared. The horses and carriage veered hard right, trapping the soldier and his mount between the conveyance and a building. Too late, the soldier tried to slow his animal, but horse and rider were caught in a tumble of horses and carriage.

Raeven didn't stay to watch the debacle. Instead, she whirled around and rushed back to where she'd left Bastien. To her relief, he was hobbling toward her.

"Are you all right?" she asked.

At the same time, he called, "Are you mad?"

She slowed her horse and offered him a hand. "I might be. Get on. Hurry."

He didn't argue. He took her hand, swung up behind her, and grabbed on to her waist. Warmth flowed though her when his hands were on her again. It had been so long since she'd felt his touch. But she pushed down the stabs of arousal and spurred her horse back the way they'd come. She didn't think the soldier would be any threat to them, but she didn't want to take any chances. As soon as she saw a narrow alley, she cut through it and emerged on a busy street on the other side.

She slowed the horse to a walk and hoped they didn't look too conspicuous. The last thing she needed was to try and explain herself to the watch.

"Might I ask where we're going?" Bastien said in her ear. She shivered and gripped the reins tighter.

"Berkeley Square." Wherever that was. Wimberley's coachman had given her directions, but those were from the docks. Now she was hopelessly turned around.

"What is in Berkley Square?"

She wanted to see his face when she told him, so she turned in the saddle and smiled. "It's where your brother Julien resides."

His face remained perfectly blank for three long seconds, and then he blinked. "What did you say?"

She had to turn forward again, but she was still smiling. "I said it's where your brother Julien resides. I have it on good authority he and his wife live at Fourteen Berkeley Square."

Bastien's grip on her waist tightened. "Is he expecting us?"

"No. And, I have a confession."

"*Merde.*"

She couldn't stop grinning. It was so *good* to have him with her again, even if it was only for an hour or so.

"What's the confession?" he asked.

She turned to face him. "I have no idea where Fourteen Berkeley Square is, and I'm afraid if we don't find it soon, half the soldiers in London will be after us."

To his credit, Bastien only closed his eyes and muttered, "*Merde.*"

Eighteen

JULIEN WAS ALIVE. NOT ONLY WAS HIS BROTHER ALIVE, Bastien thought, but he was alive and had been living in England for all these years. Bastien had asked a jarvey to point them in the direction of Berkeley Square, and if they'd followed the directions correctly, he and Raeven were only a few blocks away.

In a few moments, he would see his brother again.

Bastien hoped he didn't bring half the British Army down on Julien. By now, the soldiers at the prison would have noted Captain Cutlass was late in arriving and would be searching for him. When they found their compatriots and heard the story—assuming the two men were able to tell the story of Bastien's escape—they'd scour London looking for him. Bastien knew his time with his brother would be short. He intended to search out a vessel as quickly as possible and return to Gibraltar. The *Shadow* stopped there yearly, and he would surely see Ridley and the rest of his crew again soon. As long as he steered clear of the British Navy, he'd be free to carry on as before.

In front of him, Raeven turned her head to peer at him. Her hair brushed against his cheek, and he smelled cherries. He tightened his hands on her waist and thought how hard it would be to leave her. But this life of running and hiding was not a life he wanted for her. She belonged somewhere safe. Her father would keep her safe. Perhaps he'd marry her to some respectable Englishman, and she'd have a dozen children. He'd like that for her. He'd like to know she was safe and well, married and a mother.

He couldn't give her that life.

"That's it," Raeven said. "That's Berkeley Square, and I believe that's number fourteen."

The house was an enormous tower of white. Lights blazed in the windows, making it appear a beacon in the darkness. Bastien realized he was holding his breath as Raeven stopped the horse in front of the town house. The trees in the park were bare, but the last of winter was behind them, and Bastien could imagine the place when surrounded by verdant leaves and a rainbow of flowers.

Raeven glanced back at him, and he forced himself to breathe.

"Are you ready?" she asked.

"As I'll ever be." He dismounted then helped her down, as well. She felt warm and soft in his arms. He'd missed holding her. He would miss holding her.

He'd wanted to marry her, but he realized now how selfish an idea that had been. He was a pirate with several prices on his head. He could never give her a family and home like the one they stood before.

He started up the walk and felt Raeven hesitate beside him. "What's wrong?" he asked.

She glanced down at her black breeches and the belted black shirt she wore. "I look a fright." Indeed, her hair was streaming down her back, and she had scrapes on her hands, dirt on one cheek, and there was a tear in the material on her thigh.

She looked beautiful.

"We make quite a pair." He glanced down at himself—his torn coat, his dusty breeches, his bloody shirt. He wasn't sure if the blood was hers or his or one of the soldier's. He took her hand. "Come on. Let's scare the servants."

She shook her head but followed him with a laugh. At the door, he lifted the ornate lion's head and banged three times. Bastien could have sworn he heard the echo of the knocker in the silence. A moment later, the door creaked open, and an equally creaky butler stood in the entryway. "May I help you?" The butler's eyes skimmed over the pair of them, and the disdain showed clearly on his face.

"We're here to see the duc," Bastien said.

"The duc and duchesse are not home at present. If you'd care to leave your card"—his tone indicated he doubted they possessed cards—"I will give it to His Grace at the first opportunity."

"What's your name?" Bastien asked.

The butler raised his brows. "Grimsby, and yours?"

"Bastien. I suggest, Grimsby, you go get the duc. We'll wait for him in the parlor or the drawing room. Better yet"—he pushed his way past this Grimsby—"we'll wait in the dining room. Miss Russell and I are famished."

"Sir!" Grimsby argued. "You cannot shoulder your way into this house. I will call the footmen and have you bodily removed."

Bastien stood nose to nose with the butler. "And what will Julien say when he hears you've had servants lay hands on his brother?"

"Brother?" Grimsby sputtered. "You are not the comte!"

Bastien's eyes narrowed, and he grabbed Grimsby's shirt and jerked him close. "Armand. Is Armand alive? Is he here in London?"

"N-no!" the butler squeaked as Bastien lifted him off the ground. "His lordship is at his estate in Southampton."

Bastien's fingers slipped, and he released Grimsby and turned to Raeven. She looked as shocked as he felt. "Did you know about this?" he asked.

She shook her head. "No." She reached out, touched his sleeve. "Bastien, both of your brothers. They're both alive."

Bastien heard a sharp intake of breath and turned to see Grimsby staring at him. "You… I didn't see it before. But you look just like the comte."

Bastien nodded. "I'm his twin. Now, where is Julien? I don't have any time to waste."

Grimsby swallowed. "He is not at home. The duchesse and your mother—"

"My *who*?"

Grimsby jumped back even as Bastien reached for him. Grimsby stuttered, "The dowager duchesse, sir— er, my lord. They have all gone to Lord Astley's ball. They left the little boy at home, of course…"

Bastien reached behind him, searched for a chair, and when he didn't find one, sank down onto the floor. "My mother. And I have a nephew."

Raeven knelt beside him.

"I don't know what to say," he told her. "I don't know what to do."

She nodded. "I do. We go to this Lord Astley's and find them. We know the soldiers are looking for us, and we might be able to trust this butler, but we might not. I'd rather keep moving than sit here and wait for the soldiers to turn up."

"Madam," the butler said stiffly. "I do not know what kind of trouble you are in, but I assure you, I would never betray one His Grace's family members. I—"

"All the same, Grimsby." Raeven stood and faced him. "Tell us how to reach Lord Astley's ball. We'll see the duc for ourselves."

Grimsby's gaze swept over her. "Madam, you cannot attend Lord Astley's ball dressed in this fashion."

"It's no good, Grimsby." Bastien stood. "You won't talk her out of it, and I agree with her. We'll go to the ball."

Grimsby sighed. Loudly.

"Give us the direction," Bastien ordered.

❧

Raeven could hear the strains of the orchestra even as they stood outside the glittering town house. She had thought the Valére house enormous, but this was even larger, even more ornate. She stood beside Bastien on the lawn and watched the carriages pull into the drive. Women dressed in silks and velvet, jewels sparkling in the glow of the torches, stepped regally from each conveyance.

She looked down at her men's clothing and blew out a breath. "Perhaps this was not such a good idea."

"We have little choice," Bastien said. "We can't trust the butler, and I want to see my family before I have to go into hiding. Maybe they can help hide me."

Raeven nodded. "You're right." She bit her lip as another well-appointed carriage clattered up to the house. "How should we do this? Walk in the door there?" She gestured to a door where two liveried footmen were assisting a woman in a white gown and diamonds from her coach.

Bastien considered then shook his head. "I think we go in the back. Perhaps there's a terrace."

Raeven smiled. "Good idea. One other problem. Once we're inside, how will we find your brother? You haven't seen him in years. Will you recognize him before we're spotted and thrown out?"

"I'll know him," Bastien said. She glanced at him, and his expression was pure confidence. "And we'll move quickly."

They scaled the gate and entered the back garden. Fortunately, the terrace was well lit with Chinese lanterns strewn in long lines. Several couples walked arm and arm, and several had veered off the path. Bastien and Raeven almost stepped on one amorous man and woman. Raeven apologized profusely before Bastien grabbed her arm and pulled her away.

They climbed the stone steps to the French doors leading into the ballroom. Raeven was thankful for the dark because it masked their tattered appearance, but they still garnered more than their share of curious looks. Raeven ducked her head. Bastien took the steps two at a time, and Raeven hurried to keep up, but when they stood before the French doors and she glimpsed the dazzling ballroom, she balked.

She had been to balls before. She had worn pretty gowns and her mother's jewels. She had spent an hour pinning her hair and applying subtle rouge. But she had never seen a ball like this one. The men and women looked as though they were kings and queens. The ladies' dresses alone awed her. She had never seen so many rich fabrics or sumptuous styles. Jewels flashed, fans waved lazily, and the women all but glided across the ballroom floor.

The men were almost as impressive. They stood straight and regal, their navy coats brushed to perfection, their cravats stiff, and their gazes imperious. She wanted to shrink rather than walk before those imperious glances. She had never felt so much the sailor's daughter as she did now.

"Raeven, let's go," Bastien urged. When she looked at him, she saw no trace of worry on his handsome features. But then he belonged here, among these gods and goddesses. One glimpse of him, even in torn breeches and a dirty coat, hair loose about his shoulders and a smear of dirt or blood on one cheek, and he looked a part of the ensemble before her. Even in disarray, he was regal and imperious.

But, of course, he did belong. He was no pirate's son. He was the son of a duc—he was a marquis—and when he stepped through the French doors, he would only be reclaiming what was rightly his all along.

She, however, had no place here. And when Bastien stepped through those doors, she knew she would lose him. She'd thought to hold on by rescuing him from prison. She'd thought to hang on by bringing him to his family. But now she could see she had only widened the chasm between them. She had known it was there, but she had never acknowledged it until now, when it gaped, wide and inaccessible.

"Perhaps you should go alone," she said, aware her voice trembled slightly. She cleared her throat. She was not afraid—not of the *ton*, not of Bastien's brother, the duc, not of losing Bastien. She would go on.

Bastien scowled at her. "Don't be ridiculous. I'm not going to leave you here." He grabbed her arm. "Hurry."

And with one yank, he pulled her into the glittering ballroom. She squinted at the bright lights from the chandeliers and lowered her head again, feeling strangely self-conscious. At their sudden appearance, she could hear the hum of conversation dim then hush. From the corners of her lowered eyes, she saw heads turn, women lean to their partners to whisper, and muffled exclamations.

Oh, how she wanted to disappear!

Instead, she raised her head and looked directly in the eyes of those they passed. Let them stare. Let them whisper. She didn't live her life in stuffy ballrooms. She had seen the world. She tried to let them see her defiance in her gaze. She wanted them to know she didn't care if they mocked her.

A man stepped out before Bastien, and before he could speak, Bastien said, "The duc de Valére. Where is he?"

The man looked surprised then gestured toward the house's interior. "I believe he's with Lord Astley in the library. Some matters of business to discuss."

"Good. I'll join him." And Bastien, still holding her hand, plunged onward. The orchestra was still playing and people were still dancing, but Raeven was very much aware they were the main entertainment at the moment. Like the Red Sea before Moses, the guests parted as she and Bastien made their way across the ballroom.

But one woman stepped into the breach. She was smiling tenuously. "Armand?"

Bastien stopped, and Raeven felt the tremor of shock course through his body. "No," he managed.

The woman stepped closer, and Raeven studied her. She was beautiful—tall with dark hair coiled elaborately on her head, dark eyes, and full lips. She was slim, her willowy figure accented by the wispy white gown she wore. And, like the other women, she sparkled. No one would ever call the diamonds at her neck and ears garish, but they whispered wealth and taste.

She nodded and moved closer, almost touching Bastien now. "No, you're not Armand. He's... you're... You must be Sébastien." Her eyes glowed, and the smile she flashed was as bright as the lights in the chandelier. "Oh, I cannot believe it!"

Bastien's fingers tightened on Raeven's, and then he released her.

So soon, she thought. She'd hoped he would hold on just a little longer.

Raeven watched as the lovely woman in white

offered her hand and Bastien took it, kissed her gloved knuckles. He looked as though he'd been born to do such things. "I am Bastien," he said. "And you are?"

"Sarah, the duchesse de Valére. I'm Julien's wife." She spoke quickly, her voice a little breathless.

If Bastien was surprised to meet his sister-in-law, he didn't show it. He drew Raeven forward. "Your Grace, this is Miss Russell."

Raeven took the woman's gloved hand, and Sarah squeezed her fingers reassuringly. "Pleased to meet you, Miss Russell."

Raeven watched as Bastien casually took the duchesse's arm and give her a charming smile. "Would you take me to your husband? I'm in something of a hurry."

Sarah nodded. "Trouble?" She waved a hand. "Of course there is. It seems to follow you brothers like a hungry puppy. This way…" She gestured for them to follow then turned back and gave Bastien a quick hug. "I'm sorry, but I simply can't believe you're here. I'm so thrilled. Your brother will be—oh! But your mother. She will want to see you. We *must* seek her out." She looked from guest to guest. "Can someone find the dowager…?"

"No." Bastien shook his head firmly. "My mother will have to wait, I'm afraid. We haven't any time to waste."

The duchesse nodded, her expression more grave now. "Very well. But I'm going to have to answer for this later," she said as she led them past the staring guests. No one made any pretense of not watching them now. At some moment Raeven couldn't pinpoint, the music had stopped and the last vestiges of the ball halted. She could feel heat creeping up her neck and cheeks, but she ignored it and held her head high. So what if she looked like a street urchin?

She could set, reef, and furl a sail.

She could fight with a sword, rapier, cutlass, and dagger, and wasn't a bad shot with a pistol.

She could plot a course halfway across the world. And be sure her ship actually reached its destination.

What could these men and women do but stand about, dance, and look pretty?

Finally—*finally*—they left the ballroom and stood in the house's large foyer. To Raeven it seemed cavernous as a tomb with its high, domed ceiling, marble statues, and stark, imposing walls. A footman or butler materialized immediately and bowed to the duchesse. "Your Grace, how may I be of service?"

"I need to see my husband. Is this the library?" She gestured to one of the closed doors.

"Yes, Your Grace. Shall I announce you and your... companions?" His tone had just the slightest sneer of derision, but Sarah ignored it.

"No. We want to announce ourselves," she said, more than a hint of excitement in her tone.

She went to the door, knocked briskly, and opened it.

❧

Bastien held his breath as the door swung open. He heard the duchesse—strange to think of anyone but his mother as the duchesse de Valére—call out something. Perhaps a greeting. And then the two men inside swung around to face them. The men were well dressed in all but matching coats, breeches, and pumps.

They both held crystal glasses filled with amber liquid. Bastien had never seen one of the men.

And when his gaze met that of the other, the years fell away.

The duchesse moved to the side, and Bastien stepped forward. He opened his mouth to say something. He thought he might say something amusing or pithy, but no words came.

Instead, he watched his brother hand his glass to the man he'd been speaking with, take two steps, and then enfold Bastien in a firm, hard embrace. Bastien stood immobile, hardly knowing what response he should make. An hour or so before, he had not known his brother was alive, and now here was Julien, in the flesh, hugging him fiercely.

Julien stepped back, put his hands on Bastien's shoulders. Too late, Bastien realized he should have embraced his brother in return. "I knew you were alive," Julien said in French.

The voice.

The voice was almost the same. Older, deeper, but Bastien knew that voice. "I've been looking for you, looking for Captain Cutlass."

Bastien had a thousand questions. He wanted to ask about his twin, their mother, his father, his nephew, this Sarah, how long Julien had been searching for him, how he had known Bastien survived, how Julien survived...

Instead, he said, "I think most of the soldiers in London are searching for Captain Cutlass. Raeven and I just escaped those transporting me to Newgate."

He reached for Raeven and noted, again, she stood

behind him, off by herself. She seemed to want to shrink away, to avoid notice. He took her wrist and pulled her forward. "This is Raeven Russell, daughter of Admiral Russell. She aided my escape, and I imagine her father has noticed her absence by now."

"That doesn't give us much time to reminisce. I take it the navy may be after you, as well?"

Bastien shrugged. "I'm a popular man at the moment."

Julien laughed. "If that's another way of saying you're in trouble—again—my answer is this seems like old times. And, once again, dear brother, I am going to come to your aid."

Bastien bristled, just as he had as a child. "I can handle myself. I only stopped to say hello before making my escape."

"Oh!" The duchesse gripped his arm. "But you can't leave now. You haven't even seen your mother."

Lord Astley, who had been standing quietly near the bookshelves, stepped forward. "I'll fetch her. I think it best if I inform the servants we might have military company. If the soldiers knock on my door, Valére, you can be assured we'll do everything we can to stall them."

"Thank you," Julien said. When Astley was gone, Julien gestured to the couch and chairs clustered on one side of the room. "Now, quickly, tell me everything."

Bastien led Raeven to a chair before taking one himself. "It's not an easy matter to fix. You won't be able to snap your fingers and right the wrong."

Julien sat on the couch across from him and smiled. "These days, I have more than fingers to snap. Start talking."

So Bastien did, and for the first time since Maine's betrayal, he had someone at his back again. He was not on his own. Bastien could handle himself, but he couldn't stop the smile that rose to his lips when he thought of his older brother looking out for him again.

Nineteen

EVERYTHING HAPPENED IN A WHIRLWIND. ONE MOMENT Raeven was at some lord's ball, and the next she was ferried back to Berkeley Square in a carriage so sumptuous she was afraid to sit on the squabs, lest she dirty them.

She had argued now that Bastien was back with his family, she should return to the *Regal*, but Bastien wouldn't allow it. She thought Julien might have agreed her return to the *Regal* was best, but he didn't protest when Bastien told her no. And so she found herself in the lavish carriage with the dowager and the duchesse de Valére.

Before she and Bastien had parted, Raeven had witnessed the reunion between mother and son. The dowager had rushed into Lord Astley's library and practically mowed Bastien over with the enthusiasm of her embrace. It was difficult to believe the stately woman seated across from her now was the same woman who'd cried and babbled and hugged Bastien until he must have felt more loved and adored than any other man on earth.

The reunion had made Raeven cry, had made her ache for her own mother, the mother she had never known.

Now she looked at the duchesse and Bastien's mother. They looked back. Both women were kind, but Raeven knew they didn't quite know what to think if her—the tart their precious Bastien had thrust upon them. They hadn't called her a tart, and perhaps they hadn't even thought of her that way in their minds, but she felt like unwanted rubbish. She wanted to go home, go back to the *Regal*. She didn't want to wait for Bastien to dismiss her. Didn't want to be humiliated.

"We shall send word to Armand and Felicity immediately," the dowager was saying as the carriage turned another corner. "Armand will want to see his brother."

It seemed she was expected to make some response, so Raeven said, "Naturally."

Silence. She cleared her throat.

"Ah, and who is Felicity?"

"She's the comtesse, Armand's wife. They've been married only a year."

"I see." Raeven could see the questions forming in the ladies' minds. Would Raeven be the next… what was the wife of a marquis called? She didn't know, but that's what they were wondering. Would she be Bastien's wife, or was she just a temporary diversion?

She was saved from the subject when the carriage slowed and the footmen opened the doors. Once again, she looked up at the beautiful town house, and once again, she was met by the butler, Grimsby, at the door. If he was surprised to see her again, he didn't show it.

It seemed to Raeven half the staff was awake to greet the duchesse and Bastien's mother, though it was practically the middle of the night.

"Mrs. Eggers." The dowager gestured to an older lady who immediately stepped forward. "We have two guests with us. My son Sébastien is on his way home, and this is Miss Russell." The housekeeper's gaze flicked to Raeven and then back to her employer. Raeven wondered what the staff thought of her. Wondered if she looked as much like a street urchin as she felt she did. The dowager continued, "We will need... two rooms prepared."

Raeven felt her face heat, knowing the dowager had probably guessed her relationship with Bastien was more than merely friendly. But it would have been unthinkable for them to share a room when not married.

The dowager was giving more instructions as to which rooms, how they should be prepared, and the possible arrival of Bastien's brother Armand and his family, but Raeven was not listening. She wished she had waited and returned with Bastien and his brother Julien. He had urged her to go on without him so she could rest, but she didn't feel tired. She felt unsure and uncertain and wished she were back in her cabin on the *Regal*.

"Miss Russell." The dowager took her arm and led her into a small parlor. It was feminine and inviting, with pastel paintings, moldings on the walls and ceilings, and dainty chairs upholstered in pink and white silk. It also faced the street, and Raeven found herself staring out into the square, hoping Bastien would arrive soon.

"You needn't worry about him," the dowager said, sitting delicately in one of the chairs. She wore an amber silk gown that swirled about her like honey. To Raeven's eyes, she looked too young to be the mother of men like Bastien and Julien, but then what did she know of mothers? "Julien will take good care of him. Julien takes good care of us all." She glanced at the duchesse, who was standing in the parlor's doorway. "Go ahead and check on little Etienne, Sarah. You won't feel easy until you do."

The duchesse smiled, and Raeven realized Etienne must be her son. "I'll be back down in a moment."

The dowager waved a hand. "Go to bed. I shall make certain Miss Russell is settled."

The duchesse, who looked tired, nodded. "I'll see you at breakfast, Miss Russell. It was a pleasure to meet you. And thank you."

Raeven frowned. "Thank you?"

"For bringing Bastien home. You don't know how much this means to Julien. He's never stopped looking for him, never given up hope. Now his family is complete again." She looked at the dowager, a sadness flickering in her eyes. "Or almost. Good night."

When she was gone, silence, except for the crackling of wood in the fire, filled the parlor. Raeven stared out the window again, and when she turned back to the dowager, the older woman's gaze was far, far away. When she spoke, her voice was quiet and distant. "I never believed." There was anguish in her tone. "It was easier for me, I suppose, to believe the twins dead. The idea of them being alive somewhere without me—" Her voice broke.

Raeven felt tears sting her eyes, and she went to the woman, knelt before her. "There was nothing you could have done. Bastien told me the story of his escape. He thought you perished."

The dowager shook her head, and a single tear escaped down her cheek. "All those years alone." She looked at Raeven. "But then he wasn't alone. He had you."

Raeven swallowed. She hadn't exactly comforted Bastien. In the short time she'd known him, she'd tried to kill him numerous times, seen him shot, betrayed, and imprisoned. "W-we haven't known each other very long," Raeven said.

"Really? Bastien said you'd met last summer."

When had he said that? Raeven stood. "Yes, well. It was a brief meeting initially." She'd tried to carve him open in that tavern in Brest. "We met again a month or so ago in Gibraltar."

The dowager smiled. "And you brought him home."

"Actually, my father did. I don't know if you understood, Your Grace, but Bastien is under arrest for piracy. The navy would like nothing better than to see him hanged for his crimes."

The dowager waved a hand. "Julien will fix that."

Raeven shook her head. "I don't see how."

"You will." The dowager leaned back and assessed her. Raeven shifted from foot to foot and wished she had taken one of the chairs. "You love him."

"I beg your pardon?"

"Bastien. You love him. You are an admiral's daughter, and yet you risked your own life and freedom to help my son. Why would you do such a thing unless you loved him?"

"It doesn't matter," Raeven blurted. The dowager raised her brows, but Raeven couldn't seem to stop talking. "He doesn't love me back—or at least he hasn't said as much. He did say he wanted to marry me, but that was... before." She gestured to the delicate parlor. "And even if he wants me now, it will never work."

"Why?" the dowager asked quietly.

"We're from two different worlds. I belong with my father on the *Regal*. He needs me. I'm all he has."

"And yet earlier it sounded as though you considered my son's proposal of marriage."

Raeven opened her mouth, closed it again. "It wasn't exactly a *proposal*."

The dowager lifted her brows.

"That was before," Raeven tried to explain. "Now." Again she gestured helplessly to the room, to the dowager, sitting there looking so stately. "I don't belong here, in this world."

"You belonged with the pirate, not the nobleman."

"Yes—no. I—I don't know. I don't know that we ever belonged together. I—"

The housekeeper opened the door. "I'm sorry to interrupt. Miss Russell's room is ready. Shall I show her up?"

The dowager looked at Raeven, and she glanced out the window one last time. Still no sign of Bastien. "Yes, please." Suddenly, she was tired. So tired.

Bastien came to her in the night. She'd known he would. She did not know how he would know which room, but she knew he would find her.

She was dozing when he slipped into bed beside

her, when his warm arms came around her and he pulled her against his nakedness. She was naked, as well. She hadn't bothered with the night rail the maid she'd dismissed left on the bed. It was frilly and delicate—everything she was not.

"Mmm," Bastien murmured in her ear. "You're warm." He kissed her neck. "Soft." His hand cupped one breast, but before he could go any farther, she turned in his arms to face him.

"I was worried about you."

He traced her cheek with one finger. "As you see, I'm in your bed, safe and sound."

"The soldiers?"

"My brother is dealing with them. Apparently, he's richer than the King. He's going to buy the navy a ship or three on the condition they forget all about Captain Cutlass."

"Will they accept?"

"They have little choice." He pulled a lock of her hair to his nose, sniffed. "Cherries. Captain Cutlass is no more. There's only Sébastien Harcourt."

"Marquis de Valére."

"*Ma belle*, you make it sound like a crime. It's a title, nothing more."

How she wished that were true.

Suddenly, he lay back on the pillow, stared up at the ceiling, and smiled. In the dim light from the fire, she could see his face. He seemed so happy. "I never dreamed of this. Never dreamed I'd be sleeping under my brother's roof. Never dreamed I'd see my mother again." He glanced at Raeven. "She looks the same. She's still beautiful."

Raeven nodded. "She's very beautiful."

"And I have a nephew. They named him Etienne, after my father. I'm an uncle."

Her heart ached at his happiness. She was glad she had been a part of it, however briefly.

"Armand and Felicity—that's his wife—will come tomorrow or the next day. Julien told me Armand was imprisoned for years. I wish I'd known before. I wish—"

She put a finger over his lips. "You can spend your whole life regretting. You have them now. You have me now."

His hand curled in her hair again. "Yes, I do, don't I?" He pulled her mouth to his and kissed her. "And what do you suggest I do with you?"

She shook her head, slid on top of him. "It's what I'm going to do with you this time."

"Oh?" He groaned when her breasts rubbed his chest.

She leaned forward, captured his wrists and anchored them to the pillow. She knew he could take back control whenever he liked, but for the moment, he seemed content to allow her to lead.

She lowered her mouth to his, touching his lips lightly. She'd missed his lips; she *would* miss his lips. She brushed hers softly against his, letting her tongue dart out lightly. His fingers curled, and she nudged his mouth open, kissing him more deeply.

He'd been drinking brandy. He tasted of it and of the wild pirate she loved. Their tongues mated, and she felt as though the world around them rocked. She knew they were on solid land, but when she kissed him, she could almost feel the swell of the sea. He smelled like the sea, like the salty ocean, the clean, crisp air.

She felt his arms tense and strain, knew when he realized he was still pinned to the bed. Knew when he accepted it and stilled. She broke the kiss, bent to taste his neck, to trail her tongue over the stubble on his jaw.

"*Mon coeur*," he murmured.

Her heart stuttered. Did he mean it, or was it simply an endearment? Something said in the heat of this moment?

It didn't matter. None of it mattered anymore.

She lifted her head. "I'm going to need my hands."

"Oh, really?"

"Mmm-hmm. I'm ordering you not to move."

"Yes, Captain." He was grinning, amused by her, but when she scraped her teeth along his shoulder and down his chest, she heard his quick inhalation of breath. She ran her fingers over the muscles of his chest. She was reminded he might be an aristocrat, but he hadn't lived the life of one. He was hard as steel, and his muscles tensed and rippled under her fingertips. She looked up at him, saw he was watching her as she was watching him. She let him see her while she admired his broad shoulder, his sculpted chest, his slim hips.

And then her eyes slid lower.

"Now what, Captain?" His tone was too easy, too light. She lowered her mouth to his erection, touched her tongue to him.

"More of this?" she asked.

"You're the captain."

She smiled. His voice had been hoarse and strained.

She touched her tongue to him again, ran it up and down the length of him. When she looked up, his hands were clutching the pillow. He saw her looking at him, reached for her, but she held up a hand. "I didn't say you could move."

"Raeven—"

"Shh." She bent again, this time taking him into her mouth. She heard his groan as she tasted him, felt him tense beneath her. She teased him, liking the control, knowing he was on the fringe of losing his.

"Raeven!" His hands clutched her shoulders.

She looked up, shook her head. "I didn't say—"

"I need to be inside you. Now. Take me or I'll—"

She didn't wait for him to finish. She straddled him, lowered herself slowly over his hardness, and took him inside her.

She had wanted their lovemaking to be passionate but playful, but now when she looked down at him, she couldn't keep her emotions in check. Her heart swelled as she moved over him. He cupped her neck, brought her lips to his for a tender kiss. She returned it and allowed him to reverse their positions.

He moved slowly, gently, taking his time. He kissed her sweetly, and she had to swallow to keep the tears from spilling over.

When she found release, it was slow and warm. She sighed her pleasure, and he sighed with her.

He held her a long time—their bodies pressed together, their hearts beating together. Just when she felt his arms relax, felt him fall into sleep, he whispered, "Raeven."

❧

He woke alone. He was not in the room he'd been given. That room had been dark and masculine in color and décor. This room was much smaller and brighter. The walls were papered in yellow and the windows covered by white and yellow curtains. He lay in a small brass bed, the white coverlet tangled about his feet.

Bastien sat, looked about the small room, and knew she was gone.

He didn't need to see her clothes missing. He didn't need to ask the staff if she'd gone down for breakfast. He didn't need to search for her in the garden or the library or any of the other rooms.

She was gone.

He felt her absence and could have cursed himself for not seeing this coming. She'd been different last night, and now he realized it was more than fatigue or eagerness to be with him again. She'd been saying good-bye.

"Merde." He sat just as her door opened and a maid stepped inside.

"Good morning, Miss Russell—oh!" She gaped at his nakedness and hastily backed up. "I'm sorry. I'll come back."

"Don't bother," Bastien growled. "She's gone."

"Yes, my lord." The maid closed the door, and Bastien pulled on his breeches and shirt and stalked out of the room.

Julien met him in the hallway, rolled his eyes. "You might try being discreet. This isn't a pirate ship."

"I wish it were. It's harder to escape."

"Escape? Who's escaped?"

"Raeven. She's gone."

"I see."

Bastien brushed past him. "No, you don't. I need to go after her. I'm going—"

"Nowhere." Julien grabbed his shoulder, held him fast. "It's going to take several days to negotiate with the navy, and until then, you're by no means safe from Newgate. If word leaks that Captain…" He paused, looked about. "That you are here, the public will clamor for your execution. You have quite the reputation for harassment of British ships."

"Exaggeration. One or two skirmishes with the British Navy, and everyone's out for your neck."

"Yes, well, yours isn't safe yet. You're not going anywhere until I say you can."

"Oh, really?" Fury welled inside him, aimed more at himself than his brother, but Julien was standing there. "I'll go when and where I want."

Julien crossed his arms. "Fine. But don't come back here."

Bastien blinked.

"You think this is just about you? You've been on your own so long, you don't consider anyone else. Your being here puts me, *ma mére*, your whole family in jeopardy. Armand and Felicity will be here soon. You endanger them, as well."

Bastien scowled. "If I'm so dangerous, why the hell did you bring me here?"

"You're my brother. But I have a wife and child to protect. The Foreign Office would like nothing more than to find reason to accuse me of treason, spying. They've tried it before. These negotiations with the navy are delicate and need to be kept from public scrutiny. I'll undertake them, and I'll win, but I need you to give me time before you show yourself in public again."

Bastien fisted his hands. "And Raeven?"

"She left you." The implication was clear. For the first time, Bastien felt himself doubting. Perhaps she didn't love him. Perhaps she'd saved him only out of guilt. She'd lost Percy and couldn't bear the responsibility of losing another person she cared about.

He knew where she was. She'd gone back to her father, back to the *Regal*. And wasn't that where she belonged?

The hell if it was.

"I'm going after her, Julien," Bastien said. "So you'd better hurry those negotiations."

Julien looked grim. "I'll do my best."

Bastien nodded. He'd give his brother two days, and then he'd go get Raeven. He only hoped he wasn't too late.

Twenty

RAEVEN STOOD ON THE DECK OF THE *REGAL* AND watched the men ready the ship for departure. They'd been docked for a week, and she'd spent six nights without Bastien.

Six long, lonely nights.

And he hadn't come for her. She hadn't really expected him to come, but that didn't mean she hadn't hoped, hadn't longed, hadn't wished on every measly star she could spot in this hazy-skied city. And the reality was Bastien wasn't coming. He had his family now, had his title, and soon would probably have a rich, titled wife.

A marquise. Yesterday she'd asked Fitzwilliam Wimberley for the title of the wife of a marquis, and he'd given her a strange look and then the answer.

She didn't care if he gave her a thousand strange looks. She didn't care if the whole crew watched her with sideways glances. She knew she was just standing on the deck, not doing anything, not helping as she always did. She knew she was red nosed from crying. She knew she was clutching her stupid skirts to keep them from tangling about her ankles in the wind.

Why had she worn a skirt or brushed her hair? It wasn't as though anyone cared what she looked like.

A warm hand settled on her shoulder, and she spun around with a yelp. Her father tightened his grip to calm her. "I didn't mean to startle you."

"It's my fault. I was thinking of something else."

"You were thinking of him. The pirate."

"No, I..." She looked down at the deck. "Yes, I was."

Her father nodded, seemed resigned. He studied the men on the yardarms. "I was surprised when you returned the day after we docked. I thought you might run away with him. I certainly made sure you had the opportunity."

Raeven gaped. "You thought I would—what do you mean you made certain I had the opportunity?"

"He should have had an escort to Newgate of at least six soldiers. I detained four of them. I didn't think even you, Raeven, could outwit six soldiers."

She stared at him, and when he looked down at her, he laughed at the bewildered expression on her face. "But why would you do that? Why would you help when you knew I might run away with him?"

The admiral sighed, shook his head. "Because, dear daughter, you love him. He makes you happy. God's nightgown, it pains me to admit it! You and a pirate. A rogue!" He clenched his jaw and took a deep breath.

Raeven was relieved when his color returned to normal and he didn't begin coughing. He'd been coughing too much lately.

"But you're not my little girl anymore. You love him, and as difficult as this is for you to believe, I do want you to be happy."

The admiral had never been a man to show much affection, especially in front of his crew, but now Raeven wrapped her arms around him. "Oh, Daddy! Thank you." She buried her face in his blue coat. It smelled like him—oakum, boot polish, and the sea.

He stiffened at her sudden embrace then awkwardly put his arms about her. Finally, she released him, stood back, and gave him a teary smile. "But you're not going to lose me to a pirate. He's found his family again. He's home where he belongs." She looked about the *Regal*. "So am I."

Her father shook his head. "You'll always have a home here, but this ship is no place for a young woman. You need a husband, children."

She was shaking her head, but he ignored her.

"Earlier this week, I asked for a few months leave from my post."

Raeven blinked in surprise. "You what? Why?"

"I wanted to spend some time with you on land. See you settled."

"And your health—"

"Is fine." He waved away her concern. "But my request was denied. It seems the seas are heating up again. The Admiralty doesn't think this peace with Old Boney will last much longer."

Raeven nodded. She was glad. Battles and action would keep her mind off Bastien.

"And that's why I've hired a new purser."

Raeven sucked in a breath. She'd known this was

coming, known one day a replacement for Percy would be found. She would be forced to accept her friend was never coming back. She cleared her throat. "Who is he?"

He nodded to someone who stood behind her, and she turned and looked into cobalt blue eyes. Bastien, wearing navy dress, saluted her. She stared at him, turned to her father, and stuttered, "What is this?"

The admiral shook his head. "It's exactly what it looks like. He came here this morning, asking for your hand in matrimony."

"What?" She turned to stare at Bastien, who only shrugged.

"I told the rogue no, of course. I'm not giving my blessing to any bloody pirate."

"And I told him I'm not a pirate anymore." The sound of Bastien's voice, the lilt of his accent, washed over her. It was years since she'd last heard his voice. "I've joined the navy. I knew you were in need of a purser."

Raeven shook her head. "Is this some sort of joke?"

"No." Her father looked tense. "I have orders from the Admiralty to accept him for Mr. Williams's position. Apparently, money can buy more than freedom."

"It's not just my brother's money," Bastien argued. "I *am* an excellent seaman."

Raeven simply stared at him. "You can't be serious."

He looked her directly in the eyes. "I am very serious. I have signed on as purser on the HMS *Regal*. I know I can't ever hope to replace Mr. Williams, but I will carry out his duties to the best of my abilities."

"Why?" she asked. "Why would you do this?"

He cocked a brow. "Why else, *ma belle*? You left me. I figured I would have to come to you. I asked for your hand in marriage, but your father refused to give his consent."

The admiral cleared his throat. "But I would not be overly dismayed if you married against my wishes."

"It would mean abandoning my post," Bastien drawled.

"I think we will find a way to make do."

Raeven's head was spinning, and her heart thudded in her chest. "I don't understand," she told Bastien. "You have your family now, your title, your—"

He took her hand, and the admiral muttered under his breath and moved away. "But I don't have you, *mon coeur*. I need you, *mon amour*. Without you, the rest is meaningless. I want you to be my wife."

His wife. "Your marquise," she whispered.

He grinned. "Yes, that's right."

She shook her head. "But I don't know anything about being a marquise. I don't know anything about ducs and mansions and fancy balls."

"Then we'll learn together. Or, better yet, we'll build a ship and sail it around the world. I think you and I would suffocate if we were confined on land too long."

He was right, and she could imagine sailing the world with him. Just the two of them, making love under the stars…

"But you don't want to marry me…"

He sighed. "Are you going to force me to bend a knee? Again? Very well."

And to her astonishment, he knelt before her. This

gesture generated calls from the *Regal*'s crew, most of whom had given up all pretense of working and were openly watching the scene. Bastien ignored them. "Raeven Russell, will you be my Mrs. Cutlass, my marquise, my petite cabin girl…"

She frowned and looked away. He took her hand in his, and when she looked back, his eyes were dark, his expression tender. "My heart, my love, my wife? Raeven, will you have me, a so-called pirate and a self-confessed rogue, as your husband?"

She couldn't breathe. She couldn't think. She couldn't stand. She knelt beside him and wrapped her arms around him. "Bastien, I love you."

"*Je t'aime, ma belle.* I love you." He pulled back, held her by the shoulders. "But you haven't answered the question, and I confess I'm eager to know if I'll be forced to wear this uniform much longer."

She laughed. "No. I mean, yes, I'll marry you, and no, you won't have to wear the uniform." She grinned. "Unless you want. I think it suits you."

He looked at her with something akin to horror, and she laughed again. It felt so good to laugh, felt so good to be back in his arms.

The sound of boots behind them had her looking over her shoulder. Her father stood grim faced. "Am I to congratulate the happy couple?"

Raeven leaped up. "Yes!" She hugged him hard, realizing as she did, this was good-bye. She pulled back. "But will you be all right without me? Will you take care of yourself?"

He straightened. "I'll be fine." To her surprise, he leaned down and kissed her cheek. "I'll be happy knowing you're well taken care of." He gave Bastien a warning look. "Now, get the hell off my ship. The next time we dock, I'll expect to see grandchildren."

Bastien gave a mock-salute. "Yes, Captain." He turned, swept her into his arms, and carried her, laughing, down the gangplank and back onto land. When they stood on the deck, he lowered her, and Raeven looked up at the *Regal* then into Bastien's eyes.

"I love you," she said. "I always have. From that first moment in Brest, I loved you."

"I know."

She frowned, but he reached into his coat and pulled out a paper.

"What's that?"

"A special license. My brother has all sorts of connections. My family is waiting at the church now. Are you ready to be married?"

She gaped. "*Now*? Today? I–I'm not dressed, not—"

He put a finger over her lips. "I love you just the way you are, and yes, now. Today. I want you to be mine legally before you change your mind."

She swallowed and nodded. Life with Bastien would never be predictable, never ordinary. She could think, or she could hold her breath and dive in.

She inhaled and prepared to jump.

Epilogue

It was the worst pain she had ever felt. She'd screamed until her throat was raw and only a hoarse croak would come out. Bastien stood beside her, held her hand throughout the ordeal. She'd told him to leave, told him he wasn't supposed to be in the room, but he'd been steadfast, and after the pain became unbearable, she was glad to have his hand to clamp onto.

She wanted to say she forgot the pain when the midwife presented her with the howling baby girl. She took the baby in her arms, stared down at her red face, the shock of black hair, and the muddy blue eyes. Raeven didn't forget the pain, but she did fall in love.

Instantly. Irrevocably.

She looked at Bastien and knew he felt it, too. She held the baby out to him. "Your daughter."

He blinked. "You want me to hold her?"

"Don't you want to?" She almost laughed at the look of pure terror on his face.

"Yes, but—"

"Then here."

He took the squalling baby carefully in his arms, looked down at her, and immediately she ceased crying.

"There," Raeven said. "She likes you. What shall we call her? Elizabeth? After my mother?"

He nodded, still staring, enraptured, at his daughter. "*Bon jour*, Elizabeth. *Bienvenue*."

The midwife had barely finished her duties and the linens scarcely changed when the first knock came at the door. It was Sarah. "Raeven, can we come in now? Just Felicity and Rowena and I."

Raeven smiled sleepily at Bastien. The baby was curled in one of his arms, and he had the other wrapped securely around her shoulders. "Your family," she murmured.

"Allow one in, they'll all be in."

He was right, but she didn't mind. Somehow his family had become hers, as well.

"Come in, Sarah."

The door opened to admit the duchesse, the dowager, and the comtesse. All three of the women crowded around the baby and cooed.

"What have you named her?" Rowena asked.

"Elizabeth," Raeven told them.

"Oh, I adore that name!" Felicity, who had a daughter of her own, beamed. "Hello, Elizabeth."

"We might call her Eliza," Sarah said.

"Call who Eliza?" Julien stuck his head in the doorway. He was holding Etienne, and the little boy smiled shyly. "Armand and the admiral want to know if it's safe to enter."

Beside her, Bastien gave a short sigh. "Why don't we invite the servants while we're at it?"

"Oh, I know Mrs. Eggers wants to meet the baby," Felicity said. "And your friend, Bastien, Mr. Leveque."

Raeven smiled. "Perhaps later."

Julien and Armand stood at the foot of the bed. As usual, Armand was silent, but he gave Raeven a smile. Her father came to stand on the other side of her. "I heard you named her Elizabeth," he said. "Your mother would have been honored."

She smiled up at him. "I know you were hoping for a grandson."

"Now that I've retired, I need someone to go fishing with me." He smiled at the baby, who had begun to fuss. "But I think this little girl will have her mother's spirit. She ought to keep me busy."

Raeven took the baby into her arms, and Bastien leaned over and kissed his wife's temple. "Do you think she'll be able to sail in a few months? Our ship will be ready, and the world awaits."

"She'll have her sea legs before her land legs."

"Just as it should be," he murmured into her hair. Raeven had to agree.

Acknowledgments

There are many people who make a book like this possible. I'd like to thank Sourcebooks, especially my editor, Deb Werksman, who calmly talked me through all the title and cover changes to this book without once suggesting I grab a paper bag for my hyperventilation. I'd also like to thank Danielle Jackson, Sarah Ryan, Susie Benton, Cat Clyne, Dominique Raccah, and all the others at Sourcebooks who work so hard on my behalf. As Deb said, I got the full Sourcebooks' treatment. Thank you for not resting until we got it right. I'm extremely fortunate to have Joanna MacKenzie and Danielle Egan-Miller as my agents. They make me feel like the only author in the world. And thank you for having such a large supply of paper bags on hand.

This novel required research into ships and sailing. I'm indebted to my dad for sharing his vast knowledge of seafaring and for reading sections of this novel for correctness. I'm also grateful to Ronald Stebbins for his input. As this is a work of fiction, I've taken a few liberties, but I made every attempt at accuracy.

I use several Spanish names in this novel, and I'm appreciative of the suggestions and translations made by Gina Colion-Hernandez. Once again, Pascale Zurzolo-Champeau graciously answered my questions regarding French expressions and phrases. Of course, any and all mistakes in the novel are mine completely.

My career as an author wouldn't be possible without the support of family and friends, including my longtime friend and critique partner, Christina Hergenrader; the members of West Houston RWA, especially Sharie Kohler and Tera Lynn Childs; and the ladies of the Sisterhood of the Jaunty Quills, in particular Margo Maguire and Robyn DeHart. Madeira James at xuni.com took me on as a client in 2004, and she still designs and maintains my website. Somehow she always finds time for another update or tweak. And last but far from least, I'd like to acknowledge my husband for making so many dinners, entertaining Baby Galen, and always building me up.

About the Author

Shana Galen is the author of seven Regency historicals, including the Rita-nominated *Blackthorne's Bride*. Her books have been sold in Brazil, Russia, the Netherlands, Spain, and Turkey and featured in the Rhapsody and Doubleday Book Clubs. A former English teacher in Houston's inner city, Shana now writes full time. She is a happily married wife and mother of a daughter. She loves to hear from readers: visit her website at www.shanagalen.com or see what she's up to daily on Facebook and Twitter.

Lord and Lady Spy

Somewhere in Europe, July 1815

THE SPY CALLED SAINT HUNKERED DOWN IN THE bottom of the wardrobe she'd occupied for the last four hours and attempted to stifle a yawn.

She didn't need to crack the door to know the activities in the bed across the room were still very much in progress. She could hear the courtesan urging her "horse" onward, the woman's demands punctuated by the man's loud neighs.

Saint sighed, shifting so her muscles remained limber. She'd given up being embarrassed about three and a quarter hours ago and now wondered how much longer the game could persist.

Where was Lucien Ducos? If Bonaparte's advisor didn't make an appearance tonight, Saint was going to have a lot of explaining to do. Despite being ordered to track Ducos to France, she'd elected to remain right here.

Something told her that Bonaparte's advisor would visit his mistress one last time before leaving. It was a feeling—her intuition speaking to her. And Saint always listened to her intuition.

It had led her to this wardrobe, where she'd been treated to The Sassy Upstairs Maid, The Very Bad Boy, and now Horse and Rider. Ducos had better turn up soon—before someone decided to play Hide and Seek and discovered the wardrobe held more than clothes.

The horse's neighs grew louder, and Saint covered her ears. How much longer? She was definitely leaving as soon as the horse… was stabled.

She sighed. Oh, who was she fooling? Of course, she wouldn't leave. She'd stay as long as necessary to secure Ducos.

That was her mission.

Failure was not an option.

The horse neighed frantically, and Saint dropped her head in her hands and tried to remember why she was putting up with this. Bonaparte had escaped after his defeat at Waterloo. England—nay, Europe— would not be safe until he was apprehended and dealt with. All sources pointed to Ducos as the man who knew where Bonaparte was hidden.

Her mission was to find Ducos and make him talk.

And she'd do her duty. She'd tracked him here, discovered the name of his courtesan, and set the perfect trap. So where was the Frenchman?

Suddenly the slaps and neighs were interrupted by three loud bangs on the front door. The courtesan's house was small, the outer door located down a short flight of steps near the bedroom. In the abrupt silence, Saint could hear the housekeeper's shoes clicking through the vestibule.

"What are you doing?" the horse asked the courtesan in one of the seven languages Saint knew well. "You can't stop now."

"One moment," the woman answered, her voice tense. Saint's nose itched, and she sat forward, careful to